Chasing The Butterfly

by Jayme H. Mansfield

Amber and Hugh ~ Enjoy the journey! Jayme Mansfield

Lighthouse Publishing
of the Carolinas

Praise for *Chasing The Butterfly*

Chasing the Butterfly is an inspiring debut novel of love and forgiveness. Author Jayme H. Mansfield weaves a fascinating tale and beautiful imagery to trace a young woman's journey through war and betrayal to healing and restoration.

Henry McLaughlin
Award-winning fiction author of *Journey To Riverbend*

Mansfield weaves a story of beauty in the midst of survival and ultimate forgiveness.

DiAnn Mills
Award-winning & best-selling fiction author

Jayme H. Mansfield

CHASING THE BUTTERFLY BY JAYME H. MANSFIELD
Published by Lighthouse Publishing of the Carolinas
2333 Barton Oaks Dr., Raleigh, NC, 27614

ISBN 978-1941103371
Copyright © 2014 by Jayme H. Mansfield
Cover illustration by Kelly Berger
Cover design by writelydesigned.com
Interior design by Karthick Srinivasan

Available in print from your local bookstore, online, or from the publisher at:
www.lighthousepublishingofthecarolinas.com

For more information on this book and the author visit: www.jaymemansfield.com

This is a work of fiction. Names, characters, and incidents are all products of the author's imagination or are used for fictional purposes. Any mentioned brand names, places, and trade marks remain the property of their respective owners, bear no association with the author or the publisher, and are used for fictional purposes only.

Scripture quotations are taken from the HOLY BIBLE NEW INTERNATIONAL VERSION r. NIVr Copyright c 1973, 1978, 1984 by International Bible Society. Used by permission of Zondervan Publishing House. All rights reserved.

Brought to you by the creative team at LighthousePublishingoftheCarolinas.com: Eddie Jones, Rowena Kuo, Andrea Merrell, and Brian Cross.

Library of Congress Cataloging-in-Publication Data
Mansfield, Jayme H.
Chasing the Butterfly/Jayme H. Mansfield 1st ed.

Printed in the United States of America

Dedication

To my mother, who has always believed in me.

In memory of my father (1933-2007),
who loved his little girl with all his heart.

To my husband James, thank you for
journeying with me for this lifetime—I love you.

To Gracie, my furry and four-legged
writing companion to the end.

Acknowledgements

I'm fascinated by life's journey. Perhaps that is largely why I wrote this book. Partly, it's the view outside the window, the days and years that converge into a steady stream of memories. However, it's those with *whom* we travel—whose paths converge and enrich our lives—that make all the difference. It's to these people (and I could never list them all, but you know who you are) that I say thank you for traveling with me throughout this literary and life journey. You are a blessing!

- To the writing community who initially gave me legs to reach new milestones. My Christian Writers Guild mentors: DiAnn Mills, Yvonne Lehman, Jim Zabloski, and Jerry Jenkins. A special thanks to CWG friend Henry McLaughlin for making the initial edits and cheering me on.
- To my agent, Jessica Kirkland, and Blythe Daniel at the Blythe Daniel Agency for taking me under their wings and finding my first publishing home.
- To the kind folks at Lighthouse Publishing of the Carolinas for believing in my story and providing the opportunity. A special thanks to my editor, Andrea Merrell, for not only her keen editing eye, but her gracious teaching spirit.
- To my good friend and marketing wing-woman, Heidi Hamamoto, for keeping me afloat amidst all the to-do's and the giant learning curve. For Denille Obermeyer for her brilliance and creativity. Not to be left out, Gina and Mindy at SocialKNX for their marketing prowess.
- To artist extraordinaire, Kelly Berger, for gifting me with her cover design painting and understanding me so well. Yes indeed, our lives have come full circle.

- To my Timberline teaching buddies and dear friends who have made me laugh until I cry and helped keep my dream alive.
- To the parents, students, and staff at Aspen Academy who have supported my writing dream in so many ways. Over the past three years, you have fueled my creativity, allowed me to reach for the sky, and shared in the laughter and tears that come from great books and powerful writing.
- To my friends who continually shower my life with sunshine—you applaud my wild and crazy ideas and put up with the pace of my life. Thanks for keeping me upright. Especially Elizabeth, you are my confidante, my twin, my true friend.
- To my family. You know me so well. Mom and Mary Ann (Bones), thank you for reading the early draft and believing I had a story to tell. Pappa Tom, you were in this from the very start, stayed with me through the tough stuff, and opened my eyes to seeing the Truth.
- To my dear ones—Ian, Adam, and Graham—your laughter, energy, and endearing spirits keep me in check and enjoying what life is really about.
- To my husband, James, side-by-side, we have experienced blessings beyond belief. Our adventure continues to be written with love and the Lord. Surely, to Him be all the Glory for this wild ride we call life. I wouldn't want to be on it with anyone but you.

Prologue

Roussillon, France, 1929

Mama didn't believe I saw something wonderful on our family's voyage when we left our house in New York City and sailed far away to a new home in the south of France. Though I was only five years old, she didn't understand I experienced a beacon of light that would direct me the rest of my life.

But I knew differently. I wasn't looking west across the ocean to America or even watching the most beautiful sunset I had ever seen. I was watching God—and at that moment, I knew for the rest of my life I wanted to be part of His creation.

One

I learned to run that day … really run. My head insisted she was gone, but my heart demanded I run after her one more time.

After kneeling to gather my scattered papers, I knocked over the glass holding my new paintbrush. The blue-tinted water pooled around my knees and soaked the hem of my dress as it filled crevices between the stones on our front porch. I stood, clutching my paintings, and my feet skittered across the lawn and onto the gravel road leading to the center of town. It didn't matter that the bottoms of my bare feet stung from the jagged stones.

I couldn't stop. If I did, I'd never find her—she'd be gone. My long hair tangled and caught in the tears streaming down my face. Pushing it out of my eyes, it flew out behind me like a windstorm. My pale-yellow sundress twisted between my legs and threw me to the ground. I lay there trying to breathe, then pushed myself up, hiked my dress to my waist, and ran full stride down the center of the road. I ran with my head down, determined—running as if for my life.

My head lifted in time to see Papa's car swerve onto the soft shoulder and skid to a halt. Except for the strained car engine, there was silence. I froze, gripping the hem of my dirty dress with one hand and my crumpled paintings in the other. Silhouetted by the setting sun, he leapt out of the car and ran to me. My eyes were drowning, making it impossible to focus.

"Ella! What are you doing? I almost ran you down." Papa wrapped me in his arms. "Your feet are bleeding. Oh, dear God, what happened?"

My lips quivered and my entire body shook.

Papa held me tighter. He sat cross-legged on the road and gathered me onto his lap. He breathed hard against my neck. "Did someone hurt you? Tell me the truth."

He took my face in his large hands and pushed the tangles of hair from my eyes. My breathing slowed and there was a momentary calm, like the sea before a storm.

"She's ... gone."

"Who, Ella?"

My head shook from side to side. "Mama." I stared into his soft, brown eyes and then whispered the vicious words. "This morning she was all fancy, wearing her pretty blue dress and red lipstick." I ran my tongue over my lips, tasting the dust and tears. "I said, 'Mama, why are you dressed up?'"

"Bet she just wanted to look pretty." Papa winked.

"That's what she said. 'Ella, I want to be pretty again.'"

"Again?" His smile faded.

I nodded. "I told her she's always pretty."

Papa tucked a strand of hair behind my ear. "Yes, she's a pretty girl, just like you."

I lowered my eyes. "I heard you and Mama yelling last night."

"Your mother and I had a little disagreement. That's all. It's fine now."

"No. She had her travel case. I was coming up the path from the pond and saw her put it in the front seat."

"Did she tell you where she was going?" Papa stared hard at me and my heart broke.

"She said she was going to the market, but she didn't seem right. I asked to go with her, but she looked at me real strange and told me to go inside the house.

"Did you obey your mother?"

"No. I ran after the car when she drove away, but she wouldn't stop. I waited on the porch for her all day. When she didn't come back, I had to try and find her."

Papa squeezed me. "Oh, Lord, she didn't." His eyes filled with tears. He pressed his mouth into my hair and whispered her name as though wishing her back home. "Marie."

But his voice confirmed the truth. My arms wrapped tightly around his neck, and a damp spot formed on his shirt as the tears rushed from my eyes.

Finally, he gathered me up and stood to his full height. He turned toward the sun as it cast its final light on the hills. Like many evenings, we watched the color of the hills intensify to a deep crimson. Tonight they resembled bleeding hearts. Gradually, the color darkened and the hills beat their last bit of life.

Papa carried me back to the car. After opening the passenger door, he placed me gently on the front seat. My body was limp like the injured baby bird I tried to rescue last spring after a windstorm had knocked its nest out of a tree.

"We're going home, Ella."

"Back to New York?"

"New York?" Papa's forehead wrinkled. "Of course not. Why would you ask that?"

"Mama says this isn't our home," I whispered.

"The farmhouse is our home. Roussillon is our home."

"But you told Mama she'd be happy here." I waited for him to say something, but his open mouth was silent. "Remember? You said we'd live happily ever after in the sweet-smelling vineyards and—"

"I know. And the far-reaching lavender fields in the south of France." Papa's eyes filled with tears, but he wiped them away with the back of his hand.

As we pulled into the center of the road, I looked out the dust-tinted window in time to see my paintings spiraling on the side of the road as a gentle wind lifted them in unison. They chased in circles, trying to catch and hold on to one another. I don't know when I let them go and set them free. Perhaps it was the moment Papa also realized she was gone. I knew then my gifts for her would never be received.

As the car moved slowly down the road, I turned and knelt on the seat to watch my papers through the rear window. My paintings danced—beckoning me to return and play some day. As they floated to the ground, they waved a final time, fluttered a last breath, and then lay scattered and lifeless, like the pieces of my seven-year-old heart.

Two

Waiting for Mama, 1931

My stomach growled as the late summer sun scorched my skin, but I still wouldn't leave the front porch steps. I had sat there so long the uneven stones seemed to become part of my backside. Mama had been gone for two days and my eyes refused to stop watching for her to walk up the drive, give me a hug and kiss, and tell me how pretty I looked in my yellow dress.

She was so beautiful. Her long, dark hair was always perfectly tucked behind her ears to display milky pearl earrings, just like the porcelain doll Papa had surprised me with on my fifth birthday. Mama's skin was perfect and her lips smooth and full, yet always hiding a smile.

When we had completed our long journey from New York City in 1929 and arrived at the train station in the tiny hill town of Roussillon, my brother Jack knocked the doll out of my arms. She crashed on the blackened bricks, and pieces of her lovely face fell over the edge of the platform, scattering across the metal tracks. Jack was scolded and told to pick up the fragments, but my doll was missing too many pieces to be put back together. Papa promised he would buy me another, but I had to leave behind what was left of my precious possession. Somewhere deep inside my heart, pieces of my life were lost that day as well.

Now Mama was gone. I wanted to believe she still loved me, even though her affection began to dry up the moment our ship from America reached the shores of France. I wanted to believe I looked beautiful in my dress. It didn't matter that it was faded and wrinkled, because the day Papa gave me that dress, he said it was the same color as when the sun gently wakes the quiet hill town of Roussillon and paints its soft light on the sleepy homes.

My brothers had said very little, and it made me wonder what they were thinking after our mother simply drove away. Like me, they were probably wondering if she would ever come back—and what our family would be like without her. As I sat on the hard steps, reliving the events of the day she left, vivid images of my brothers filled my thoughts.

After Mama left that morning, I kept myself busy painting pictures of her favorite flowers while waiting for her to return. The screen door sprang open and my brothers bounded through with pears in hand and pieces of bread stuffed in their mouths. My oldest brother Charles used his shirtsleeve to wipe the juice running down his chin. He always had a silly grin. When I was little, I thought it made him look stupid. Now it made me love him even more.

But neither of my brothers knew how much our lives were about to change.

"You've been sitting here all afternoon," Jack said. "Too bad you missed the fun at the swimming hole. You shouldn't have left so soon." He held out the straggly remains of his pear and dangled it in front of my face. It swung back and forth until the ripened fruit broke from the stem and landed on one of my paintings. The juice left a stain that forced the blues, greens, and yellows into a muddy puddle. I didn't say anything to Jack about the painting. Nothing else mattered that day except having Mama come home.

"Charles, Jack, please go with me to find Mama."

Charles bent his gangly twelve-year-old body over my shoulder, picked the pear off my ruined painting, and tossed it into the yard. "Oh, she's fine. Probably stopped to talk to a neighbor."

"You have to stop being with her all the time," Jack said as he bent his arms and assumed a flapping chicken position. Sticking his bottom out, he strutted across the stones. "You follow her around like a baby chick. The other kids play with their friends, but all you do is stay home and scribble on that paper. Everyone thinks you're strange."

"What about you? Who looks strange now? Don't be so mean to your sister," Charles said. "Ella, she'll be home soon. Before you know it, Mama will be back making dinner."

He sat next to me. His tan legs revealed a hint of dark hair, and his bare feet cast long shadows on the bleached stone. I wanted to believe him when he put his strong arm around my narrow shoulders, but something in the way he hugged me told me he was scared as well.

We were silent for several minutes as I watched tiny red ants crawl in and out of cracks in the stone slabs around my feet. The ants seemed determined to go somewhere, but at the same time, they went nowhere. They just ran and ran. Perhaps they were scared to stop—scared they would never reach where they needed to go.

I wiggled my toes. "Do you think they're afraid?"

"Who?" Charles pushed hair from his eyes and glanced around.

"The ants." I nodded toward my feet. "They're so busy moving. They never stop."

"Ella, you sure think about funny things." Charles squeezed me and laughed.

"More like weird things." Jack leaned over, nearly touching the stone with his nose. Then he turned his head to the side and hovered his ear above the zig-zagging ants. "What's that?" He cupped his ear as if to hear the ants speak. "You think she's weird too?"

I glanced at Charles and he rolled his eyes.

The pretend conversation continued. "Ah, I understand. The bugs too? All the animals think she's odd?"

"That's enough." Charles' voice lowered to a menacing tone. "Leave her alone."

"But I haven't asked the ants if they're afraid of anything. Ella wants to know." Jack resumed his discussion, his lips nearly brushing the stones. Finally, he sat up. "I have their answer." He looked at us and waited. "Well, do you want to know what they said?"

I nodded, wondering if perhaps the tiny creatures had actually spoken to him.

"They aren't afraid of much, only getting stepped on by big feet or crushed with rocks." My brother scooped a handful of pebbles from the dirt along the porch.

"Did they really say that?" My eyes widened as I tried to tell whether he was bluffing.

"Of course they did." Jack stood. "And to prove it, watch this." He stomped his feet upon the fleeing ants and pummeled them with his handful of rocks.

"Stop it! Leave them alone!" I jumped up and tried to stop him, but he only laughed and continued to crush the fragile bodies.

"Knock it off!" Charles grabbed Jack by his ankle and tugged him to the ground. "Don't be so cruel."

Jack rolled over and inspected the scrape on his elbow that was already oozing blood. "You're as crazy as she is." He pushed himself up and glared at us. "You always have to be the hero." He stomped again. "Even to stupid ants." He spit on the twisted, motionless bodies of the ants, turned, and marched into the house. The screen door slammed behind him.

I leaned closer to the stones, looking for any survivors from my brother's wrath. A few ants scurried around the lifeless bodies. Now I wondered if they were both sad and scared.

"Ignore him, Ella." Charles took my hand and pulled me next to him on the steps. "He's got nothing better to do than be angry at the world for no good reason." He hugged me again and we sat, patiently waiting for Mama.

The sound of a passing car brought me back to the present, and I blinked away the tears. As long as I lived, I would never forget that terrible day and the surge of panic that hit me like a crashing wave. Beginning at my toes, it ran up my legs and into my stomach, until it grabbed my heart. That's when I gasped for air, grabbed my paintings, and went in search of my mother.

But it was too late.

Three

Leaving—New York City, 1929

"Marie, you will not use the Lord's name in vain in this home." Papa's voice bellowed, and a quiver ran up my spine.

"But, Henri, I never agreed to this." Mama's voice was muffled behind the kitchen door, but I felt the sting of each word being thrown between her and Papa. Except for darting our eyes between one another, Charles, Jack, and I sat frozen like the statues in City Park.

Even though they had called us to the dining room for supper some time ago, we now waited silently, except for my growling stomach. My brothers fidgeted with their forks and knives. I remained still and listened.

After Papa's last remark, I didn't expect Mama to have much more to say. Members of the Moreau family knew that taking God's name in vain was about the worst thing any of us could do. *Mama is in big trouble,* I thought just as the kitchen door swung open and crashed into the wall. Mama, red-faced and wild-eyed, marched toward her seat at the end of the mahogany dining table. Again, the door flew open and hit the wall. This time, tiny crumbles of plaster fell to the floor. My father moved to his chair with his chin thrust forward and eyes narrowed.

I tucked my head and studied the thin gold line encircling the outer edge of my plate. Mama's breathing was deep and quick like she had run a race, and I waited for it to slow before I peeked. Keeping my head bowed, I raised my eyes and watched Mama smooth her dark hair along the side of her temple. At the other end of the table, my father wore a face that said he was deadly serious.

"Children." His voice was raspy and strained as he settled into his chair and took stock of his family. He looked first at Charles and then Jack. Then he looked the length of the table toward Mama. She flipped her hair and pretended to look out the window, but it was dark outside. And even though the crystals shimmered in the chandelier hanging above our table, it felt dark and scary inside our home.

Papa sighed deeply, then turned his head and looked at me with those big, brown eyes. He reminded me of a puppy dog, and I couldn't help the slight smile that formed on my lips. Papa smiled back.

He cleared his throat and announced, "Children, your mother and I have exciting news." He paused, hands in the air, then followed with a finger-tapping drum roll on his plate. My brothers and I leaned forward, chests pressed against the table and eyes fixed on Papa. "The Moreau family is moving to France … to the beautiful south of France."

I squealed and clapped my hands, even though I knew little of the place except for the stories my father shared about his boyhood. Jack stuck his tongue out at me, and Charles slouched in his chair, arms crossed. Mama was silent, her face blank. She looked lifeless.

"Come on now. In just a few days, it's going to be a big adventure for you on the ship. You may even see some whales off the port side if you keep your heads up instead of staring at your shoes and pouting all day. Besides, you will love the countryside where we'll be living."

My brothers rolled their eyes and shifted in their chairs. I swung my legs back and forth, skimming the Oriental rug with the tips of my black leather shoes.

"When your grandfather—my father—got too sick to continue working the vineyard, my Uncle Paul-Henri took over the Moreau family vineyard. He was a strong, hard-working man and did a fine job making the wines well known in the lower regions of France. He passed away last month and the farm and vineyard are now my responsibility to carry on for the family."

"Or, the business could be sold," Mama chimed in. "As it should be."

Papa breathed deeply as his chest rose. "Or, we could continue a respectable family business with the workers who want to stay on, and I can accept the job to be a part of the boardwalk project in Marseilles. Most architects would dream of such an opportunity—"

"That's right. It's *your* dream with no consideration of mine." Mama's voice cut through the room like a knife.

"Let's not go over this again, especially in front of the children." He gestured with his right hand around the table. "Besides, you'll be able to pursue your singing and piano in France once we get settled." Papa's smile looked forced. "I have no doubt your talent will travel with you wherever you go."

"Mama, will you play for us tonight?" I clasped my hands in anticipation.

She was quick to answer. "Not tonight, Ella."

"But you haven't—"

"I said, *no*." Mama pretended to look out the darkened window again.

"Marie, would you like to say the blessing before we eat?" The question hung in the air, hovering somewhere between the platter of now-cold roast beef and the scalloped potatoes.

"Go ahead, Henri."

"You haven't shared grace lately. That's always been your favorite part of our meals." Papa stroked his chin. "Your prayers are beau—"

"I told you to go ahead." Mama folded her hands and bowed her head.

Not really listening to the blessing, I tried to remember the last time Mama had shared grace and wondered if she were mad at God. Perhaps she didn't want to talk to Him anymore. My stomach fluttered the way it did when Jack dared me to climb into a trunk in the attic during a game of hide-and-seek. When he shut the lid, it was perfectly dark. I thought I might die in that silent and lonely place, so I whispered to Jesus. Now I wondered what would happen to Mama if she stopped talking to God altogether.

After our food was blessed, Mama meticulously carved my roast into small, then even smaller pieces. Her eyes glazed over with tears, but she was quick to blink them away before they could roll onto her cheeks. Her skin was so beautiful—the color of the pink rose that bloomed earliest in our garden.

Breaking the silence, Papa lifted his crystal glass to propose a toast, hesitated, then set it down. Whenever he was about to share a story, his head would tilt slightly, then he'd squint an eye and pause, probably going somewhere back in time.

"You know, I was about your age, Charles—yes, I was nine years old, when I ran around that small hill town. My parents—your grandfather and grandmother—grew a beautiful vineyard. They produced one of the finest wines in the Petit Luberon area, and they taught me to spot the perfect color of grapes that were ready for picking. I knew harvest time had come when the vineyards were speckled with deep purple. I'd follow my father up and down the long rows. Whatever he did, I did also. It was like a game of *Simon Says,* except without talking."

"Oh, I love to play *Simon Says,*" I said excitedly. "Let's play it now."

Placing his forefinger to his lips, Papa shushed me and smiled. "My father was very quiet when he checked the vines. He needed all his senses on the job. First, he'd lean into a fat cluster of grapes and gently cup it in his big, strong hands, careful not to pull it from its vine. He'd squint his left eye like he was looking through a captain's telescope, and study the purple balls lying in his palm." Papa squeezed his left eye shut as his opposite brow rose. He lifted an invisible cluster of grapes from his plate. "Standing next to him, I'd gather my own cluster close to my left eye and gently roll the grapes back and forth. We'd watch the sunlight brush over the grapes as they changed from purple to red. It was magic."

"Pink too?" I asked.

Jack sneered at me from across the table. "Not pink. Grapes aren't pink."

"Next, your grandfather would bend over and place his nose right in the middle of the cluster. He'd shut his eyes and take in a bear-sized breath through his nose. If the grapes were ready, a big grin spread across his face."

"What would he do if the grapes weren't ready?" Charles' blue eyes fixed on Papa.

As if temporarily knocked from a dream, Papa glanced at Charles. "Then he'd carefully put the cluster back in the vine like he was tucking it in for a nap. I'd follow him back to the house and he wouldn't say a word. I knew he was waiting on the grapes with a special kind of patience you have only when you trust. The next day we'd be back in the vineyard repeating the same steps until the grapes were ready for us."

"What did he do when the grapes were ready?" Jack grinned, revealing the most recent space from a lost tooth.

"If he was happy with the grapes, the best part was about to happen." Papa folded his arms on the table. My brothers and I leaned closer to hear his secret.

Papa whispered, "If Father was pleased with the grapes, he'd choose the fattest one, pluck it, and pop it into his mouth." Delicately, Papa plucked the fattest grape from his imaginary cluster, rolled it between his fingers, then popped it into his mouth.

I watched him savor the sweet juice, licked my lips, and tasted the same sweetness that was waiting for us on the other side of the ocean in a sleepy town in the south of France.

"The hard work came when we'd pick the grapes and carry the heavy baskets into the cellar. My father taught me how to turn the fat, purple grapes into a bottled treasure." Papa tilted his head to the other side. He seemed to look back in time with a sadness I hadn't seen before. "Then he began to lose his strength."

"Well, it was a good thing your mother had the sense to insist they leave the farm and move to America. That stubborn land would have put him in the grave before his time." Mama started to push herself away from the table, but stopped. "She wasn't a dreamer like your father."

I looked at Papa, then followed his serious eyes across the table as they met hers glaring back at him.

My father circled his forefinger around the opening of his glass, apparently continuing his thoughts as if he had one foot in America— the other already back in France. "I told my mother I could take over— that I was almost a man. I can still hear her voice. It was soft and sad. *'Mon fils, au fond de ton coeur tu es deja un homme. C'est un probleme. Je veux que tu restes un enfant pour le moment. Et surtout, c'est aussi la volonte de Dieu. Seul un coeur d'enfant peut faire l'experience de Ses merveilles. Malheureusement, l'enfance ne dure pas.'"*

"Papa, that sounds beautiful." I looked at my mother, hoping to see a wide smile spread across her perfect face. "Doesn't it sound wonderful, Mama?"

She ignored me, gathered the linen napkin from her lap, folded it lengthwise, and laid it alongside her plate of untouched food. I followed her stare across the expansive table and beyond Papa, who sat at the far end. Behind him, an ornately-carved, cherry mantel hovered over the fireplace. Glowing embers ebbed and flowed beneath the remains of charred logs as an occasional flame shot up in defiance of the dwindling fire.

Mama's eyes rested on a large, white-faced clock atop the mantel—a family heirloom—by which she typically scheduled her day. But tonight, the only sound was the clock's incessant ticking, a painful reminder of the cold silence of the evening.

"Mama?" Either she pretended not to hear or her thoughts had taken her too far away to recognize my plea.

Charles stopped wiggling and focused on the man sitting quietly at the end of the table. "What does that mean? What you spoke in French?"

Papa placed his large hand over Charles' forearm and stroked his smooth skin. "I have never forgotten what my mother spoke. She said, 'My son, you're a man at heart. That's the problem. I want you to be a child for now. More importantly, so does God. When you have the heart of a child, you can truly experience His wonders. Sadly, childhood doesn't last for long.'"

Jack was silent. He frowned and clanged his fork against the gold-rimmed, china plate. Papa gave a stern look to my younger brother. "And a seven-year-old boy should be able to find plenty of adventures in Roussillon, just like I did."

Charles' eyes filled with tears. "But we'll never see our friends again. No one will know us there. They'll think we're odd." He blinked and pushed the cut pieces of roast back and forth with the tip of his ivory-handled knife. "I can't speak French. The kids will laugh at me."

Jack clanged his fork even louder.

Papa pushed his chair away from the table and stood. He threw his napkin onto the table. "Do you see what I mean now, Marie? I should have been speaking French to the children since the day they were born. You insisted on them being completely American. Now look where that's gotten us. They have a French father, and they can't speak the most beautiful language in the world." He ran his fingers through his dark, neatly-trimmed hair.

"The children have been better because of it. They are Americans." Mama fixed determined eyes on her husband.

"Even though they were born in America, you mustn't forget I was born in France. You, my children, are part of me." Papa surveyed the perimeters of the dining table.

"Henri, this isn't just about you. They were born *here*, not on the other side of the Atlantic. You may be French, but at least your parents, God rest their souls, had the good sense to come to America for the chance of a better life."

"Marie, I'm well aware of my birthplace and ancestry. Besides, I don't need to be reminded of my parents' mistake to leave France."

"Then we would have never met."

"How true." Papa's tone softened. "And we wouldn't have our lovely family."

"Of course. But in case you have forgotten, I'm one-hundred percent

American, born and raised in this great city." Mama crossed her arms, straightened her back, and narrowed her eyes until her perfectly shaped brows nearly touched above her petite nose.

Papa stiffened and shoved his chair into the table. Utensils rattled on the plates and water spilled from the crystal glasses, making small puddles on the dark wood. "How could I forget?" Papa's voice mocked Mama, and a terrible knot rose in my stomach. "You remind me every day of your proud nationality and how awful I am to take my family away from this enormous, over-crowded, unsafe, and bleak pit called New York City."

Papa paced in front of the dying fire, his large hands shoved into his pockets while his pronounced steps drowned out the ticking clock. "No, Marie, what you fail to remember is that I love my family and am desperately trying to provide us a peaceful, safe, and beautiful place to live that has a promising future for all of us."

"For you, Henri. Only for you." I caught Mama obviously trying to contain a smirk as she gracefully sipped from her wine glass. She seemed to enjoy watching Papa become angry and agitated, and then I remembered how she spoke disrespectfully to the Lord.

Our food grew even colder, like the damp, gray air that hangs in the city before new grass appears in the park. An uneasy silence hovered in the room. Even Jack stopped clanging his fork. The last ember smoldered, flickered its last life, and a chilling draft crawled up my spine.

Finally, grabbing hold of the top rung of his chair, Papa's protruding knuckles whitened. "So to this ruined meal and to my children, I say, *bonsoir*. But to you, Marie, I say good evening." He headed toward the front door and snatched his coat and hat from the rack in the entryway. Securing his coat to ward off the spring chill, he reached for the doorknob.

I slid from my chair and scurried after him, reaching for the cuff of his free arm. "Papa, I want to go with you."

"Not tonight, Ella. I'm going to the office to finish some work. Stay home with the others and get ready for bed." He grabbed the knob and tugged open the large door. The leaded glass adorning the door reflected the glowing streetlights.

"No. I mean I want to go to France with you."

He closed the door and rested his forehead against the glass. With the slightest movement, I tugged his coattail. A sound rumbled in his throat and I wasn't sure if he chuckled or suppressed a cry. I tugged harder, and this time he turned around and looked down at me.

Standing toe to toe with my father, I tipped my head back, my long hair brushing against my waist. He was massive to my littleness, but when he smiled, I knew he was my friendly giant.

I called up to him. "I want to go with you to the most beautiful place in the world."

As though descending from the top of a great mountain, Papa knelt and looked into my eyes. His own eyes softened as he blinked away a tear. "Then I'll take you there. I promise it is as beautiful as you. God knew what he was doing when he made Ella Moreau and Roussillon."

Perhaps Papa's French blood pulsating in me had overpowered Mama's love affair with Americanisms. So, at the age of five, I dreamed of the place Papa wove into wonderful stories.

I imagined myself walking through shoulder-high fields of intense, fire-orange poppies, moving slowly, unscratched from their twisted, prickly stems. Their tissue-soft petals would flutter like millions of crimson butterflies around my face as they were about to take flight. The force of so many beating wings lifted me high above the fields. An enormous satin lake would appear to move below, fluctuating its hues between ginger orange and blood red. The waves would ripple as I was carried by the wind to some faraway place. A place named after a magical mixture of ochre, vermillion, and red rock—Roussillon.

Four

Arriving—Roussillon, 1929

I didn't lose my sea legs until we left the port city of Le Havre, made a brief stop in Paris, and concluded the train ride to the Luberon region in the south of France and to the east of the La Durance River. When the train arrived in Roussillon, I made my way to the open door and stepped into our new world.

"Ella, you could have grabbed your own luggage. It's still sitting on the seat." Jack lumbered off the steps, followed by his case thumping the concrete with each stride. "Gosh, all you've carried is that dumb porcelain doll."

"She's not dumb, Jacque. You don't even know her." I clutched my doll to my chest.

"My name's *Jack!* Don't ever call me anything else." He spat, barely missing my shoe.

"Papa said your name is Jacque now that we live in France, and if you spit again, I'm going to tell on you." I took a big step backward in case his aim improved.

"We don't live here yet. We're still travelers until we move in that million-year-old house." My brother made an awful noise in his throat, and I jumped behind his suitcase. "Maybe that old farmhouse has already crumbled and fallen apart. When we get there, all there will be is a big pile of rocks. We'll have to dig a hole in the pile and live like animals in a cave."

"Papa would never make us live like that." I smoothed my doll's pink, satin dress and held her tighter.

"Well, you'd better get your clothes before the train leaves or else you'll have to wear the same underpants for the rest of your life." Jack tipped his leather case on its side and plopped down, elbows on knees, chin in hands, and assumed the same grumpy expression he'd worn most of the journey.

Charles and Papa finished lowering the last pieces of luggage onto the platform. Papa handed me my small case and winked. Large crates holding Mama's vanity, an ornately-carved bookcase, a portion of Papa's select library, and a few other larger household items were being unloaded from the freight car at the end of the platform. The missing item was Mama's piano. It was too difficult and expensive to move. Papa promised to take Mama to the city as soon as his new job as assistant architect on the boardwalk in the port city of Marseilles was underway. There, she would be able to choose a beautiful piano and have it delivered to Roussillon.

She watched the silhouette of men lifting the crates and balancing heavy loads on dollies as if waiting for an old friend to disembark. But as the steel doors closed and latched, Mama wiped away tears with a lace handkerchief.

Shortly before we left our tall, brick home in New York City, and after the few boxes and other items that would travel to our new home in France had been delivered to the train station, Mama sat at her piano. She walked her slender fingers along the white keys, stepping up to the somber black notes, up and down again until she reached the end. Then she played a song I had never heard. It was a sad song … a final, broken-hearted good-bye. She didn't seem to notice I was in the room. If she did, it didn't matter. She was surely thousands of miles away in a place reserved only for her dreams.

Even though we had traveled for weeks across the ocean and days by train, Papa seemed to have a renewed energy in his gait as he effortlessly lifted the largest piece of luggage from the platform and marched toward me.

"We're here. I can hardly believe it." Papa's outstretched arms seemed to hug his beloved homeland. He glanced around the cavernous depot, bordered by a brick wall on one side and coal-stained grasses and rocks along the length of the track. "Isn't it beautiful?"

"It's ugly." Jack stood and kicked the side of his trunk.

"It's fine. I'm sure we're not going to live at the train station." Charles gave his younger brother a warning look and stepped forward. "Are you ready to go, Papa?"

"Yes, I'm ready to escort my beautiful wife." He held out his hand to Mama. She hesitated, then placed her slender hand in his outstretched palm.

I had hoped Papa's gesture and Mama's response was a peace offering. They didn't speak much to each other over the course of our travel, only words of necessity, not words of love. Whenever Papa talked about his boyhood home, Mama would quietly leave. Sometimes I'd find her on the ship's main deck leaning against the back railing, looking west— toward America.

Reflecting back, I remembered what I wanted to tell Mama on the ship and why her silence was so painful. I wanted to tell her what happened early one evening when I was on the upper deck feeling the cool breeze comb my hair with its gentle fingers. I wanted her to know I, too, was looking toward the west—but I saw something much different than she did.

The remnants of the day's last clouds were painted across the sky, and the sun hovered above what appeared to be the edge of the earth, exhausted at the end of the day. An intense mixture of purple and red faded to hues of pink and orange. The sun gradually settled itself on the horizon like a gigantic burning ball. It descended ever so slowly, sinking into the deep water without a sound. Then, just as the final, fire-orange sliver rested on the water's edge, an electric green light burst along the horizon, and as quickly as it had happened, the sky turned black.

"Amazing, wasn't it?"

I gasped and spun around. A dim silhouette of a man who was as wide as he was tall stood in front of me. His silver hair danced above a dark face.

"The Green Flash. It was better than I had ever imagined possible." The man stepped to my side, leaned his heavy chest against the railing, and peered into the night hovering above the water. "It's said only a few people are lucky enough to witness it in their lifetime. The great author Jules Verne claimed it to be an old Scottish legend that, 'If one were to peer into the light of the Green Flash, they would gain the power to read the very souls of other people they met.' You saw it, child, didn't you?"

"Yes sir."

"Ah, a polite little girl. Polite and special."

"Special?"

"Of course. I've been waiting my entire life to see the Green Flash.

But you've seen it as a child. You've received the gift early. Yes indeed, the best present ever."

"I like presents."

The moonlight shone on the side of the man's face. His skin hung loosely like the elephants I'd seen at the Central Park Zoo. He smiled at me. "I like them also." Looking into the speckled darkness, the man whispered to the stars. "Thank you."

I was silent, wondering if the stars would answer him. Wondering whom he thanked. A chill ran through my body and my teeth chattered. I pulled my coat tightly around my shoulders. My parents would be looking for me.

"Good night, sir." I moved away from the railing.

His voice called after me. "Do you know who gave us this wondrous gift?"

I hesitated, wanting to hear the answer, but knowing I would get in trouble for not staying with my brothers. I began to run.

"Do you know, special little girl?" His voice carried on the night breeze and seemed to rest on my shoulder, whispering in my ear.

I stopped and turned to look at the dark outline of the stranger, his wild, silver hair still blowing in the breeze. "Sir, I think so."

"Do you?" He walked toward me, rocking from side to side, each step an obvious effort.

My heart raced. There was no hint of daylight, and the deck was empty of the usual crowds of passengers. My instincts told me to run back to our cabin and say I got confused, went down the wrong hallway. But I couldn't stop staring at the old man as his face emerged from the darkness. His labored breathing hinted of tobacco mixed with the salty ocean air.

"I must know if we saw the same thing. I need hope at my age. Tell me, little one, tell me what you saw."

"God gave us the Green Flash, sir. I feel it in my heart."

His eyes glossed and he blinked several times. Taking a handkerchief from his pant pocket, he dabbed the corners of his eyes and sniffed. "You are not only polite and special, but you are wise, very wise for such a small girl."

"Ella!" A shrill voice pierced the air.

"I have to go." I turned and ran in the direction of the voice. The sound of high heels thumped toward me on the planks.

"There you are. We've been looking all over this ship for you."

Grabbing my shoulders and lifting my chin, Mama peered into my eyes. "Where have you been, young lady?"

"I've been right here, looking at the stars." I pointed upward. "Aren't they wonderful?"

"Stars? Ella, that's the last thing I would have been looking at. You had us all worried. You were supposed to be with your brothers." Mama took a firm hold of my hand and, with a jerk, pulled me alongside. "You'll stay close to me from now on," she muttered as I tried to keep up with her hurried pace. "Stars. Staring at the stars. What am I going to do with this child?"

"Mama, I saw something beautiful. That man saw it too." I was breathing hard.

"What man?" She glanced at me, still keeping her pace.

"That man right there." With my free hand, I pointed over my shoulder.

Mama halted and I bumped into her hip. She spun us around. "I don't see anyone."

I squinted and tried to find his odd shape and messy hair silhouetted by the moon. "He was right there. We were talking about how beautiful it was. He asked me who gave it to us."

"You're not making any sense. No man is standing there." She squeezed my hand harder. "You are going straight to bed."

With a final tug, Mama turned and led us across the upper deck.

Five

Life without Mama, 1931

It had been two years since the Green Flash. And even though the happiness and life in Mama seemed to dim each season since we had arrived in Roussillon, the mysterious light never lost its brilliance in my mind. So, as soon as fear surged in me and I wanted to cry out for my mother, I would retreat into my memory and fix my eyes on the Flash.

The first days without her left me motionless. I sat in the open doorway and leaned against the rough, wooden frame. The peeling, green paint scratched at my bare shoulders. I looked beyond the front steps, imagining Mama rounding the last corner of the curvy road leading from the market and walking up our drive. Inside our kitchen was what remained of my family. We hadn't lit a fire since late winter, and the stale smell of cedar ash still lingered from the pit. My brothers were lying on the worn rug in front of the cold fireplace side by side on their backs with hands tucked behind their heads. I followed their gaze to the yellowed water stain that crept across the ceiling like a spider and wondered if they would ever wrestle and laugh again.

Papa sat at the kitchen table with his face in his hands, elbows bracing the weight of his head. The only movement was the heaving of his chest. The saddest sobs would come from the deepest parts of his gut. After a few minutes, the sounds would stop and he'd sit frozen, except for an occasional tear that ran down his tanned face and dripped onto the worn pages of his Bible. Could a person actually die from a broken heart? I wanted to wrap my arms around him and squeeze hard, just like he had held me in the middle of the road a few days ago. I wanted to tell him we'd be fine, but I had never been a good liar.

A truck plodded down the dirt road that stretched the length of our vineyards. The chalky dust stirred up by the tires gathered into a ghost-like plume, then settled back to the earth as if never disturbed. Even the air didn't move. It hung its August heat over all of us, weighing us down like a suffocating blanket.

I don't know how long we would have stayed in our spots. Perhaps we would have shriveled up and died there—eventually found by some unfortunate visitor who would tell the neighbors we had died of broken hearts. But Papa, after a particularly long period of silence, finally stretched his arms in the air, rotated his head from side to side, and took in a deep breath. He stood, straightened his back, and surveyed the room with sleepy eyes as if coming out of a long, winter's slumber.

"Children, we're going to the pond. It's time for a swim."

He seemed very matter-of-fact, especially in light of our recent family tragedy. Without a word, the rest of us methodically stood from our static positions. We followed our father down the drive, onto the path that led through the thick grove of twisted olive trees, and across the tall field scattered with abandoned grapevines. The last of summer's deep, purple grapes bent the vines unmercifully toward the ground. Golden grasses tickled beneath my chin as a gentle breeze played them back and forth. I tucked loose strands of hair behind my ears. Determined not to lose sight of Papa's rhythmic march, I followed closely behind … my own Pied Piper.

At the top of the hill, we looked down and focused on the small pond we walked to nearly every summer day. But today it presented itself differently. Ripples weaved across the surface of the water, beckoning us to come closer. The surrounding oak trees fluttered their leaves, applauding our arrival to the beloved swimming hole. Papa was the first to cast off his trousers and dive into the cool water. I had seen him plunge in a hundred times in his briefs, but panic surged in my stomach until I saw his slicked-back hair emerge and break the surface.

"Ah, it's wonderful, children. Come in and join me."

"Me first." Charles tugged off his own trousers and splashed in alongside Papa.

"Well, aren't you getting in?" Jack gave me a sneer.

"Of course I'm getting in. I have to take my clothes off first. Go ahead." I tried to sneer back, but he was much better at giving nasty looks.

"Just peel them off and jump in." He grabbed my shirt and tried to pull it over my head.

"Leave me alone! I'll get in when I'm ready." I pulled my shirt back down and with my best attempt at strong-arming him, shoved Jack toward the pond. He lost his balance and slid down the slippery, moss-covered side of the pond, plunging backwards into the water.

"Your little sister isn't so little any longer. You'd better start being nicer to her." Papa swam toward Jack who was spitting out a mouthful of pond water and wiping a streak of mud from his forehead. Strong arms grabbed him from behind, lifted his slight body from the water, and spun him around, making a spray of water with his outstretched feet.

Charles joined them in the shallow water of the pond. The threesome looked up at me as I stood in the grass above the water's edge. They winked at one another. Then in a flash of unified movement, they splashed relentlessly until I was soaked from head to bare feet. When I didn't respond, they stopped and we stared at one another. No one moved or said a thing. Water dripped down our faces—but it wasn't mixed with tears this time. It was here, in that still moment, where we would find refreshment and begin to define our new life without Mama.

Six

Marie Moreau—Paris Train Station, 1931

Leaving had to happen quickly. I didn't want to lie, but how else could it be done? I insisted Charles and Jack take Ella to the swimming hole while I went to the market. They would come home sunburned, tired, and hungry. That would help them fall asleep easier the first night.

That was my plan, but now the image of dear Ella, desperately chasing after me in the rearview mirror, will haunt me for the rest of my life. My foot lifted off the accelerator to slam on the brake. But then, with tears swelling in my eyes, I realized I was crying more for myself than her. The only choice was to speed away. My family would be better off without me.

A small amount of money and my American citizenship papers were stuffed in the bottom of my bag. I took only what was needed to ride the train into Paris, then on to Le Havre. From there, I would get a ticket to cross the Atlantic by ship. To make the passage faster, I'd dream of returning to my beloved New York harbor. By morning, Henri would probably find the car parked at the train station. He could ask the cashier which train I had taken. Then, he would finally believe it was necessary for me to go to ever be happy again.

Before leaving the house, I caught my reflection in the dresser mirror. With determination, I completed my final act. Rummaging in my bag, I pulled out my boldest, red lipstick and slid it across my lips. It empowered me to see someone different in the mirror.

I looked at the frame sitting on the dresser and ran my fingers across the tanned and smiling faces of my children. The photo was taken last summer after Henri came home with the mare. The children cheered, then threw their arms around their father's waist and squeezed him until he begged for mercy. Henri was the children's hero. They were so happy, so innocent.

My hand traveled to another picture—Henri and me. We stood in front of the house, our new home. Henri was handsome as he flashed his smile, held a bottle of wine high above his head, and presented a bouquet of sunflowers to me—my favorite. But it was obvious. My forced, strained smile was a reflection of the unhappiness that had begun to taint everything in my life.

* * * * *

It's miserable in this station. The air doesn't move, and it seems I'll wait eternally for a train that may never come. When can I get out of this city? Paris. What is the attraction of this place? This country? The Roussillon sun was so hot it seemed to burn a hole in my soul. No god would have made that place. The wind whipped and pulled my hair. It stung my eyes and deafened my ears. It robbed me of my singing voice—the beautiful voice that defined me—the voice that was for others to envy and bring me fame.

If I pull the brim lower over my face, I can fade into the dismal backdrop of this rat-hole. Are these people looking at me? No, they're staring into some forgotten dream they can't reach. They're stuck here just like me—wanting to go away, anywhere but here.

I'm not like these pathetic people. I have a place to go. A home—a place that knows and belongs to me. America. New York City. I never should have left. How foolish to think I could go thousands of miles away from home to follow my husband's dream. How could Henri and the children expect me to be happy when France wasn't a part of my dream? They don't know who I am. They don't understand what it means to be a daughter of a successful New Yorker—the only child of Franklin Thomas Evans and Anna Elizabeth Evans. My father had such plans for my life with his connections in New York. He was the only one who ever truly believed in and shared my dream that I would become a famous musician. No one knows what I gave up along the way—the opportunities that slipped away.

There's no shame in my decision. Let these comatose people watch me strut the platform as I hypnotize them with my beautiful black hair swaying to the rhythm of my heels clicking on the cement. They don't know they're witnessing the return of the real Marie Moreau.

Finally, lights burn through the haze. The massive engine vibrates the soles of my feet. I shake with growing excitement.

These people are so rude. Can't they stare at someone else? I'm not the only person who's ever had to make a tough decision. They've surely hurt a few people along the way.

Nothing deters their looks—their judgments. They keep staring at me. I feel it through my skin. They know what I've done. Is it that obvious? Does my face reveal so blatantly the worse thing a mother could ever do—leave her family?

Seven

Fever, 1931

It came on quickly. My body burned as winter's frost robbed the landscape of its life.

"Get me another damp cloth and then stay away from her." Papa motioned Charles away.

"But, Papa, I want to help," Charles said.

"I don't need everyone sick. Stay with Jack and keep him busy."

"But—"

"Do what you're told." Papa's voice made me jump. He didn't sound himself today.

"Yes sir." Charles' voice cracked.

"I'm sorry, Charles. You're only trying to help. We just need the doctor to get here."

"I'll watch for him."

I gazed at my brother in the doorway. He smiled at me then disappeared into the kitchen.

Papa pushed damp strands of hair off my forehead, but my head pounded at the slightest touch. "You'll feel better soon, *mon ange*." He kissed my cheek. "God takes care of his angels."

"I feel …" The words caught in my throat and my eyes filled with tears. "I feel awful."

"I know." Papa stroked my hand. "But you're a tough little girl. Remember those tears chase the fever and hurt away."

"Mama used to say that." I looked at Papa and wished Mama were sitting next to him.

"Yes she did, child."

"I'm forgetting what Mama looks like."

"Oh, Ella …"

"I know she looks like the photo in my bedroom, but I can't see her in my head. Can you see her when you need her?"

Papa leaned back in the chair. He looked older and had the same sad expression that had settled in the day Mama left. "Yes, I pretend she's here. I listen for her voice in the kitchen and out in the yard. Sometimes I imagine she's walking up the drive. At night, I look for her face before turning out the lights."

"Papa, don't worry. I'm not going away."

He stroked my cheek. "That's right, you're not going anywhere."

Charles appeared at the foot of the bed. "Dr. Levin's here."

The familiar round-faced doctor approached my bedside and dabbed his pink nose with a worn handkerchief. "Hello, Henri. It's really cold out there. Roads are getting icy. Got here as soon as I could." Dr. Levin patted Papa on the shoulder, then placed his palm on my forehead. "Ah, our sleeping princess is awake."

The doctor had come to our home in September after Jack upset a hornets' nest. Later that night, he cried for Mama. Now I knew how he felt. I wanted Mama next to me, holding my hand, giving me butterfly kisses with her long eyelashes, and telling me things would be better soon. But Mama wouldn't come. She was somewhere far away and couldn't hear my silent cries.

After Doctor Levin checked my raw throat, listened to my heart, and confirmed a high temperature, he gently pushed aside the blanket. The air sent a chill throughout my body.

"Henri, do you see her knees and ankles? They're hot and swollen."

Papa stepped next to the doctor and stroked my arm. "Her wrist is swollen too."

"Ella, besides your throat, does anything else hurt?" The doctor narrowed his eyes.

"It hurts all over. Hurts to move." I slowly raised my hand to my chest and a lump formed in my throat. "It hurts really bad here." I didn't want to cry, but couldn't help it.

"Shhh, it's all right." Papa laid a towel across my forehead and I began to sob.

"Papa, what's wrong with her?" Charles sat at the foot of my bed.

"Charles, I need you to stay away." Papa's voice was stern.

"But I need to be with her."

"Your sister needs sleep. Let's all let her rest." The doctor pulled the blanket up to my chin, zipped his black bag, and gave me a wink. "Be a good princess, little Ella, and have sweet dreams. I'll be back to see you tomorrow."

Outside my door, as the men spoke in hushed tones, I closed my eyes and drifted away into a fevered dream. Alone in a small boat in the middle of an endless ocean, the waves were furious as they tossed the boat. I huddled on the rough, wooden floorboards clinging to a rope dangling from the side. My tiny body ached as it slid back and forth across the boards, deep splinters gathering in my bare legs. Cold seawater spilled into the boat, yet it stung as though I were submerged in boiling water. I pulled myself from the floor and peered across the unsettled water. In the distance, a large ship was approaching. I was excited that I would soon be rescued. But as the ship neared, it turned abruptly. Standing at the port side railing was a woman. She wore a flowing yellow dress, and her long dark hair circled around her face in the wind.

"Help me!" I cried out, frantically waving my bruised arms in the air. But the ship passed by. With one giant gust of wind, the woman's hair lifted away from her face.

It was my mother.

"Mama!" I shouted. The ship glided past me as though cutting through soft cream. "Come back ..." The brutal salt water attacking my face choked out my words.

Suddenly, the ship appeared much closer to me, close enough to reach out and touch its side. My hands lifted toward Mama, wanting her to gather me into her arms. Reaching higher, I could nearly touch the hem of her dress. Her lavender perfume was carried by the wind.

"Mama, save me."

She leaned over the railing and looked directly into my eyes. She called out to me, but I couldn't hear her voice above the crashing waves. Then she simply raised her white-gloved hand and waved as the ship floated away, farther and farther, until it vanished.

I stared into the last glimmer of sunlight as it met the black sea. My boat continued to struggle against the waves, trying to toss me into the darkness. I finally surrendered and fell to my knees, hanging on to the side of the boat. As I peered across the heaving ocean, an intense green light suddenly flashed across the horizon. As soon as it occurred, it disappeared and everything was black. It was surely the same streak of light I had seen on my journey across the Atlantic. Now, the boat was still and my hair hung limp on my damp face. A peace washed over me, and I was no longer afraid.

"Papa, she's finally waking up. Come quick."

I forced my eyes open and saw Charles at my side.

Papa placed his hand on my forehead. "The fever's down." He stroked my wrist and lifted the edge of the blanket. "She's not as swollen either. Her knees look better. Ella, how are you feeling? You've been asleep all day." He tucked the blanket around me.

"Bet ..." I tried to force out the words but my throat was dry. Papa sat on my bed and rested me against his chest. He lifted a cup of water to my lips. I sipped and allowed the cool water to slip down my throat. "Papa, I saw ..." My voice cracked and he gave me another drink.

"What did you see?" Charles leaned closer.

"I saw the Green Flash."

"The what?" Charles glanced at Papa.

"The Green Flash ... on the ocean. I was going to fall into the water, and Mama wouldn't come back for me. She went away on a big ship and left me in the dark."

"You were having a dream." Papa held me tightly. "It's all right now."

"No, Papa. It was real. The waves kept knocking me over. It was scary. See, feel my hair." I touched the damp hair alongside my face.

"Honey, your fever is breaking." Gentle fingers brushed the hair away from my face.

"What else happened?" Charles' eyes widened.

"Charles, please. Let's not—"

"After the light, the waves stopped. I wasn't scared anymore."

"Did you see Mama?" Charles moved to the edge of my bed. "Did she come back?"

"No. But she was beautiful. She was wearing a yellow dress."

Papa stood and walked to the window. He was silent for a few moments as he gazed out the glass, and I wondered if I had made him sad. But he turned toward us and smiled. "Marie was always pretty in yellow."

"She tried to talk to me but it was too loud."

Papa plopped on the bed and gathered Charles and me in his safe arms. "Maybe she was trying to say she still loves you."

Eight

Andre, 1935

We were doing our usual chores—feeding the horse, filling the water trough, and throwing feed to the chickens when he appeared at the end of the drive.

"Looking for someone?" Papa stepped from the open barn door and approached the dark-haired boy.

"Sir, I'm looking for work."

"What kind of work, son?"

My brothers and I ran to stand next to Papa.

"Anything, sir, but I know how to tend vineyards." The boy straightened his thin body.

"Well, you can see I've got my own workers here, but we could use some extra help with the harvest." Papa extended his hand and the boy eagerly accepted. But unlike a regular handshake, he took the boy's hand, turned it palm-side up, and ran his thumb over the calluses too defined for a boy. "It's hard work but I see you're use to it."

"Yes sir. I'm a hard worker, just like my father."

Papa surveyed the boy. He wore a dirty undershirt, outgrown tan trousers, and leather sandals that had walked too many miles.

"Where have you come from, son?"

"Italy, sir. My home is, uh … was … the grape-growing region west of Florence. I've worked with grapes all my life."

"And where is your home now?"

"Wherever I can find work."

"You seem young to be traveling around by yourself."

"I'm fourteen, sir. Almost a man."

"Me too. Well almost." Jack stepped forward and offered his hand. "I'm Jack and this is my brother, Charles."

"Hi. And who's this?" The boy nodded at me. Although his face was dirt-stained, he had the most beautiful green eyes and smooth, tan skin.

"I'm Ella. I'm eleven." I shrunk behind Papa.

"I'll work for food and a place to sleep. A barn's fine if that's what you can offer."

"What's your name?"

"Andre."

"You've got a surname?"

"Donato, sir."

Papa stepped toward Andre and placed a large hand on his shoulder. Leaning down, he looked directly into the boy's bright green eyes, surrounded by a tangle of hair the rich color of vineyard soil. Papa studied the young face the same way he reads the pages of a favorite book.

Finally, Papa turned and walked toward the house. After a few steps, he stopped. "You know a man named Joseph?"

The boy's hands were curled into white-knuckled fists pressed tightly against the sides of his thin thighs.

Papa turned and pointed his long finger toward Andre. "You look just like him."

Andre pushed away a tear with the back of a clenched fist.

"I knew your father. Heard what happened to him. This place isn't Mussolini's territory—it's mine."

Andre cleared his throat. "Thank you, sir."

"You won't sleep in the barn. Come with me."

The boy followed Papa's great strides to the front porch. The rest of us trotted behind, taking in the arrival of the stranger from Italy.

Nine

Growing Up, 1937

The grapes had been harvested months ago. Metamorphosed into rich wine that now waited in dusty bottles in the cool cellar, they would remain in darkness until the appointed time for their debut.

Andre remained at our home through the passing seasons. He became like family instead of the lanky stranger who had appeared at the end of our road almost two years ago. He and Papa often walked the vineyards until the last light of day, talking, nodding, sometimes laughing, and a few times even weeping. Andre became my extra brother. The three boys spent long days at the swimming hole, jumping from the highest branches, then dunking and splashing each other until Jack got angry and stomped home.

Almost thirteen now, I didn't go to the swimming hole as often. My desire was to spend as much time as possible with my paints and brushes. Often, in private moments of painting, I'd notice Andre watching me from the vineyards or sitting quietly nearby. I pretended not to see him watching. However, I'd smooth the back of my hair and tuck the loose strands behind my ears, wondering if my old dress—that had shrunk above my knees—looked ridiculous and ill-fitting on my skinny body. But why should I care? Andre was basically a brother now. With those thoughts, a feeling of shame would wash over me, leaving my cheeks warm.

"It's amazing how your paintings make even winter vines come alive." Andre curled tighter in the wicker chair that remained on the front porch through every season.

"They look dead to me." Jack gave Andre a teasing punch to the arm. "They're all twisted and brown."

"I'm going to twist you." Andre grabbed my brother and wrestled him to the ground.

"Don't knock my table." I dipped my brush into the water bowl and flicked it at the boys as they laughed and rolled on the cold stones.

"Ah, Ella, you take your painting too seriously. Have a little fun." Jack threw another punch at Andre who quickly pinned him until Jack called a truce.

"Your paintings are amazing. I wish I could paint like that." Andre released my brother from the ground. "Maybe you *should* take it seriously. Do you want to be an artist?"

"I am an artist. I paint every day."

Jack plopped himself onto the chair. "You paint *all* day. You never do anything else. Papa lets you get away without doing any work around here."

"That's not true. I do help around here." I dipped my brush, determined to continue my painting. "And I don't paint *all* day."

"But how can you paint the same things over and over? Don't you get tired of all this?" Jack cocked his head toward the vineyards. "It looks the same, year after year. The same grapes grow and die. The same orange flowers cover the hill. Then they bend over and die. The same sun rises. The same sun sets. It never changes."

"Can't you see it? They're never the same. Just when I think I've painted the fields every way possible, the light catches them differently, and I'm sure I've never seen anything so beautiful in all my life."

"We know what's beautiful." Jack nodded at Andre. "You know the new girl in town I'm talking about."

"Sure, she's real good-looking, but you're talking about a different kind of beauty." Andre ran his finger along the faint pencil marks I had sketched on the paper.

"Well, that's the kind of beauty I like. But don't get any ideas, Andre. She's mine. I might go see her right now." Jack pounced from the porch and started down the drive.

Andre tossed a shriveled apple at him. "You don't even know her name."

"I will soon." My brother picked up the apple and threw it full speed. We ducked behind the table that unfortunately took the full hit. Rotten apple bits sprayed across my painting.

"Ella, I'm sorry for egging him on." Andre tried to wipe the stain from the paper.

"It's fine." I removed the paper from its clip and shook off the remaining bits. "Something can still be made of this."

"You need to find a better place to paint. It's dangerous out here with that crazy brother of yours. Plus, he has good aim." He smiled and winked, and I smiled back.

"Andre, can I ask you something?"

"Sure." He settled himself back into the chair. "What do you want to know?"

"Is she really beautiful?"

"Who?"

"The new girl." I clipped the paper back on the easel and randomly swirled colors from my palette.

"Yeah, she's really pretty. We saw her at school yesterday. Her family moved here from up north. We heard her mother talking to the teacher about how things are changing and getting bad, especially closer to the big cities."

I turned to face him. "What do you mean getting bad?"

"They say the Nazis are getting more power in Germany, and Hitler isn't going to stop there. People are getting nervous he may want France."

"He can't just decide he wants France. It's not his."

"Ella, anything can happen." A terrified look spread across his face—one I hadn't seen since the day he arrived and Papa had asked about his father.

I knelt in front of him and held his hand. "What happened to your father?"

After a long silence, Andre barely whispered. "They took them away."

"Who?" I squeezed his hand.

"Mussolini's thugs." A strained voice replaced his whisper. "They came to our villa in the night and took both of them."

"Them?"

"My father and grandfather." Andre's jaw tightened.

"Why would they do that?"

"Because they told people they didn't agree with him."

"With Mussolini?"

"They wouldn't join him. I wouldn't either."

"But you're only a boy."

"Old enough." Andre stood. "That's why they told me to run."

"What about your mother?"

"She died when I was five. My father and grandfather raised me."

"I'm sorry. It's hard not to have a mother." A familiar pain surged through me.

"Yes, Ella." He lifted my chin. "I see your sadness, except it's a strange thing."

"What's strange?"

"It's not there when you paint. You seem happy, kind of peaceful. It's like you're doing what you're supposed to do." Andre looked into my eyes as if trying to read my mind.

"I think painting is what I'm supposed to do. It seems right."

"For me it's working in the vineyard. It's not like painting or making anything beautiful like you do, but it feels right, like I'm supposed to be out there." Andre stood and surveyed the rows lining the front and southern sides of our property.

I joined him on the stone step. "But you are making it beautiful. You and Papa help it create itself over and over each year."

"You're right. But even without us, the vines would grow again each spring, and the grapes would be fat in the fall like the wild vines down by the creek."

"But they wouldn't make one of the best wines in the region without you."

"True. Ella, what is it about you?"

I frowned as he gazed at me intently. "What do you mean?"

"You're different."

"I know. My grumpy brother keeps reminding me of that." I closed my paint tin and cast bluish gray water from my bowl onto the dirt. It disappeared into the thirsty ground.

"No, in a good way. You notice things around you, beautiful things. Then you turn them into paintings. It's like you capture them."

"Capture what?"

"All the things God makes. You know, his creation."

"I have to." I lifted a paintbrush and smoothed the damp bristles between my fingers.

"What do you mean?"

"You'll think I'm strange."

"I won't. Tell me."

"Promise?"

He nodded and relaxed his shoulders as he waited.

"If I don't paint those things …"

"Go on. Will something happen?"

"Yes."

"What, Ella?"

I squeezed my eyes shut. "They'll disappear."

"What will disappear?" Andre stepped closer and I opened my eyes.

"Everything I love. I must keep painting or God will get mad and take things away."

"He wouldn't do that. God doesn't work that way."

"But he already has."

"Has what?" I felt the slight touch of Andre's fingers on my hands.

"Taken something away."

"What did he take, Ella?"

"He took away my mother." Andre slipped his fingers through mine as I confessed my fear. "I have to paint for him." I leaned closer. "I've never said this, not even to Papa. You've got to understand. I'm the one who's captured. Everything that's beautiful to me, everything I love, will go away if God is not pleased with me. Do you understand I can't risk that?" I folded my fingers around his and searched for the answer in his soft green eyes. "So maybe the only way to be right with him—you know, to keep bad things from happening—is to paint for him."

Andre stepped back and rubbed his chin. His face scrunched in deep thought. "Then you should keep doing it. Get as good as you can get. But do it to make yourself happy, and maybe God, but not everyone else." He jumped off the porch.

"How do you know so much?" I called to him as he jogged toward the road.

"I don't." He stopped and looked straight at me. "But I do know something else."

"What's that?"

"You're beautiful when you paint."

Andre ran full speed down the road until he rounded the curve past the cypress trees. I was glad he couldn't see my face. I knew it was bright red because my heart was racing wildly.

Ten

Discovered, 1939

"Papa? Boys? What's going on?" I set the bag, heavy with fresh bread, cheese, and fruit, on the kitchen table and made my way down the hallway toward the closed door. The pounding of a hammer and grinding saw vibrated the wooden floorboards.

"Wait!" Jack grabbed the back of my blouse and pulled me to a quick stop. "You can't go in there yet."

"In the storage room? Why not? Let go of me." I pushed his arm away, but he grabbed me around the waist and squeezed. "Stop it."

"You can't go in. I've been appointed as the guard." He squeezed me harder and laughed.

"Guard what?" I couldn't help but laugh myself. "My fifteenth birthday present?" I raised a curious eyebrow. "It must be something big."

"No, they're prisoners of war. You can't go in there. It's too gruesome for a girl."

"Silly, that's all you ever think about."

"What, girls?"

"No, you goof, war." I tried to wiggle free but he held fast.

"Well, that's the only thing in the news and on everyone's mind. Now stay put or I'll have to put you under house arrest." He pretended to cuff my hands.

"Someone save me from this horrible German," I called out.

"German." A vicious glare replaced his teasing smile. "How dare you call me a German."

"Sorry, I was only kidding." The look on his face scared me.

"It's not funny. I'll be leaving soon to go kill Germans." He dug his thumb into my hand. "We're all going. Charles, Andre, and my buddy Remy."

"You can't do that." I pulled my hands away.

"Wanna bet? As soon as I figure it out, we'll be gone. They're calling up men every day."

"But you're only boys."

"Ella, where have you been? Haven't you noticed we've all grown up? Oh, I know. You've had your head buried in those paints all these years." He leaned against the wall and showed a smug grin.

"That's cruel." I crossed my arms and glared back at him. "I have noticed you've grown up. You're right. You're nearly men, especially Charles. He's already eighteen."

"Well, I know you've noticed my buddy, Remy. I've seen the way you look at him and try to act cute when he's around."

"That's not true. He's been our neighbor forever. I can't help it that your friend likes to see my paintings." I started for the closed door but he grabbed my arm. "Let go."

"Listen to me."

"No, you listen to me. At least Remy encourages me to paint like Charles and Andre do. Not like you, who thinks it's a waste of time."

"Stay away from him, Ella. He has more important things to think about than a girl like you. I don't want you to drive him away too."

His words were like a shot in the stomach. "What did you say?"

He released my arm and mumbled, "I didn't say anything."

"Yes you did. What was that supposed to mean?" I gathered my courage and stepped closer. Standing tall, I was nearly eye-to-eye with him. "Who have I driven away?"

I asked, not sure I wanted to hear the answer.

"Let it go. It didn't mean anything." He turned and started down the hall.

"Do you think I'm stupid? I know what you meant."

He stopped with his back still toward me. "It's been eight years, Ella. Let it go." His shoulders slumped. "And don't follow me."

Jack walked toward the kitchen as I leaned against the wall and tried to push the answer from my mind.

The storage room door opened slightly and Andre peeked out. "Oh, you're home. How long have you been standing here?"

"Only a minute. What's going on in there?" I stepped toward the door.

"Not so fast. Hold on." He disappeared behind the closed door.

Even though my curiosity was piqued, I was about to return to the kitchen to begin lunch when the door opened again. Papa slid his body through the half-closed door, a wide smile spreading across his face.

"Close your eyes and take my hand." He reached his leathered hand toward mine.

"What can be such a secret in the storage room?"

"You'll see. Now shut your eyes or I'll have to blindfold you."

Papa led me into a silent room, and the scent of lavender filled my head. He took me a few steps further, then turned me slightly to the right. I felt the warmth of sunlight on my face as he whispered in my ear, "Okay. Now open your eyes."

"Oh, Papa." That's all I could say. In front of the open window loomed a tall wooden easel. Resting on its rim was a large, blank canvas. I ran my fingers across its stark vastness, my fingers following the ray of sunlight stretching itself toward the edges. I leaned over a table next to the easel and breathed the lavender sprigs overflowing a slender vase.

"There's more. Look around." Papa beamed as he talked.

I was either a bit light-headed from the intensity of the lavender or dreaming. A narrow, sage-green table ran the length of the far wall. An ivory linen cloth hung evenly off each side, displaying a delicate scallop along the edges. The soft glow from a milk-shade lamp warmed the newly painted pale-yellow walls. That glow was from the same lamp that had perched on Mama's dresser for as long as I could remember.

"I'll get you a new lamp the next time I'm in Marseilles. One that puts out better light for painting in the evening." Papa switched the light off.

"It's fine. Really, it's perfect." I stepped toward the lamp and turned the small, brass knob, then glanced up at three rows of shelves. One was filled with glass canning jars, some empty, while others held an array of paintbrushes, pencils, and palette knives. "New brushes?" I scanned the various lengths and shapes as they stood dutifully like soldiers ready for their first assignment. Touching their tips, my fingers traveled over round, flat, and fan-shaped bristles. Some were full and soft, others thin and stiff.

"I hope they're the right ones. Andre and I picked them out from Monsieur Caval's store catalog. It's amazing what you can order from that book." Papa removed the longest brush and tickled my chin with the coarse bristles. "He said these are for art, not painting barns."

So enthralled with the transformation of the storage room, I had forgotten Andre was present. With a swish of air and a white flash, he pulled a sheet from the far corner.

"Ta da! *Pour vous, mon amie.*"

"For me?" I gasped and covered my mouth as a giggle escaped. Stacked against the wall was an assortment of new canvases of every imaginable size. The largest measured evenly with Andre's height, down to petite frames that would fit in my palm.

"We bought the canvas on a big roll. Your brothers have been helping me make frames and stretch the canvas out in the barn for weeks. We thought you'd catch us for sure." Andre proudly flipped through the neatly organized canvases.

"It was a miracle to get the canvas," Jack said as he stepped into the room. "You know the war is heating up and things like that need to go to the war effort."

"Thank you for helping make the canvases." I tried to hug him but he shrugged.

"No problem. Andre needed the help."

Andre looked out the window. "The rest of the surprise should be here any time."

"There's more? I don't know what to say." I stood on my tiptoes and kissed Papa's cheek. "Why did you do all this?"

"He's here. Close your eyes again." Andre dashed down the hallway.

"Who's here?"

"Charles is back. He's not going to like that we let you in the room without him." Papa covered my eyes with his large hand.

I heard steps running down the hallway toward the room. "Hey, why'd you bring her in already?" Charles sounded out of breath.

"We couldn't keep her out. She threatened to kick down the door." Andre laughed.

"Not true, Charles. Now let me see what's going on."

"Give me a second." Paper rustled, metal clanged, and wood thumped as my anticipation grew.

Papa removed his hand, and I blinked a few times to regain my focus. A large, white enameled tray sat on the green table. In the tray were two neat lines of paint tubes side by side. One line was oil paints, the other watercolors, each with the labels facing upwards. I studied the writing and whispered their names.

"Look up on the top shelf, Ella." Charles tapped me on the shoulder, momentarily rocking me out of my song. "I hope it's not too high for you."

"She's pretty short. May need a step stool." Jack came alongside me.

"No, I can reach it." My hand stretched to the top shelf and touched the ragged edge of a stack of watercolor paper. I lifted the top sheet and felt its perfect texture. Holding it to the window, I read the watermark.

"Arches. Papa, we can't afford this. I've never had paper so beautiful."

He crossed his arms and nodded. "That's for me to worry about. The vineyard's been good to us this year. There's more on order. Chalk and oil pastels should arrive any day. Charles will go back to town and pick them up at Caval's."

"I've never tried those before, but have always wanted to." My eyes traveled around the room, taking it all in—the paint, brushes, pencils, stack of paper, canvases in the corner, and the easel. For a moment, I imagined myself standing in front of it, brush in hand, fresh paint on my smock, pondering which color to use next. Only this morning I had set a basket of apples on the storage room shelf where the long table now stood. By the hands of those I loved the most, the room had been transformed into a new world—my world.

"What's happened to the storage?" I was beginning to wonder if this had been a dream.

"In the kitchen." Andre latched the window as a gust of wind swept into the room. "We've made a mess of the cupboards, but you can straighten them up when you have time."

Charles picked up a hammer and thumped it against his palm. "And since we're experts with tools, Papa's assigned us to build a shed off the side of the house."

"I don't know what to say to everyone." A lump grew in my throat. "Thank you, thank you a million times. I can't believe this is my very own studio." The four of them stood in a row, the most important people in my life. I blinked my eyes and my mind took a photograph, capturing the moment, never to let go.

"The only problem …" I shifted my weight.

"Did we forget something?" Andre surveyed the table.

"Not at all. You didn't miss a thing." An uncertainty washed over me, and I felt a blush cover my cheeks. I pretended to look out the window. "It's just that all of this is for a real artist. An artist who sells her pieces."

"I see." Papa began to pace the floor, hands clasped behind his back.

And with a sly grin he added, "We'll need to discuss that over dinner tonight. We have a visitor joining us."

* * * * *

The knock came just as the last plate was put in its place. Papa had instructed me to set the table with our best linens, silver, and crystal—none of which had been used since Mama left.

"*Bienvenue*, Stefan." Papa embraced the short man wearing a long, gray woolen overcoat.

"Ah, so good to see you again, Henri. Marseille is never the same without you."

"Here, let me take your coat and hat. Come in and meet the family."

The man was bald, with large ears and a long nose under which he wore a reddish mustache. His appearance almost made me chuckle when he entered the kitchen and took my hand. The late October night air had chilled his hands, but when he spoke, his voice seemed to warm the room.

"*Bonsoir*, you must be Mademoiselle Ella."

"I am. Welcome to our home."

"Ella, this is Monsieur Lenoir. He is a Parisian but has lived in Marseilles for some time."

"Yes, I've been in the south since just before you arrived from America. How many years has that been now, Henri?"

"Nearly ten years, Stefan, though it seems like I've been here a lifetime."

The front door swung open and the boys entered, each holding a bottle of wine. They laughed and shouldered each other, trying to be the first to the kitchen.

"*Garçons*, manners. Please." Papa outstretched his hands on the door jam, halting the boys. "Our guest is here."

"We know, we saw his auto on the drive." Charles called out from the rear. "Did you see it? It's a Packard."

"That's right, young man. It's a 1937 Packard 12. It took a ride across the Atlantic all the way from Detroit, Michigan. I'll take you for a spin in the morning." Monsieur Lenoir smiled at me. "I'll take all of you if you'd like."

"Sons, a proper introduction of yourselves is necessary." Papa released them through the doorway where they set the finest vintage wines from the Vineyard du Moreau on the table. "This is my former business colleague and good friend, Monsieur Stefan Lenoir."

"Pleased to meet you, sir. I'm Charles Moreau." Charles shook the man's hand.

"I'm Jack. Seventeen years old, sir."

"I can see that. Pleasure to meet you, young man."

Andre stepped forward and offered his hand. "I'm Andre Donato. I'm seventeen also."

"Wonderful. A home full of strong, handsome boys and a beautiful daughter." Monsieur Lenoir's mustache lifted above his wide smile.

"He's not our real brother." Jack gestured toward Andre. "He's from Italy."

"I can see the difference. Hmm? I once knew a man named Donato. Which part of—"

"Here, let's go to the sitting room near the fire and have a glass of wine." Papa directed his friend across the room. He looked back and eyed Jack, a warning to watch his tongue. "Boys, go to the barn and bring in enough wood for the evening. Ella, bring in a tray of cheeses and a bottle from the table. You can join us."

I thought Papa would want to speak privately with Monsieur Lenoir, but I was curious to find out who this man was and why he came from Marseille to visit us. As I entered the room, I heard Monsieur Lenoir speak.

"Henri. I'm sorry. I didn't mean to say—"

"It's all right. No one knows for sure where a man stands these days." Papa poured his friend a savory Cabernet, bearing the label used since Papa's grandfather, Charles Moreau II began the vineyard in the 1850s. "His father and grandfather disagreed with Mussolini and both disappeared one night. They told the boy to run and he ended up here." Papa gazed at the fire. "He's a son to me now. I love him."

"He's the son of Joseph Donato, isn't he? Looks just like him." Monsieur Lenoir joined Papa by the fire. "An expert vintner. Made the best Italian wine I've ever tasted."

"Indeed." Papa lifted his glass and stepped away from the fire. "What news have you been hearing in Marseille? The north is surely under pressure. Everything, everyone for that matter, is changing so quickly."

"You know I will always be a Frenchman, a free Frenchman for sure. There's trouble coming in from all sides, but we'll hold fast. Hitler is destroying Czechoslovakia."

"And making Poland nervous." Papa breathed in the rich aroma of the wine.

"Indeed, while delusional Mussolini stomps around in the south. Such a mess, it is. To make matters worse, the franc has tumbled, and I'm feeling it in the building business."

"Not by the looks of your automobile." Papa motioned a toast to his friend.

"True enough. I had it sent over a few years ago, but now I'm taking precautions with my earnings. Not as much extra to play with in Paris, especially in the art galleries."

At the mention of the galleries, my ears perked. I had heard of the high-priced galleries dotting the Champs-Elysees and the receptions filled with the bourgeois gawking over works by Picasso, Matisse, Legar, and Utrillo.

"Good old King George VI assures us we would be in better shape if we'll side with him." Papa refilled the glasses.

"I'm not sure who to believe, but sharing a bed with the Brits doesn't sit well with me. Gives me indigestion just to think of it." Monsieur Lenoir chuckled. The tips of his large protruding ears turned rouge. Our guest turned toward me. "Speaking of art galleries, I understand you are an artist."

My heart jumped, and I felt the familiar blush redden my face. "Well, I do like to paint. I paint whenever I can."

"What do you like to paint, my dear?" Monsieur Lenoir sliced a piece of Roquefort and popped it into his mouth.

"I like to paint lots of things, sir. The vineyard when the sun is low in the sky, the poppies and sunflowers in the fields, the twisted olive trees and the straight cypress trees. Sometimes I paint our barn and the animals sleeping in the sun, or huddled together when it's cold. Oh, and then there are the sunsets and sunrises. I never get tired of painting those."

"You must awake early." He smiled and winked.

"Yes, that's when I can see what the light is going to do to the vineyard and the hills."

"Hmm. You seem to see things like an artist. You even talk like an artist." He sliced another piece of cheese and held it on the tip of the knife. "Tell me, where did you get your training?"

I glanced at Papa, not sure what to say.

"She's never had lessons. No training." Papa swirled his wine, concentrating on its concentric path.

"Henri, you must be kidding. I've never seen work like that without some instruction." Monsieur Lenoir scooted forward in his chair.

My eyes widened. "You've seen my paintings?"

"Yes, I thought you knew. Do you know why I've come here?" He glanced at Papa.

"Ella, I sent Monsieur Lenoir a few of your oils and watercolors. I knew he had an extensive collection of art and knows talent."

"Which did you send him? What if they aren't good?" I felt slightly dizzy.

"They are more than good, Ella. My favorite is a field of poppies with two people walking far in the distance as if they are engaged in deep conversation and will continue walking until the sun rests. Perhaps it is a mother and daughter."

"Papa, where did you find that piece?" I approached his side.

He took my hand. "It was in a stack of watercolor paintings in your closet. I leafed through them and that one stood out to me. It moved me. Something about it grabbed my heart, and I wanted to find out if it did the same for someone who knows quality art."

"But that one wasn't for anyone to see. It's a silly picture of people walking in an overgrown field." I couldn't help it. I began to cry.

"My dear, Ella. What a fool I am." Papa pulled me onto his lap as he would a small child. "I just now realized who the people are. I was blind not to know—so engrossed with the colors I didn't even notice."

"I'm missing something here. Will one of you fill me in?" A serious look replaced Monsieur Lenoir's jovial expression.

"The two people in the painting are Ella and her mother. You remember my wife, Marie?"

"Of course, the beautiful American woman." He set his glass on the table and folded his hands. "I heard what happened but didn't want to pry. I'm sorry to have touched on a sensitive subject."

"Not your fault, Stefan. I shouldn't have been so blind." Papa offered an apologetic smile toward me.

"But despite that, Ella, you have a highly unusual talent. You have an artistic gift that's only given by God. You need to do something with that gift, and here in Roussillon you won't get the recognition you deserve." The visitor lifted his glass. "I propose a toast to Ella Moreau. The newly discovered artist in France, and for that matter, all of Europe."

Papa raised his glass. "To Ella. May God use this talent through my daughter for his own wonderful purpose."

"Young lady, I'd like to be the first to purchase one of your works." Monsieur Lenoir leaned back in his chair and crossed his short legs.

"Really? Do you mean it?" I stood and straightened my dress.

"Absolutely. It would be an honor. And, if I might add, a good investment. I know your work will sell. In fact, it will be in high demand. There hasn't been such a young girl … how old are you, may I ask?"

"I'm turning fifteen tomorrow."

"Ah, then an especially good reason to celebrate. There hasn't been a young lady with pronounced artistic talent to grace Paris in a long time."

"Paris?" I nearly shouted.

"Couldn't she paint from here?" Papa grew serious.

"She'd never get the attention here, especially beginning her career. She needs to be in the *La Ville Lumiere*."

Papa shook his head. "But she's too young to go on her own."

"I'm nearly sixteen, Papa."

"Now is not the time to go to the city—too much unrest. The threat of the Germans coming as far as our beloved city is all too real." Monsieur Lenoir took my hand. "But when it settles down, and let's pray for that to happen soon, I know the perfect person to take you in."

"And whom might that be, dear friend?" Papa retained his serious look.

"Madame DuBois, the grand patron of the arts."

Papa coughed and looked startled. "DuBois?"

"*Oui*, Emelia DuBois. Did you ever meet her in Marseilles? On occasion, she has stayed at our home."

"I don't believe so." Papa took a long sip from his glass.

"She's Parisian by blood, but all of France knows her, at least those who know art. She owns one of the most successful galleries in all of Europe and can smell talent like your daughter's better than a king's best hunting dog." His mustache danced as he sniffed. "In fact, I'm surprised she hasn't already ferreted her out from your provincial hiding spot." Monsieur Lenoir stood and stretched his short body to all of its five feet. "By the way, the scent from the kitchen is tantalizing."

"Of course." Papa stood and stretched to his full height, nearly touching the ceiling with his hands. "And after dinner, Ella can show you her work in the studio."

I hugged Papa with an excitement I had never felt before.

"You're the best father ever."

Eleven

It was the third day of June. The family gathered in the kitchen as the Germans bombed Paris. We listened as the crackly radio announced that, for the third time in seventy years, Paris was a city under siege. Only days prior, nearly two-thirds of the residents had fled the city by whatever means possible. Paris became a city devoid of life.

Again, our lives were about to drastically change. Papa hadn't cried, at least not in front of us, since Mama left. Now he sat at the same table, holding his head and weeping.

"Papa, you scare me when you cry like that." I turned down the radio and rubbed his back.

"*Mon cherie*, you have no idea what this means. When La Ville des Lumieres is defeated, there is no France. She is *le coeur*. Even though I am provincial, the city of lights is our country's heart."

Charles pulled out a chair and plopped himself next to Papa. "Our army will surely push the Germans out."

"It will take much more than the French army. We're still depleted from the last war." Papa shook his head and swiped at the tears.

"It's time to announce my intentions." Jack crossed his arms. "I'm enlisting first thing in the morning. Remy, Andre, and I agreed we'd go as soon as there was real trouble."

"You're not serious?" Papa narrowed his brows as he studied my brother. Then he shifted his stare to Andre. "Do you want to go too?" Andre was silent and cast his eyes toward the floor.

"Who would like some pastry?" I interrupted.

Papa snorted. "The three of you aren't even of age."

"I'm eighteen in a month. Andre turns the end of the summer. They'll take us cause they need us." Jack's smug attitude had returned and I hated him for it. "Remy's been eighteen since Christmas. Besides, the other boys—I mean men—at school are doing the same."

"Andre, you're not really going, are you?" Without even thinking, I had cut the cherry pastry into several pieces, divided them onto plates, and served one to Andre.

"No thanks." He looked away.

"You didn't answer me." I held my position and pushed the plate toward him.

After a long silence, he accepted the dessert and looked down at me. He had grown taller over the winter and was now easily a head above. "They'll probably make me go anyway."

"That's not an answer. It's not true either."

"They won't make you go, Andre. You're not a French citizen." Papa stood and paced around the table, a motion he reserved for moments of deep thought or concern.

"But you, Charles." Papa stopped and rested his hand on Charles' shoulder. "They might very well be calling you up any day. You're old enough now and even though you were born in America, you have dual citizenship. You'll be on the records as eligible."

Charles hadn't said much up to this point. He ran his fingers over the stubble covering his chin. "I figured that."

"Oh, Lord. What's a man to believe?" Papa began to pace again, this time speaking aloud to God. "We're called to love and protect country. You can't ask that I sacrifice my three sons. I love France but I love my sons more."

Jack straightened as though reporting for duty. "Papa, it's not your choice or God's. It's mine. Remy and I will be leaving by the end of the week. Whoever else is in can join us." He glared at Andre. "I think you're getting cold feet. Am I right, *brother*?"

Andre slammed his plate on the table and stormed from the room. I started after him but Charles grabbed my arm.

"Let him be, Ella." The usual pink in Charles' cheeks had been replaced with a lifeless gray, probably the same hue as the poor Parisians who, hours ago, watched their city burn and turn to smoke and ash.

Twelve

The Pond, 1939

No one spoke much the rest of the day. Each of us seemed to ponder which move the others would make, like pawns in a giant chess game. Each person's action would affect the entire family in a crucial manner.

The spring mistral, with its pouring rain and raw winds, had swept through southern France for a week with a vengeance. Behind our house, the irrigation creek had swelled and overflowed its banks. Strong winds voluntarily closed unhooked shutters on both levels of the house and knocked a large branch from the tallest oak tree onto the fence, crushing it beneath its massive weight.

But today was unusually hot for early summer, and the heat added to the emotional weight each of us bore. Even painting didn't lighten my mood. I sketched a vase with flowers, but each line and curve felt contrived and unnatural. Scrubbing with the stub of a gum eraser returned me to blank paper, devoid of inspiration.

"No luck?" Charles stuck his head through the doorway.

"Not today. I just don't have it." I set the eraser and pencil on the side table. "Too much on my mind."

Charles was handsome, tall and strong like Papa, but most importantly, he had the same heart. Charles was compassionate, sensitive, and fiercely protective. His heart had ached for Mama over the years, especially when we were younger, and I heard him cry at night. But as we grew up, Charles was so intent on helping Papa take care of us, helping to fill the hole in our lives, that he sacrificed acknowledging his own pain.

As he stood in the doorway that afternoon, my mind studied every detail of his face so as to never forget him. Strangely, he stood silently, neither of us speaking for a long time. Either he was also memorizing me or was providing me time to draw him perfectly into my memory.

"Let's go swimming," Charles finally interrupted. "It's too hot to stay in the house."

I hadn't gone in the water since last summer. Usually, I'd walk the short distance through the meadow with the boys with the intention of swimming or at least wading in the shallow part of the pond. I always brought my sketchbook, palette, and brushes, or box of pastels just in case a perfect image or lighting would present itself.

The boys initially teased me to join them in the cool water by splashing or threatening to throw me in. But soon they would become engrossed in their own games of dunking, racing, and swinging from the dangling tree rope and forget about me sitting on the bank. Over the long summer days, I had drawn and painted so many pages in my sketchbook of the boys playing in the swimming hole that when the pages were flipped through quickly, the images formed a motion picture.

"Get your suit on and come with me. Just you and me." Charles smiled his broad smile. "But here's the deal … you can't bring your art stuff along."

"Why not?"

"Cause you're getting in the water or I'll throw you in."

"Bully." I tried to look serious. "Okay, I won't bring it, but I'm not getting in if the water is too cold. The rains have probably made it freezing."

"Fair enough. Meet you in the yard in five minutes." Charles disappeared down the hall.

When we reached the top of the hill just before descending to the pond, we surveyed the scene. The orange poppies gathered once again in clusters on the other side of the hill, announcing spring was turning the corner toward summer. The cattails emerged near the edges of the pond, their brown bodies poised with yellow-spiked flowers on top. In the fall, the soft bodies would burst open and fluffy seeds would take flight across the pond and hang from the overreaching willow trees nearby.

I squinted toward the pond. "The water looks murky."

"No excuses." Charles took my hand, and we ran down the hill toward the sandy bank.

Charles kicked off his shoes, unbuttoned his shirt and pants, and tossed them aside, revealing striped swim trunks. "Come on, Ella. You're not going in with your dress on, are you?"

"Don't worry. I have my suit on underneath. Just don't rush me." I slipped my shoes off. The rain had muddied the bank, and my toes squished in the muck.

"I'm going in." Charles waded into the pond, balancing himself with his arms outstretched as he navigated the slippery, moss-covered rocks. "Wow. It is a little chilly." He waded out further, plunged under, then popped up and shook his dark brown hair like a wet dog.

"Charles, it's too cold. Do I have to?" I held my ground on the sloping bank as the water lapped over my toes.

"I'm already getting used to it." He bobbed up and down as he floated farther from me. "Have a swim with your biggest brother, just for old time's sake."

I nodded, pulled my sundress over my head, and laid it on the grass. The first step into the pond wasn't bad. But when the water reached my stomach, I gasped and caught my breath. Charles held his hands in the air and motioned for me to continue. The rocks felt slimy, and I tried to avoid the sharper ones as I slowly stepped toward him. I couldn't see the bottom since the rain had churned the water and turned it dark green.

Just as the water rose to my chest and shoulders, I tripped over something jagged and slipped under the water. My foot was caught, and I kicked and flailed my arms. My chest hurt as panic swept over me and stole my breath.

"Ella!" His voice was muffled as his arms wrapped around me and pulled my head above the surface. My hair was tangled around my face. Charles pushed it out of my eyes and mouth. "It's all right. I've got you."

"My foot was caught." I began to cry. "I couldn't breathe."

Even though I was fifteen, Charles cradled me like a baby and held me to his chest. "You must have tripped on this branch. I can feel it with my foot. The winds probably knocked old branches off the trees this spring." He held me tighter as I shivered. "You know, Ella, you can stand here. The water won't be over your head." He grinned and released me back in the water. "Let's go out farther where it's deeper, and we won't step on things. Come on, take my hand."

As we swam toward the deeper water, my body warmed while my

legs and arms propelled me toward the center of the pond. The sun had traveled to the west and shone through the tallest trees. It warmed my face as I swam alongside my brother. Occasionally, we would stop to float on our backs and watch the clouds change shapes. Then, we'd flip over and tread water while we talked of nothing important.

My arms and legs were tired, and I was getting hungry as dinnertime approached. "I'm ready to go back to the shore. Are you?"

"I'll take a few swings off the rope before I go. Do you want to try?"

"Definitely not. Last time I got a rope burn all the way up my leg."

"Then swim back to the shore, dry off, and watch me. I'll show you some tricks."

I swam back toward the muddy bank to retrieve my clothes as Charles headed in the direction of the grove of trees. Years ago, Papa had tethered a braided rope nearly midway up one of the trees and around a thick branch that sprawled across the water. It was the perfect spot to reach, straddle the branch, and gather the rope from beneath. Then, we'd walk to the opposite end of the branch until the rope was stretched out. Always cautious, I would sit on the branch, hold on to the rope, and scoot myself slowly off as the rope tightened and sailed me over the pond until I let go and splashed into the water.

The boys, on the other hand, perpetually tried to outdo one another. They would gather the rope, grab it up high, jump off the branch and release from the most lofty point possible. Sometimes they'd land feet first, but often their tricks ended in a belly or back flop.

I reached the shore, wrung the water from my hair, and sat on a large, warm rock, watching Charles as he reached the other side and climbed the tree. Once he was on the extended branch, we waved at one another just before he launched himself out over the pond and landed with a terrific splash. I stood and clapped as he emerged.

"Bravo!" I yelled across the pond.

"Wait. There's more." He swam back to the shore.

Charles performed several more heroic feats before I laid back on the rock and shut my eyes. The swimming had been both invigorating and exhausting. I lay there for quite some time, and then turned onto my belly for my back and shoulders to catch the late day's sun. I ran my fingers through the mix of tall and short grasses standing in front of my face. A ladybug navigated a slender blade. I placed my finger in its path as it continued its quest and stepped onto my skin. It crawled along my finger until it reached the back of my hand, but must have felt me quiver from the tickle because it opened its spotted case and took flight. I propped myself on my elbows and watched it disappear into the thick bushes covered with red berries.

Resting on the closest bush, no more than an arm's length from me, was an extraordinary butterfly. It was a large, yellow and black Monarch, its spotted wing pattern perfectly symmetrical. The wings were poised together, pointing toward the sky. Its legs twitched and its antennae tilted side to side as if it were waiting for an important message. Perhaps having received a response, it separated its wings, gracefully raised and lowered them a few times, then silently departed the leaf.

I tiptoed after the butterfly as it flew up the embankment flitting this way and that. I was mesmerized by its silent beauty—its unique design and perfection. It hurried along the worn path that meandered around the pond. I followed a few steps behind, slowing down when it hovered above a flower or encircled a tree before continuing on its journey. Finally, it left its course and flew into the open, soaring over the tall grasses and poppies growing wild in the field. It rose higher and higher until it disappeared in the sun's rays. With my hand above my eyes to shield the brightness, I hoped to catch a final glimpse. But it was gone, continuing on its way in a most glorious manner. I wondered why God had given such a beautiful creature a brief life.

The dirt path led back to the embankment that surrounded the pond. Heading toward the pond, I looked across the water to find Charles. The rope hung limp from the branch and the surface was still.

I cupped my hands to my mouth. "Charles. Where are you?" My eyes scanned the branches of the swinging tree and the grass-covered bank. "Charles," I called out again, but only a slight breeze in the leaves answered. Possibly, he had returned home without me. But then I saw his clothes and shoes still cast aside near the bushes. I tried to call his name again, but no sound emerged. My voice had been stolen and only gasps came out of my mouth.

In a panic, I ran to the water's edge, the cold water lapping over my bare feet. Only then could I scream his name, over and over. "Charles! Charles! Charles!" I started into the water but an overwhelming fear stopped me from going farther. I spun around, forcing myself through the slick mud and back to the grass. Running along the path leading to the other side of the pond, low hanging branches pulled at my hair. I swiped them out of my way, then left the path after the curve and jumped through tall grasses and cattails to reach the water's edge.

"Charles. If you're hiding, this isn't funny." I looked behind me, hoping he'd appear from the trees. Stepping toward the water, I leaned over and caught my dull reflection. It startled me and I retracted back. I walked along the edge just beyond the trees, slipped in the mud, and caught my balance.

"I'm sure you walked back home. You were hungry and thought I had gone home first." I bit my lip as a sick feeling rose in my throat. "You left your shoes and clothes because ..." I started to shake, "you boys always leave things lying around."

I could climb the embankment, head home, and find Charles sitting at the kitchen table enjoying several slices of the pastry no one had an appetite for earlier in the day, or I could glance in the dark water a last time. I started toward the rise, stopped, and looked over my shoulder.

Then I saw him—face down in the water, his hair rhythmically swaying on the surface.

"Charles!" I screamed and ran along the path to where the small creek exited the pond. Jumping in the water, I swam to his side and grabbed his arm. "Oh my God, what's happened?" My feet barely touched the bottom as I tried to brace myself and turn him over, wrapping my arms around his waist and lunging backwards. He flopped over, his weight pushing me under the water. I surfaced and saw through blurry eyes, his face. "Charles! Don't do this!"

My screams went unheard as I cradled his body in the water as he had held me only a short time before.

* * * * *

Panic resurfaces whenever I relive that day. It always will. Any reasoning was gone at that moment. I thought of letting myself go under as I held him—using his weight to hold me down until I died. Then I thought about Papa and couldn't bear to think what would happen if he found both of us drowned. I imagined him falling over and dying on the edge of the pond where he played as a boy and rested with his own children after a long day's swim. Besides, I didn't want to lose him too, even though it didn't make sense since I'd be gone.

I've prayed to God to help soften the memory, even erase it from my mind, especially because part of me still believes it was my fault.

If I hadn't chased the butterfly, Charles wouldn't have died.

Thirteen

Goodbye, 1939

On the same smoldering day, I buried one brother and watched the other leave for war. I wanted to hate God, yet begged Him to protect what was left of my family.

Earlier that morning, I had sat in the front pew of our tiny church running my fingers over the aged-wood bench, smoothed to a velvety finish from years of parishioners perched on the very spot. My mind pictured faceless people, filing into the church and sliding across the pews in rhythmic succession. Some came to share in the joy of a wedding or baptism. Others came to a funeral, filled with sorrow and leaving thousands of tears that soaked into the intricate grain of wood. Many came on Sundays to make requests of God—petitions for forgiveness and healing for broken hearts. There were some who came to bask in His grace and replenish their souls. I wondered ... how many came simply to be in His presence?

I sat between Papa and Jack as we mourned the death of Charles. Andre had volunteered to speak to the small congregation on behalf of the family. As his hands gripped the sides of the podium, his voice wavered when he spoke of the day he first met Charles and of the unusual assurance he experienced that they would become brothers. During several pauses, I thought Andre would not be able to continue. But he shut his eyes and turned his palms upward as if receiving a gift. With voice cracking, he leaned over the podium and shared another story. And although part of me wanted to relive the memories of Charles, each image pierced my heart and thickened the lump growing in my throat.

Andre concluded by opening the large black Bible on the podium, a constant fixture in the church over the years since we came to Roussillon. He flipped through the pages and stopped. "This is from Jeremiah 29:11-13, a Scripture that many of us know. It meant a lot to Charles." Andre cleared his throat. "'For I know the thoughts that I think toward you, saith the Lord, thoughts of peace, and not of evil, to give you an expected end. Then shall ye call upon me, and ye shall go and pray unto me, and I will hearken unto you. And ye shall seek me, and find me, when ye shall search for me with all your heart.'"

Andre surveyed the congregation until his eyes met mine. "You may be wondering why I shared this Scripture with you at a funeral. It doesn't seem fitting, does it?" He hesitated and held my eyes. "I believe the Lord, and Charles too, want us to keep living. You know, keep hoping and ..." His voiced cracked. He glanced across the silent gathering, nodded a polite thank you, then descended the steps and joined us on the front pew. Sliding next to Papa, Andre slumped forward, finally releasing a torrent of tears for the brother we all loved. Papa wrapped his arm around Andre. I grabbed Jack's hand and he squeezed mine in return. Then he released my hand and dropped it onto the wooden seat that had held too many broken souls.

As the pastor continued the service, he spoke of Charles' stolen and brief life. Not just Charles, but all of us had been robbed. My fingers twisted the fabric of my dark dress, lying limp along my thighs as an unwelcomed anger swelled in my throat. I wanted to scream and run from the suffocating walls of the normally peaceful and comforting building. But I was trapped. Half of me lamented the loss of Charles, the other mourned the loss of myself—fading away like the veil of the morning fog slowly lifting over the rolling hills of Roussillon. I wondered if God had enough love, if He was big enough, to discover a sliver of life left in me.

I squeezed my eyes and pictured myself where two paths diverged. One path led to the overbearing guilt and sadness enveloping the pond where Charles and I last shared life's fragility. The other path was shrouded with a terrorizing blackness as Jack, with his best friend Remy at his side, strode into the unknown. It was clear I couldn't venture down either path. Behind me was the past—a place where I could go only in memory.

I blinked and found myself again on the front pew of the old stone church, in time to join the last words of the concluding prayer and hear my papa's weeping.

We buried my brother in the small cemetery next to the church. Papa looked a hundred years old as he stared into the deep hole in the moist ground as the casket was lowered, probably wishing he would be the one returning to the earth instead of his son. I surveyed the gathered group of family and neighbors. A few of their eyes met mine, and I wondered if they thought I was the one who was meant to drown, not beautiful Charles.

A wrinkled woman stepped next to Papa and nudged him with her elbow. She cradled a tremendous cluster of burgundy peonies like a precious newborn. She was the woman who sold flowers on the third Thursday of each month when the traveling market came to our town.

Mama and I had seen her when we walked to town our first week in Roussillon. Mama complimented her on the beautiful flowers, then the woman had leaned toward me and extended a single, cobalt delphinium. She whispered in my ear, "Food is for the body, spices are for the mind, but flowers are for the soul. God made them all, but never forget the flowers." Mama smiled and bought a large bouquet— burgundy peonies—so fragrant they made my head swirl.

Now, standing in the damp grass, Papa nodded and accepted the gift from the woman. He buried his head in their scent that wafted across the void in the ground between us. The fragrance was so powerful, I imagined the aroma reached all the way across the ocean to America where we thought Mama might be, unaware her child had died. I breathed in deeply and then watched Papa methodically drop each stem into the earth.

* * * * *

"I don't care what you say." Andre squared his shoulders and frowned.

Pointing an accusing finger, Jack circled Andre like a prowling tiger. "You're scared, that's it. You aren't enough of a man."

"You don't get it, do you?" Andre grabbed Jack's shirtsleeve and tugged him off balance.

"Let's go. Right here. Probably long overdue." My brother positioned his fists and Andre did the same. "I should have beat the tar out of you the day you stepped onto our property."

"Stop it!" I stepped between the boys who had outsized me for several years. "You're both acting crazy."

"Is that what this is about?" Andre lowered his fists and glared at

58

Jack. "It has nothing to do with me changing my mind about signing up. You hate that I ever came here."

"Maybe." Jack lifted his fists again. "All I know is you aren't my brother. The only one I ever had was better and braver than you'll ever be. You should have drowned instead of him."

Andre stumbled back as if receiving a punch to the gut.

"Jack!" I shoved him backwards.

"Suit yourself, chicken." My brother stuffed his hands deep in his pockets. "But you're going back on your word. You said you were going with Remy and me."

Andre visibly steadied himself. When he spoke, his voice sounded like a growl. "But that was before Charles. How can you leave your father and sister alone? For God's sake, your brother got buried this afternoon. You must have been born without a heart." Andre wiped the sweat from his temple. "Maybe *you* should have been the one we buried today."

I braced my hands against Jack's chest, but he only looked at me with the same infuriating smirk.

"You don't have to hold me back, Ella. He's not worth the fight." He kicked at the dirt. "You either. Go on over there and stand next to your boyfriend."

I staggered back. He might as well have slapped me. "Enough from both of you." My voice shook. "It's an awful day. Nobody's going anywhere." It seemed too long that we waited in silence.

Finally, my brother spoke, though he sounded like someone I had never known. "Remy is meeting me at the train station in an hour. I'll be gone before dark." He turned and walked toward the house.

"Jack …" I called after him. But even though just a few steps from me, he had already traveled hundreds of miles and thousands of years away.

Fourteen

Prayer, 1939

It was late summer, yet Andre, Papa, and I withdrew as though retreating to our own winter hibernation. We gathered at dinnertime, and the men worked side by side in the vineyard, but little was spoken. Individually, we wrestled with the dark presence that had engulfed our lives since Charles' death and Jack's departure.

"Papa, share what you're reading." I offered him another serving of fresh asparagus, but he waved it away. His cheeks were shallow and the massive, strong man I knew had reduced over summer's time. We hadn't heard from Jack, but considered no news a hopeful blessing.

"Which book are you reading?" Andre leaned over the table toward Papa's open Bible.

"Habakkuk." Papa smoothed the rippled pages with his calloused palm and twisted the frayed, satin bookmark around his forefinger.

"I miss hearing you read." With my hand on Papa's shoulder, I felt his tense muscles and wondered if he was still wrestling with God.

Since I was a small girl, Papa had read a portion of Scripture to our family most evenings. When he took breaks from his work in the vineyard, he could be found on the front porch, feet propped on the railing, stretched back in the wicker chair, Bible open. Within a short time, his Bible would be resting across his rising and falling chest as he slept peacefully in the late afternoon sunshine.

But the day he lost both of his sons, Papa did something I never imagined possible. That evening, behind his closed bedroom door, he was talking and sobbing at the same time. I carefully budged the door open and peeked in.

He was on his knees beside his bed, face contorted and wet with tears. As he often did, he was talking with God. But then a fear washed over me as Papa's tone changed from seeking comfort from his beloved Lord to a voice of anger and hatred. In a single motion, he grabbed his Bible from the nightstand and threw it across the room. It hit the pale blue wall and landed with a thump, splayed facedown on the hardwood floor. Through the crack in the doorway, I watched a few forlorn pages flutter onto the wooden planks. Then Papa slumped, pulled his knees to his chest, and rocked like a child. I quietly closed the door and leaned my head against the wall.

I didn't know what to do, so I listened to my father sob until the hallway was enveloped by night and silence. And though darkness filled the hallway, the image of Papa fighting with God never left my mind. There was no way to extinguish its forbidding glow.

Andre's voice brought me back to the present. "Tell us what it says." He sat back and crossed his hands behind his head. "Or I can read if you'd like."

Papa cleared his throat and breathed deeply. "I'll share. I suppose it's time. It's Habakkuk 2:20. 'But the Lord is in his holy temple; let all the earth keep silence before Him.'"

"Any particular reason for that Scripture?" Andre smiled at Papa. "It's beautiful, isn't it?"

"The Lord gave it to me today. He wants us to believe …" Papa rubbed his hands and paused. "He wants us to know he is in control."

"Not us," Andre added.

"Surely not us." Papa shook his head. "Thank the Lord for that. In his own way, and I suppose in his own time, he'll take care of all this mess."

"Do you mean the war?" I sat by Papa and noticed his attempt to make amends with God. Once torn from his beloved Bible, several pages had been tucked back into their divine placement. They jutted slightly from the worn edge, a subtle reminder of Papa's humanness— anger toward the Lord and doubting his truth, then seeking forgiveness and returning to the greatest source of love.

Papa closed the well-worn book. "Yes, I mean the war, but not just that. He wants us to know he'll take care of the mess our lives have become." He looked very weary. "I struggle with God. I don't know why he's allowing us so much loss. But I have to …" He looked from Andre to me, "we have to believe he loves us and has a plan." He rubbed his hand across the black leather. "I don't see any other way."

"And in the meantime, we have to keep praying for Jack. I feel sick when I think about our last words with each other." Andre shut his eyes. "Lord, please keep him from harm and bring him home safely."

"He must feel awful too. It was a horrible day." I reached across the table and touched Andre's hand. It felt good to touch his skin, and my fingers wanted to linger. Many times I had imagined Andre holding me. I would hug him until we found comfort in each other's arms.

Andre forced a smile. "I just hope we can be brothers again."

I slid my hand off his and back into my lap, feeling foolish for thinking of him in any way other than a brother.

"*Bonsoir,*" a voice called from the porch. A weathered face appeared at the open door.

"*Bonsoir*, Monsieur Patin. Come in."

Remy's father entered and extended his hand.

"Auguste, good to see you." Papa gathered the man's hand. He studied his face and relaxed when our neighbor displayed a broad smile.

"A letter came from Remy today. It is the first we've received. He's fine." Auguste nodded quickly as if agreeing with himself. "Have you heard from your son?"

"No word yet. We're hoping that's good. It's the letter from the military that we don't want to receive." Papa motioned the farmer further inside.

"No, we don't want one of their vehicles pulling up to either of our homes, although I'm not sure if they do that anymore. Too many lives have been lost."

"What else did Remy say?" Papa poured a glass of red wine and handed it to Auguste.

"*Merci.*" Auguste sipped the wine and licked his overgrown mustache. "Can't believe our sons are in the same unit. It's a large one. They aren't bunking, but he sees him most days. He mentioned they've seen action but didn't go into detail. Probably afraid his mother wouldn't want to know what's really happening."

"Better left unsaid." Papa poured himself a glass.

"Remy had a request, Henri." Auguste stepped closer and lowered his voice. "He asked me to come to your house and ask a favor of you and Andre."

"Really?"

"What does Remy need, Monsieur Patin?" Andre leaned into the conversation.

"He wants you to pray for him." Remy's father rubbed his eyes with dirt-stained fingers. "I've never been a praying man, but my son knows he needs prayer. I could feel the fear in his words."

Papa placed his arm around our neighbor. "We all need prayer, my friend. I have some talking of my own to do with the Lord."

"Me too, but I don't feel right talking to him. I don't have the right words, you know?"

Papa chuckled. "He knows we aren't perfect. I'm a good example of that. But he knows what we're trying to say even before we have the thought." Papa led our neighbor into the living room and offered him a place on the sofa. Andre and I moved our chairs forward as the four of us formed a small circle.

"I've been so angry with God this summer that often I refused to talk with him."

"Your family has been through hell, Henri."

Papa nodded. "It's felt like it for sure. And as hard as it's been, I know in my heart we need God like never before, even though I keep trying to sort this mess out on my own account. He may be the only way we'll survive this."

"And he already knows exactly how everything will work out." Andre took my hand and held it between us. "All we can do is trust him."

I squeezed Andre's hand, thankful that he was safe from the dreadful images of war we saw in the newspapers and heard over the radio. But an ever-present fear occupied my mind and laid claim in the pit of my stomach. I felt the need to constantly look over my shoulder to keep watch for an unknown danger.

With our best attempt, our huddled circle prayed. Even Auguste offered some words to the Lord, and when we finished, he thanked us for the time together and promised to return soon.

Over the next few months, the leaves turned a myriad of warm colors, the air cooled, and eventually we woke to a thin blanket of white. Auguste and his wife, Eloise, came to our home each Sunday evening. Occasionally, they brought news from Remy. He confirmed Jack was as well as could be expected, considering the days were long and grueling and the food often sparse for all the soldiers. He mentioned that my brother spoke very little, and never of home. Remy always asked for prayers.

And so we prayed for all of us.

Fifteen

Burden, 1940

The New Year presented itself like an unwelcome stranger. Each evening, the cold winter air mixed with chilling news streaming over the radio. The previous August, the Germans had coupled with the Russians, and now they bullied those in the north. Russia invaded Finland in November shortly after Germany occupied a portion of Poland. Russia and Germany divided Poland between them as if the country was their prey, killed and waiting to be scavenged. Denmark and Norway fell in the spring. Then, without a fight, Estonia, Latvia, and Lithuania were added to the spoils of war.

The days lengthened, and the soil in our vineyards softened as new growth pushed from the earth. North of Paris, German Luftwaffe aircraft filled the skies like a swarm of mosquitoes. German tanks, the *panzers,* roared ahead of the unified ground troops as they fixed their devilish eyes on Western Europe.

"Papa, come listen." I waved to him to join us in the kitchen as the weary radio announcer's voice continued the sad news.

"After nine days of fierce fighting, the Germans hold the port city of Dunkirk, laying hold of the Channel coast. Reports are coming in that several thousand British, Belgium, and French troops have been rescued by the British Royal Navy. News from the front informs us hundreds of small boats, including fishing boats, joined the rescue. The number of casualties is unknown at this point."

The radio crackled. I turned the knob to the right, the left, but the static increased.

"Turn it off." Papa slumped into a chair. "It's too much."

"Remy's last letter said his unit was at Dunkirk." Andre paced around the table like an unsettled tiger.

"Maybe they got reassigned to another place." I glanced between the two men, hoping for a reassuring nod.

"Probably not a chance." Papa smoothed the tablecloth with his palm, and then slammed his hand on the table. I jumped and Andre stopped circling the table.

"Why hasn't he contacted us? He doesn't have the decency to think about his family?"

"Papa …" I stepped toward him.

"No, Ella. I mean it. The boy has hardened. Something happened to him a long time ago … the day your mother left. He was never the same after that."

"None of us were." I held Papa's forearm through his faded work shirt. "It's been hard for all of us." Brown skin hung loosely over protruding veins as weathered fingers intertwined with mine.

"Papa, what do you think life would be like if Mama hadn't left?"

He stroked my hand with his calloused fingers. Age was creeping in and leaving its mark, but even with the passing of winter and a reprieve from the vineyard, Papa's hands were never idle and eternally bore the signs of hard work.

"It's my fault." Papa hung his head, shaking it slowly from side to side. "I loved your mother and as crazy as it is, I still do. I never showed her enough."

"You were good to her, though. Right?"

"Sure, I treated her with respect. Provided for her. You. The boys. Told her I loved her often enough. She beamed whenever I told her how pretty she looked." Papa smiled, enjoying a brief, happy memory.

"What went wrong, Henri?" Andre settled across from us and leaned in.

Papa was silent, probably waiting for another memory to surface and speak for him. He finally rested his eyes on me. "I made her give up her dream. No one should do that." He seemed to look through me into another time. "And no one should ever take another's dream away."

"What do you mean, Papa?"

He blinked a few times and then looked at Andre. "My wife dreamed of being a famous singer and pianist. She had the talent, that's for sure, and the family connections to help move her dream along." He dropped his head. "But only in America. New York City. She believed that was the only place on earth for her to fulfill her dream."

"She could have performed here, in France." A sudden anger swelled in me at the thought of my mother's selfishness.

"I agree." Papa took my hand. "But she would never see that. Besides, she loved America more than she would ever love France."

"Or us." The words slipped out and stung.

Papa squeezed my hand. "I don't know what to say to that. But somewhere deep inside, I believe she still loves us, or at least she loves her children. People do crazy things to hold on to their dreams."

"Do you still have dreams, Henri?" Andre asked.

"Sure I do. I'm already living part of them. By the way, why have you been calling me Henri?" Papa stared at Andre. "That started right after Jack left."

Andre averted his eyes.

I'd wondered the same thing, though I suspected the reason.

"Andre, what's wrong, Son?" Papa extended his hand across the table, but Andre folded his arms and rubbed his shoulder. "It's fine. We're all on edge." Papa stood, stretched, and headed for the front door.

"Henri," Andre called after him.

Papa stopped and turned. "Yes?"

The young man stood and approached Papa. They were nearly equal in height, though Papa's stature outweighed Andre's slim, muscular build.

Andre's voice quivered. "I'm not sure …"

"Sure of what?" Papa raised an eyebrow.

"If I deserve to address you as my father."

"Of course—" Papa stepped toward Andre.

Andre held out his hand. "No, I mean it. Just before Jack left, we got in an argument. Would have been a fist fight if Ella hadn't been there." Andre glanced at me. "He told me he should have run me off the property the day I arrived. Maybe he should have."

"Nonsense." Papa widened his stance, placing his hands on his hips. He looked like a man ready to protect his fold. "You became part of this family the day you came. You know that, don't you?"

"I know you didn't have to take me in. You've raised me like your own. For that I'll always be grateful." Andre straightened himself, trying to match his stature to Papa's. "Henri, I said a terrible thing to Jack. I told him he should have been the one in the grave—not Charles."

Papa cocked his head and squinted. "Those were harsh words, Andre. I'd like to believe spoken only out of anger."

I stepped alongside Andre and placed my hand on his lower back. His muscles tensed. "But, Papa, Jack said some hateful things to Andre. I hope it's all forgotten."

"No chance. That's why he hasn't written home. He hates me, and now his only true brother is gone." Andre's eyes moistened and his face twisted. "The worst part …" He began to cry. "I meant what I said."

Papa wrapped his arms around Andre's heaving shoulders and held him close. "My son," Papa whispered in Andre's damp hair. "I love you." He bent over Andre and gathered me in with the other arm. "I love all of you. Somehow we have to keep living. We've got to hold on to the joy of the Lord and hope that good will still come." Papa bear-hugged us. "I just wish I could make it different and bring everyone back home."

We remained as one long enough for Andre's heavy breathing to subside. I felt Papa's heart beat calmly beneath his denim shirt. I remembered climbing into his lap when I was little, snuggling my head against his chest, and listening to the methodic thumping of his heart. It was a soothing sound—hearing life pulse through that big heart.

Finally, each of us blinked as we released one another.

"One more thing." Papa met Andre's eyes. "There's plenty of forgiving to do."

"What do you mean?" Andre shifted his weight from one worn work boot to the other.

"If you haven't already, you need to go to the Lord and ask for forgiveness about what happened between you and Jack. Then, you need to forgive yourself and realize we're all capable of hurting those we love the most. Finally, when Jack gets home from this nightmare of a war, you two need to forgive each other." Papa walked to the front door. "On second thought," he called over his shoulder, "write him a letter. Maybe you'll have a better chance getting a letter to him than us getting one from him." He pulled the door shut behind him.

Andre's eyes fixed on the closed door. "I love you, Papa." He followed the big man out the door, walking tall. A heavy weight had surely been lifted from his shoulders.

Sixteen

Broken, 1940

The invading summer heat chose not to leave when daylight disappeared. Regardless, I couldn't sleep while Papa's words replayed in my mind. *Somehow we have to keep living. We've got to hold on to the joy from what the Lord's given us and hope good will still come.* It took me a few days to digest what Papa meant, or at least what I thought he meant.

I resolved to preserve what the Lord had given me by doing what I did best—painting. By capturing the remnants of joy from fading memories and fleeting moments from my past, those images could be created in my art. Perhaps by securing certain pieces of my past on canvas and paper, my dreams could be painted into reality. I'd pray and paint for the chance of happiness and—possibly—even love.

Andre had accepted Papa's challenge to send Jack a letter. For several days, I watched him walk the rows in the vineyard, stretch out in the tall grasses under the olive grove with his Bible, and hide alone in his bedroom with a dim light escaping under the door late into the night.

I wanted to walk with him, and even imagined lying next to each other in the soft, swaying grasses as we watched the weightless clouds meander by. I dreamed of going to him in the night and the two of us holding one another in the darkness.

But he seemed content. I understood his contentment because when I retreated to my studio, dipped a brush, and stroked it across the canvas, the Lord and I began our dance. I talked and prayed. He listened and calmed. I painted His beauty. He brought me peace. Those moments consumed much of my day and night. They provided solace and kept my fears beyond the paned window, far away over golden grass hills and green forests of the day and into the blackness of night. Andre was most likely finding comfort in his own manner. It was not me, but the Lord whom he needed the most.

One day Andre emerged from the barn and called to me as I swept the porch.

""I'm heading to the post office and then meeting Papa at the hardware store to help with supplies. Be back before lunch." He jogged down the drive, then stopped. "Need anything in town?"

"No, I filled the pantry a few days ago." I continued sweeping the stone slabs, then added, "Not sure if Monsieur Caval has any left with the shortages, but can you get me sheets of paper? Any kind would be fine. It would be a miracle, but watercolor paints too. Let me get some money." I ran into the house and returned to find Andre, one foot propped on the front step, a hand extended for money, the other hand holding a sealed letter.

I pointed to the letter. "Do you think it will reach him?"

"Don't know, but it's worth a try. I've prayed a lot over this letter, and God will get it to him if it's meant to be. I'm sending it to the address Remy's parents gave me." He grinned, reminding me how handsome he had always been and how becoming a man fit him so well. "Which colors do you want?"

"Anything that reminds you of here."

"Where?" Andre looked around.

"Here, silly. I have some serious painting to do, so whatever you can get your hands on will be appreciated." I handed him the francs and felt a reoccurring tingle that continued to surprise me when he was near.

He winked. "I'll see you soon."

He ran to the road, his stride long and smooth, shoulders set back with confidence. His dark hair, grown a little longer over the winter, fluttered alongside his tanned, defined cheekbones. *What am I thinking? He's my brother.*

But not by blood. The last thought came rushing in, and I felt heat creeping up my neck.

Andre stopped at the edge of the drive and called back, "What was it you wanted? Bread and cheese?"

"That's it." I laughed and shook the broom in his direction. "Now get going, slow poke." Perhaps God brought him to us for many reasons.

Could God have brought him for me?

He ran until he disappeared around the curve. Suddenly, I was overwhelmed by the fear that chased *me* as I ran after Mama many years ago—the same dreadful fear that taunted me along the pond's edge last summer. Its intensity and reality was so great, I spun around, yanked the screen door open, and darted into the house. The door slammed like a giant fly swatter as I ran down the hallway toward the back of the house. Fumbling with the doorknob to the studio, I whimpered like a hunted animal. Finally, the door opened. I slipped inside and twisted the lock.

My heart pounded as I slumped against the wall and slid to the floor. With my arms crossed tightly across my chest, I held myself and stared at the closed door. A haunting voice, my own conscience, reverberated in my mind.

You'll lose him too, foolish child. Everyone you've ever loved leaves you.

"That's not true." My voice wavered.

Your mother and Jack chose to leave you.

"I couldn't stop them." My voice had somehow separated from my body, scolding me for my imperfections.

Charles left you too. He didn't want to go, but you let him drown.

"No!" Like a child having a tantrum, I screamed and kicked at the legs of the towering wooden easel. "I didn't mean to leave him alone!" I shouted in defiance as the easel teetered and fell toward my head. I covered my face and yelled, "I was only chasing the butterfly ..."

My eyes slowly opened and tried to focus. A damp stream trickled along my temple and a dull pain pulsed across my head. I wiped my hand on my forehead and peered at my fingers. A deep red smudged my hand. Had I been painting? It resembled alizarin crimson, the same color that punctuated the centers of the poppies covering the fields.

I pushed myself to my knees and the room swayed. Through blurry eyes, I noticed my easel crumpled next to me, a jagged crack in one of its legs. A large canvas lay cockeyed on the floor, splattered with green paint that still oozed from a dented can near my foot. Directly above my head, another can rested on the precipice of the jilted shelf. I crawled toward the center of the room and surveyed the disaster. More liquid dripped down my face, passing over my lips and tasting of blood.

"Papa! Andre!" I called out, then remembered I was alone. With a bloodied hand on my paint table, I pulled myself up and hung on to the wall. My wet fingers slipped on the doorknob, but they finally unlocked the door. My feet followed the hallway toward the bathroom.

A gasp escaped at my reflection in the vanity mirror. "What have I done?" Grabbing a towel, I pressed it gently on the gash along my hairline and felt my knees go weak as I heard truck tires grind over the pea gravel and come to a stop. Two doors slammed. I heard voices and tried to call out as I lay on the bathroom floor. My head pounded like a bass drum.

"Help," I whispered, tasting stale blood on my swollen lower lip.

The familiar whining of the screen door, then boots on the hardwood floor gave me the needed energy to call out. "Papa."

"Ella, that you? We're home with a truck full of supplies."

I groaned and pushed up on my elbows. Footsteps sounded down the hallway.

"We have a surpri—"

My father's face paled as he peeked in the bathroom. "Oh, Lord! What happened?" He knelt next to me.

I wanted to cry but my head hurt too much. "I fell."

"More than that happened. Andre!"

The screen door snapped and Andre appeared. "Ella?" The shock in his voice was scary. He looked as if he hardly recognized me.

"Here. Help me get her off the floor and into the bedroom." They hoisted me under each arm. Like a rag doll, my legs wobbled.

I steadied myself against the sink. "I'm alright now."

"That's what you think." The two men half walked, half carried me into the bedroom.

"Let me sit on the edge of the bed. I don't want to lie down." I lurched forward as nausea swept over me.

"Get a cold towel," Papa barked. Andre disappeared into the hallway, then reappeared in a flash. "Lie down, Ella." Papa's voice was serious and I followed his order. A cold cloth was placed on my forehead and covered my eyes. Another pain shot through my skin and I winced.

"She's got a good gash, Papa. Looks like we need the doctor."

"And a split lip too." Papa lifted the cloth, leaned over, and looked into my eyes. He cursed. The only other time I had heard him use such language was the night he and Mama fought. The next day she was gone. "Who did this, Ella?"

"Nobody."

"How'd you get all beat up?" Andre seemed confused. "I'm taking a look around." He left the room and his heavy footsteps patrolled the house like a bloodhound.

"Something isn't right here. There's talk of Nazi supporters in the south, bullying folks and even worse, but I didn't think it could be here. Was it a group of them?"

I was embarrassed at my own foolishness. "No one was here, I promise."

"Papa! You've got to come see the studio. It's all busted up."

"Stay right there." Papa pointed to the bed and hurried out.

Their voices were muffled. I couldn't make out what they were saying, but when they returned to my bedside, each held a shotgun as if marching to war.

"What are you two doing? I told you no one was here."

They exchanged quizzical looks.

"Would you please listen to me?"

Papa rested his gun and leaned it against the wall. Andre, not ready to disarm, stepped toward the window and peered out, his shotgun ready.

My father sat on the edge of the bed, the smallest movement making my head pound. "Then tell us what happened. We need to get the doctor out here to take a look at you."

How do I admit my stupidity? And worse, why was I in such a rage? "It was an accident."

Andre left his sentinel for a moment and looked over his shoulder at me.

"What were you saying about the Nazis, Papa?" I asked.

"We'll fill you in after we take care of you. We got some news in town that has everyone's nerves on edge." Papa narrowed his eyes. "Now, tell me exactly what happened."

A blush swept over me as I bent the truth and said I had accidentally bumped my easel while lifting a large canvas. "The easel tipped over, hit the shelving, and knocked a can of paint onto my head." I went on to explain seeing my reflection in the bathroom mirror and how I must have fainted at the sight of blood. "Most likely, I hit my lip on the sink when I went down."

Papa wore a skeptical look as he listened to my story. When I was finished, he wiped the dried blood from my head and dabbed my lip with the cool towel. "Well, one leg of the easel is broken, but it can be fixed easy enough. We'll get the paint wiped up from the floor. It splattered on the wall, but I can touch it up later today." He left the room and water ran again in the sink. Then he was on the phone, presumably calling Dr. Levin.

"That was quite a bump to make a mess like that." Andre stood by the open window. His gun rested at his side. "And I don't mean the bump on your head." He squinted an eye at me and seemed to look straight into my soul.

"What, you don't believe me?" My head throbbed and my heart beat faster. "It was an accident. I was clumsy."

"I believe it was an accident." He stepped to the side of the bed. "But I know you too well. You aren't clumsy. Something else happened today that you aren't telling."

He gently touched my cheek and pushed a strand of hair behind my ear. I looked into his deep green eyes and felt light-headed, not from my wound, but from an overwhelming sensation of wanting Andre to lean over and kiss my lips, soothing the pain and making it all better.

Don't fall in love with him. The voice returned. *He'll leave you.* I squeezed my eyes shut. *Something terrible will happen to him if you do.* I must have winced.

"Ella, you all right?" Andre's concern knocked the voice away.

"I'm fine. It just hurts."

Papa stepped into the room. "Doctor will be here shortly. He said to keep you quiet."

Andre gathered both guns. "I'll put these away and start unloading the truck." He winked at me and my heart fluttered. "Be back soon with your surprise."

Seventeen

Secret Paintings, 1940

Though my head was healed—stitches removed, bruises faded, and headaches less frequent—something had happened to my heart. In the weeks that followed, I hid myself in the studio, painting from morning until night, only surfacing to make meals. None of us spoke much. We each occupied our own world, though Papa and Andre shared a common fear.

"Benito Mussolini." Blood rushed to Andre's face, darkening his already-tanned skin. Water spilled on the table as he slammed his glass. "The coward has decided to come out of his shell now that the allies look beat."

"Sure, he wants to reap what Hitler has sowed. But the Italians don't know how to fight. No offense, Andre." Papa grinned and shrugged one shoulder.

"None taken. We're lovers, not fighters." The young man smiled back and I blushed, glad my father was glancing out the window.

"They barely lasted two weeks in our hills." Papa pushed aside the curtain, probably making sure a stray soldier hadn't crept onto his property. "It's a crazy time though. Since Dunkirk, things are slipping away. Now that the northwest of France is occupied by the Germans, the Nazi supporters are crawling like maggots down here." He shook his head in disgust. "I never would have believed that my own country would stoop so low."

"At least the Resistance is growing. There are plenty of true Frenchmen, even though the Vichy supporters are everywhere. Petain has turned out to be a traitor." Andre lowered his voice. A strange paranoia filled the kitchen. "You can't trust anyone now."

I blotted the damp tablecloth. "The Italians have crossed the Mediterranean into northern Africa. The Germans followed to help. It's like Hitler is everywhere." The men stared at me, and I placed my hands on my hips. "Well, I *do* listen to the radio. And I agree. The Americans need to get involved."

"Americans?" Papa slammed his fist on the table. Again, the plates and glasses rattled. "They've got their own problems." He muttered something else.

"What's that, Papa?" Andre bit into his bread.

Papa half laughed, again shaking his head. "I said they've got their own problems, including Ella's mother."

I jumped at the mention of her. "Do you know where she is?" I hadn't asked where she went since the day after she left, so many years ago.

"My guess is she's somewhere in New York. I tried to send a letter after Charles died, but it was a wild goose chase." He ran his fingers around the rim of his glass. "Not sure if her mother and father, your grandmother and grandfather, would still be alive, but I would bet that's where she went. Though who knows? Marie never got along with her mother. You probably never noticed. You were too young when we lived in New York. Your mother and grandmother, at best, tolerated one another."

"Why? Did something happen?" I tore a large chunk of the crusted bread, then divided it into smaller pieces as my hands shook. I remembered Mama's slender fingers wrapped around the tarnished cheese knife as each evening she sliced an assortment of fromage for our dessert.

"Nothing specifically that I'm aware. Marie's mother never wanted her to be a musician. Do you remember your mother's beautiful voice? She played the piano like an angel." Papa cocked his head as if listening to some faraway music.

The familiar pain surged in my chest. "Yes, it's something I'll never forget."

"Her father believed in her, encouraged her to do something with her talent, but Marie would only play privately. Sometimes on Christmas, she'd play for the family. He had even arranged an opportunity through his business connections for your mother to play at the governor's mansion. Franklin Roosevelt was the governor of New York at the time. It would have been the chance she needed to get noticed." He leaned back in the chair and rested his glasses on top of his head. "You know, Eleanor Roosevelt was Marie's favorite, her hero, so to speak. She read every article about the woman. I admit, Mrs. Roosevelt has proven herself to be quite a lady. They say she's the legs, and often the voice, for her husband, even now while he's President of the United States." Papa chuckled. "Did you know you're named after her?"

"Mrs. Roosevelt?"

"Sure. Ella Moreau. She even suggested we Americanize my surname from Moreau to Moore. Can you imagine that? Ella Moore? She thought she'd tricked me, but I knew all along."

I couldn't help but smile at Mama's sneaky plot.

"Besides, I love the name *Ella*."

"Why didn't she take the opportunity to play for the Roosevelts?" Andre's mouth was full as he spoke.

"She didn't want to cross her mother. Your grandmother wanted her to focus on being a good wife and mother. She thought chasing music would lead Marie down the wrong path. But honestly, I think Marie was scared she would fail, that she'd never realize her dream."

I settled in the chair across from Papa and met his eyes. "Was it her passion?"

"It was." His eyes misted. "I tried to encourage her. Her music was one of the things that kept me falling in love with her." He pulled a handkerchief from his side pocket and wiped his face. "But if I'm honest, I was too busy chasing my own life. So much that I dragged her away from her home and took us all the way across the ocean so I could have my dream."

"Why couldn't she have her music here?" Andre stopped eating, focused on the story of the woman he had never known.

"That's what I told myself. I figured we'd get settled, she could have a new piano just like the one she played at home, and—"

"But you never got her one." I finished his painful memory.

"No." Papa took a long, thoughtful drink of water. "I started putting all our money into the vineyard, bringing the family label back to its glory like it had been when my father ran the business. I was busy with my other job in Marseille and ..." He rubbed his hand over his stubbly chin. "And I forgot about her." He shook his head. "I forgot who she truly was."

Andre frowned. "Didn't she say something? How she missed her music?"

"She did at first." My father's eyes widened and a vacant, forlorn space occupied their darkness. "I promised to get her a piano, even take her to Paris for concerts. We'd find an instructor to give her lessons in voice and piano, though I told her she was a natural."

"None of that happened?" Andre questioned.

"Our talks, my promises, well, they sometimes turned to arguments. I wanted her to support me around here, take care of the children and the house while I was working in the city." Papa mindlessly pulled apart a piece of bread, crumbs falling onto the tablecloth. "She changed. She wasn't happy. She became hollow ... like a fallen tree in the field whose life fades away."

"Then she left." I whispered the words but their reality shouted.

Papa's eyes twitched. He looked like a man waking from a trance. "She did. I think she used her last bit of energy, and probably her courage, to leave. I didn't think she'd do it. Especially since she loved her children."

"She couldn't have loved us." My curt tone surprised even me. "She wouldn't have left if she did."

"No, she did. But she stopped loving me."

"Maybe she thought we didn't love her enough." A lump filled my throat. "I was too busy bothering her. Jack said I used to follow her around like a chicken in the yard."

"That's what little girls are supposed to do with their mothers." Papa smiled at the thought, but sadness quickly chased the moment away. "I'm so sorry, Ella. I never meant for our lives to go this way."

* * * * *

School would resume in September. I tucked myself inside my studio like a caterpillar wrapped safely in its cocoon while a hidden miracle occurred. I was determined to paint the best memories of my past and pray for my dreams of what could be.

To do this, I made a deal with God. Since he allowed those I loved—Mama, Charles, and Jack—to be taken away, then he would gift me the talent to paint images and recollections of them in a magnificent way. The paintings would preserve what was left of my memories and become reminders of what could have been. And taking a bold stance, I told God if I painted images of Andre and Papa, nothing bad would happen to them. In my mind, he owed me that. The paintings would be for his and my eyes only, hidden in the solitude of my studio in Roussillon where life would be safe—protected from the darkness crawling across the earth.

Considering the wartime shortages, it was a miracle that Andre was able to buy extra paint and paper from the supply store. Monsieur Caval had given him a discount knowing the war was consuming most people's time and thoughts. Creativity and art would have to wait until peaceful times returned.

Monsieur Caval had scrawled an encouraging note. He was glad I was continuing my artwork, even in this difficult time. He had tucked it in the bundle and instructed Andre to deliver it to me along with the art supplies. I was rereading the note when the studio door creaked.

I turned abruptly. "What are you doing here?"

"Thought you'd want some lunch." Andre set a plate filled with fresh strawberries, bread, cheeses, and a sliced hardboiled egg on the table near the window. "Sorry if I interrupted." He started for the doorway.

"No. You didn't." I folded the paper and tucked it into my pocket. "It's just that you startled me. You can stay."

Andre propped himself on the windowsill. With the sunlight behind him, his dark silhouette revealed broad shoulders angling toward a narrow waist and long legs. His tousled hair ruffled in the breeze. Though his face was shadowed, the intensity of his green eyes penetrated me—as if he were somehow reading my mind and, perhaps, my heart.

"Do you need something?" I was embarrassed at my own silly question.

"No. Just figured you were hungry." An awkward silence hung between us. He snatched a strawberry from the plate and popped it in his mouth. He peered around me. "Who's that in the background?"

I turned toward the easel and felt heat creep across my face. A faint pencil sketch of a man and woman occupied an unpainted portion of the paper. They walked along a cypress tree-lined road, hand in hand.

"Who?" I stepped in front of the image.

Andre pointed at the paper. "Those people."

"No one in particular." I swirled a brush in the jar, tapped it against the glass, and dipped it into a dollop of ochre paint. "Just people."

"Where are they going?" Andre stood and approached the easel.

"No place in particular." I stroked a light wash over the path they walked.

As he leaned over my shoulder, I felt his closeness and breathed the scent of earth and grapes. "Are they going someplace wonderful?" Then he said, barely above a whisper, "Are they in love?"

My hand jerked, leaving a yellow streak across a pointed tree. "Look what you made me do. And don't be ridiculous. Of course they're not in love." I brushed over the blemish with clear water, the earthen ochre blending in with the rich olive and warm browns.

Andre stepped away, circled around behind the easel, and peeked at me from the side of the large piece of watercolor paper. "Why can't they be in love?"

I couldn't answer. Instead, I watched the muddied colors drip down the surface of my painting as the penciled couple stood motionless in the middle of the path.

"I'd better get back to work." Andre's voice sounded far away as he started for the door.

"Andre." I forced a whisper as I continued to look at the colorless people.

"Yes?"

I couldn't look at him. "They can't love each other."

"Why is that, Ella?" He stood behind me. "Why are you so sure?" He ran his fingers down the length of my long hair. I wanted him to take me in his arms, hold me tightly, and tell me nothing awful would ever happen again. "Why can't they be together if they're in love?"

I tilted my head back into his palm and voiced the words as if they were my curse. "If she loves him, he'll …"

"He'll what? What will happen?" Gathering my hair to one side, he leaned against me, his lips brushing my neck.

I felt faint, but knew it was time to finally expose the dreaded reality that pursued me since the day I chased Mama down the dusty road. "He'll go away."

"Not if he loves her too."

"Yes, even if he thinks he loves her, he'll go away." I turned to him and studied his face, contemplating whether to reveal any more of my dark secret.

He squinted as though peering directly into the secrets of my heart. "Why would he do that? Why would he leave the girl he loves?"

"He doesn't have a choice. If he doesn't leave her, something horrible will happen to him, whether he knows it or not."

Andre shook his head. "Then why are those people in your

painting?" He reached for the paper and snatched it off the easel. "Tell me the truth." His kind eyes now glared at me.

I stumbled back and then steadied myself in defense. "Artists paint people all the time."

"Not like this." He paced around the small room in tight circles, clutching the paper. "And not like the others."

"The others? What are you talking about?"

He stopped his pacing. "You know exactly what I'm talking about."

"I do not." I started for the door, but he grabbed my hand and spun me around.

"Don't lie to me, Ella." He pulled me to his chest. "Who are those two people in the paintings stacked under the tarp?"

I pulled away and glared at him, but his stare was relentless. "Those are private. Why did you look under there?"

A hint of embarrassment crossed his face. "I wasn't looking for anything." He placed the painting back on the easel. "It was going to be a surprise. I was making more canvases for you and wanted to see what sizes you needed. I looked under the tarp and saw finished paintings."

"But you shouldn't have looked at them." I walked toward the corner of the room and tugged on an edge of the draped cloth, ensuring it covered the contents hidden underneath.

"We've been wondering what in the world you've been creating in here."

"Who?"

"Your father and I. Who else?" Andre approached the corner. "We figured you must have painted *something*. You've been in here all summer."

I widened my stance and crossed my arms. "Of course I've been painting, but what I paint is none of your business."

"Looks as though you've been painting me."

"Why would I do that?"

He stepped toward me with an odd look. "Because you're in love with me."

"You're conceited." I averted my eyes as he stepped closer.

"No. But I am in love with you." He gently turned my face. "They're the most beautiful paintings I've ever seen." He whispered into my hair, "I pray all of them come true."

My eyes looked into his, wishing to find a safe place. After a glimpse, I closed my eyes, then felt his lips touch mine.

Andre stepped back and smiled. "I'll let you get back to work." He walked toward the doorway. "Maybe someday you'll tell me about the people in the other paintings too."

I stood in the corner for a long time, staring at the vacant doorway. Finally, I lifted the edge of the tarp, peeled it back, and exposed the stack of canvases and paper. Each piece held layers of paint, encapsulating my most precious memories and providing hope for my many fragile dreams. How could I protect them? They must be hidden.

I stepped in front of the easel, stared at the sketched woman, and spoke in a whisper for the walls, my paints and brushes, the lavender-filled vase, and God to hear. "She can only love in her paintings—it's safe there." I ran my fingers over the damp paper, wishing for that moment I could step inside and run headlong down the unknown path with the man I truly loved.

Eighteen

Remy, 1940

Word of Remy's death at Dunkirk spread quickly through our small town. Neighbors and friends trickled in and out of Auguste and Eloise Patin's blue-shuttered home to share condolences and gratitude for Remy's service and bravery to defend the homeland.

Papa, Andre, and I stayed with our friends, mostly to help and support them, but also drawn to their grief, knowing word of Jack's death could arrive at any moment. Remy's letters had been our only source of information about Jack's whereabouts and well-being. We had learned not to expect letters from the one we loved.

I helped Madame Patin prepare food for the visitors. We had encouraged her to talk with the neighbors or rest, but her busy hands seemed her only respite from the pain permanently etched on her face.

Papa and Andre gathered in the front yard with the men. They spoke in hushed tones about the war and patted Auguste on his drooped shoulders. The droning news on the radio and in the papers had become relentless as battle after battle played on, and numbers of casualties for the Allies mounted. However, Germany was beginning to meet its match and, despite Remy's death, I imagined encouraging words were being exchanged that the nightmare would eventually end, and Auguste's only son's bravery and dedication to France would not be wasted.

"Did you know he had feelings for you?" Eloise wiped her hands on her appliquéd apron. "He told me the day he left for the war."

"I didn't know. I mean, we talked often." I circled the table and randomly rearranged the flowers in the vase.

"What did you talk about?" Eloise stepped to the sink and slid the newly-washed plates back into the sudsy water.

"Let me help you. Those have already been cleaned." I touched her arm.

"It doesn't matter. I'll clean them again. There's nothing else to do. But tell me, what did you talk about, if it's not too private. I want to imagine his voice."

My throat tightened as I remembered a conversation with Remy. "We talked about lots of things, you know, kids at school, his plans to go to the university and maybe become a teacher someday."

"He loved your art. Word around town is you have a God-given talent."

"Who says that?"

"Monsier Caval. He brags that he's the one keeping you painting during the war. He swears someday you'll be famous."

"Dear Monsieur Caval. Yes, he's been very helpful. It would be wonderful if he were right." I dried a stack of plates and placed them in the cupboard. "Remy was wonderful about my art. When he came over to see my brothers, he always asked to see my work. He had a way of seeing the same things I liked to paint. One evening there was a beautiful sunset over the hills. He was so excited that he came running up from the pond and insisted I grab my brush and paints and get to work immediately."

Eloise smiled. "Did you ever talk about the two of you?"

"Not really. I always thought he was handsome, but my brother made it clear Remy was his friend, and they had better things to do than be around me." I lifted glasses from the cupboard. "Jack said I flirted with Remy. Maybe I did a little." I looked at the back of his mother, hunched over the kitchen sink, and my heart ached.

"Hmmm." Eloise continued scrubbing the submerged plates. "He told me he was in love with you." She gazed out the window as if expecting her son to arrive any moment. "When he got home from the war, he wanted to spend time with you. Perhaps talk about marriage."

The glasses slipped from my hand and crashed to the floor. "Oh, I'm so sorry!"

Eloise bent over and lifted the shards off the wooden floor as I stood frozen.

"Let me get the broom." I started for the pantry but she took my arm.

"Did you hear me, Ella? He loved you."

I looked into her bloodshot and swollen eyes, but couldn't speak. I only saw a desperate mother, her eyes pleading with me to bring back a part of her son that was impossible to retrieve. Worse yet, I knew—in some remote manner—I was to blame for Remy's death on the bloody soil of Dunkirk.

Nineteen

Return and Revenge, 1945

"Where there is death, there is life." That's what Mama told me when I wept the first time I saw the rolling fields of Roussillon sunflowers slump their heads and cover their faces with withered and crumpled leaves.

I had never seen such a sight. In New York, we played on the green lawns, ran along the gravel paths, then stopped to rest on a bench and feed the pigeons bits of day-old bread. The city parks seemed endless with manicured lawns and big pots and boxes filled with bright flowers along the walkways.

Roussillon had its own magic. Fields of intense golden sunshine stretched in perfect unison. By the end of summer, the stalks towered above my head as I wove my way beneath their heavy umbrellas. But now, after standing at attention throughout the summer and dutifully following the day's light with their glorious sunshine faces, the flowers looked sad and defeated.

"The birds are having a royal feast." Mama had pretended to peck at my face and neck with her nose. It tickled and I laughed. "But the sunflowers are wiser. They know their seeds will get knocked to the ground as the birds celebrate. Then they'll hide in the soil until next summer."

"They hide?" I wiped a stray tear. "Why, Mama?"

"Because next summer, at the perfect time, the seeds will open and push new stalks toward the sky. Even though the old plants die, those tiny seeds live, tucked under a winter blanket in the dirt. They return each summer to say hello to the sun."

"And to look beautiful." I sighed, imagining their return.

Mama gazed at the stretch of land rolling upwards behind our barn and toward the narrow creek. "You're right, Ella. They are beautiful."

I slipped my hand into Mama's coat pocket and snuggled against her thigh. I shut my eyes and imagined myself a tiny seed waiting patiently through the cold winter until it would be time to push from the earth when the sun called my name.

* * * * *

"Monsieur and Madame Patin, more coffee?" I lifted the fresh pot from the stove.

"Ella, you must call us by our first names. We appreciate your manners, but you're practically grown now." Madame Patin offered her cup for a refill.

Monsieur Patin lifted his own cup. "Besides, we've been through plenty together—"

"That we've become family." Papa raised his cup as well.

I smiled at the three faces. "All right. More coffee for Eloise, Auguste, and Henri."

"Oh no you don't. I'll always be Papa to you." He gave me a light-hearted, though stern look.

I returned the look. "I was teasing. You'll be Papa even when I'm old and gray."

"Like the rest of us." Auguste chuckled, and I realized I hadn't heard him laugh since Remy's death nearly five years ago.

The back door closed behind Andre as he swung off his coat and tossed it onto the hook. "Speak for yourselves. I'm not old and gray, at least not yet. I'm freezing though."

"I'd better make a full pot." I ran the water in the sink and looked out the window. "Are we expecting someone? There's a man at the end of the drive."

"Don't think so." Papa returned to his conversation with the others about the weather.

I squinted and tried to focus on the man's face, which was mostly concealed by a tan hat. His hands were pushed deep in the side pockets of a drab green coat, and his pant legs were tucked loosely into stocky, black boots.

"He's military."

"What's that you said?" Auguste came and stood behind me. "He sure is but doesn't look like he's here on official business. Thank God for that."

The others squeezed around the sink and looked out the window, then Papa headed for the door. "I'll go see what he needs."

The rest of us watched from the open window as the man approached the house with his head down, favoring his left leg.

"Hello there. Can I help you with something?" Papa called from the drive. He walked toward the man, then halted abruptly.

When the man lifted his head, my hand jerked, and I dropped the coffee pot into the sink. The metal clanged against the porcelain. "Jack!" I gripped the edge of the counter as my knees gave way. My father ran toward his son.

Andre stood at my side as Auguste started for the door. "My God, it's really him. Come on Eloise, let's go—"

"No, Auguste. Let them go first." Eloise motioned Andre and me toward the door. Her eyes filled with tears and my heart ached. Auguste went to his wife and wrapped his arms around her. She buried her head against his chest, and they stood in the middle of the kitchen comforting each other.

I steadied myself at the window again, remembering the day my brother left for war and the horrible exchange of words between he and Andre. Though Jack's arms hung at his sides, Papa wrapped his own arms around his son, who held a dirty canvas bag that looked as though it had been dragged in dirt for miles.

Andre turned me to face him. "Ella, go welcome your brother home." My mouth was dry. "Come outside with me. He's your brother too." "I doubt he feels that way. He never wrote me back." "Maybe your letter never reached him." "Maybe." Andre nodded his head toward the door. "Go on."

I untied my apron, folded it lengthwise, and laid it over the back of a kitchen chair. From inside the screen, I watched Papa sling the canvas bag over his shoulder as the pair walked toward the house. I pushed the screen door open and slipped onto the porch, staring at the brother whom I hardly recognized. His once-rounded face was reduced to hollows beneath his cheekbones. Even without his bag, he leaned toward the right as his left leg bent awkwardly at the knee like an old piece of driftwood.

They stopped at the base of the porch. Jack tipped his hat back and forced a smile at me.

I stepped to the edge of the porch. Even though his stance was crooked, he had grown taller and we looked directly into each other's eyes. "I'm so happy you're home … and safe. You look good." Just as the last words left my mouth, I was sure he knew I was lying. He was always able to call me on fibs when we were young.

"Well, not so sure about the looking good part, but I'll take the happy to have me home." He smiled a real smile and extended his arms toward me.

I grabbed my brother's hands and pulled him close. He smelled of faraway places, danger, and sadness, but hints of him bathed my memory.

We held each other until he pushed me away and peered over my shoulder. I turned to see Andre standing in the doorway. Papa tossed the heavy bag onto the porch with a thump.

"Welcome home. We've missed you."

"Appreciate that." Jack surveyed the house, followed by silence.

"Here, let me carry your bag inside." Andre reached for the bag.

"I'll get it." Jack hoisted himself onto the porch, snatched the bag, and swung it over his shoulder.

Papa came up behind the two men. "Here, hold the door open for your brother, Andre, and we'll all go inside for a proper homecoming."

Andre and Jack exchanged uneasy glances. Andre offered his hand. "Good to have you home, brother."

Jack fumbled with his bag. "Good to be home." He shuffled through the door, and the rest of us followed, each of us looking as if we'd seen the same apparition.

In the kitchen, Eloise rose from her chair and embraced our weary soldier.

"Oh, Jack, I'm sorry, I've given you a pink lipstick mark." Eloise laughed and rubbed his cheek with her shirtsleeve.

"It's fine, Madame Patin. I haven't had a kiss in sometime." He winked. "Leave it on. Maybe it will bring me good luck."

"You still have your wit." Eloise stepped aside as Auguste took Jack's hand, shook it firmly, then pulled him into his arms. He held him a long time, probably wishing he had the chance to welcome his own son home the same way.

Papa pulled an extra chair to the table. "Let's get you something to eat and drink and tonight we'll have a wonderful meal."

"That sounds perfect. I haven't had a good meal in a million years."

Jack pulled himself up to the table and the others joined.

I placed a fresh baguette with raspberry jelly and sliced apples and pears in front of him. He tore a large chunk of bread and stuffed it in his mouth. "Let me get you some water to help that go down." I filled a pitcher and set it on the table with a glass. "I'll get the coffee going. It'll be ready in a few minutes." I retrieved the coffee pot from the sink where it laid on its side, empty and cold.

With a mouthful of bread, Jack turned toward the Patins. "How's Remy?"

There was silence. My brother glanced around the table, and then at me. "Where is he?"

I lowered my eyes and wrung my hands on a tea towel hanging limply from a drawer.

"I said, where is he?" Jack slammed his fist on the table, rattling the platter and cups.

"He's dead." Papa whispered the words, but their harsh truth screamed in my ears.

"No, he's not. I saw him when the medics took us. We talked. He was going to be fine." Jack pushed away from the table. He approached Auguste and stiffly kneeled in front of him. "He had been shot, but it was not life-threatening. He promised me he'd be fine. We'd both be all right." He held Auguste's hands and pleaded. "I told him I'd see him at home after the war and we'd go fishing together and—"

"My son died at Dunkirk." Auguste enunciated the sounds as pain etched deeper into his face with each word.

My brother's face turned ashen as though death itself crept over him. "No!" He pushed himself from the floor, knocking a chair into the wall. "You're all lying to me!"

Eloise began to cry. I stepped toward Jack and tried to touch his arm. "Please, stop."

Andre spoke firmly. "You're making this harder for the Patins."

"Stay out of this, Andre." Jack's eyes widened like a trapped, wild animal. He backed away, keeping a guarded watch on us. Then he spun around and limped out of the house, the screen door bouncing on its hinges behind him.

Papa lurched out the door after him. The rest of us remained in the kitchen, motionless, turned into stone at the whim of a wicked spell.

* * * * *

We hoped Jack would return for supper. I had prepared a nice meal of baked chicken, along with green beans and asparagus recently canned from the garden. Andre brought fresh bread from town and Papa retrieved a bottle of his premium wine from the cellar.

"He should be home anytime now. Said he'd be back before dark." Papa rolled the bottle on his pant leg, brushing away the dust and revealing a deep, burgundy glow. "A fine meal and glass of wine will do him good."

"What do you think happened to him out there? In the battles?" I set the last plate. "He scares me, Papa."

"Me too, Ella. We have no idea what he went through."

"Why didn't he come home sooner?" I circled the table, straightening the silverware.

"I suppose if they could patch a soldier up and keep him fighting, they'd keep him in the ranks." Papa rubbed his knee as if feeling his son's pain. "He can hardly walk, let alone fight. I tried to ask him about it, but he didn't want to talk."

"Poor Madame ... I mean Eloise and Auguste. Seeing him must tear their hearts out. Do you think they'll be able to come over again?"

"Eventually. They're strong people, but seeing Jack must have been like seeing Remy's ghost."

"I think they were genuinely happy to see him, but then he started acting crazy."

"Crazy?" a voice called through the open kitchen window and I jumped. "Is that what you think I am?"

I leaned over the sink. "Jack? Is that you? You startled me."

His face appeared in the window. "That's what I was taught to do." He crossed his arms and rested his elbows on the stone ledge. "I sneak up and surprise the enemy."

"But I'm not the enemy."

"I'm not so sure about that." He grinned, but the toothy smile from childhood was gone.

"Come inside and fill your belly." Papa tried to make light of the awkward exchange. "We're all ready for a good meal to celebrate my son's homecoming."

* * * * *

The evening air was chilly. We sat on the front porch wrapped in blankets and talked about simple things. The men talked about the last harvest of grapes. I mentioned some of the new neighbors who had moved down from the north.

"Trying to get away from the fighting." Jack lit a cigarette and drew a long breath.

I stared at my brother. "When did you start that?"

He leaned his head back and let out a thick plume that drifted away on the light breeze. "Everyone smokes in the military, whenever they can get a pack." He drew another long breath.

He seemed relaxed, so I asked what had been on my mind. "Do you have to go back?"

"Not planning on it." The tip of his cigarette glowed orange as it dangled from his fingers. "They don't want me back with my bum leg, even though the fighting's over." He flicked the ash to the ground. "Apparently, I'm no use to them now."

Andre looked into the darkening landscape. "Do you want to stay in the military?"

Jack fixed his eyes in the same direction, but I wondered what darkness he saw. After a long silence, he answered. "Who'd ever want to go back to hell? I figure I've killed enough Germans to last me a lifetime."

The silence was suffocating. The only noise was the creaking of Jack's wicker chair as he rhythmically rocked. Smoke exited his mouth and nose like a fire-breathing dragon.

As the last light disappeared, Papa stood and stretched. "Time for bed, everyone. There's still the extra bed in Andre's room."

"I'll be sleeping in the barn."

"That's ridiculous, Son."

"No, it's what I'm use to. Sleeping outside. The barn will be a luxury."

"But we've got a bed for—"

"The barn will do." He leaned forward and mashed his cigarette on the stone.

"Papa, let him be." Andre shot Jack a look and rose from his chair. "I'll get a blanket for him." Andre yanked the door and stomped inside.

Sleep would not come as I wrestled with images of the faceless Germans my brother had killed. I imagined him lying in mud, his leg gushing blood through torn pants as another soldier dragged him to safety. Remy's face appeared, and though covered in dirt and blood, his blue eyes gazed at me and he smiled. His voice was kind and confident. *I'll see you at home this summer. We'll walk in the fields and find you a perfect place to paint. Will you paint for me, Ella?* But before I could answer, his face faded away. I wiped the tears streaming down my cheeks, pushing damp and tangled hair from my face.

The room was still dark. I slipped out of bed and tiptoed down the silent hallway to my studio. Standing in front of a blank paper, my swollen eyes tried to focus while I created a painting for Remy in my mind. I willed the image to travel into my arms, wrists, hands, and then fingers. I painted for my childhood friend and me—again, trying to capture what was good of the past, knowing there were no future memories to make.

Eventually, light streamed into the studio. My stomach growled. Swishing my brush in a water-filled jar, I stepped away from the easel and surveyed my work. On the left side, a worn path snaked its way up a rocky outcropping. From the top of the cliff, I could gaze below to the clusters of erect pines. Beyond the forest, my eyes followed a meandering creek, navigating its way alongside our vineyard, through groves of twisted olive trees skirted with wild poppies, vanishing in the distance past hints of lavender fields.

I laid washes of earthen colors, burnt and raw values of sienna and umber, and then waited patiently for the paint to dry enough to add the details, still vivid in my mind. Many times, our childhood adventures led us to this vantage point. We never told Papa exactly where we explored since the rocks were crumbly and gave way easily. But it was Remy's favorite place. He called it his castle on the hill because he felt like a king looking over his kingdom. When I struggled to climb the steepest parts, he held my hand and called me his queen.

Once at the top, we'd gather on the same smooth slab and stare at the world below us. Never sitting for long, the boys would scurry to another ledge, toss rocks off the jagged cliffs, and listen to them tumble onto the larger rocks below. I'd remain, taking in every changing color, etching each shape and detail into my mind.

The door creaked and I was drawn back to the studio.

My brother's head peeked in the doorway. "Good morning. Thought I'd come say hello."

"Good morning to you. How'd you sleep?"

"Fine except for the barn cat nuzzling against me." He rubbed his shoulder against the door jamb.

"She was keeping you company." I smiled my best smile. "Want to come in?"

"Wouldn't want to interrupt."

"I'm at a good stopping point." I stepped aside from the easel.

"Recognize this view?"

He fixed his eyes on the painting resting on the easel. He stared at it for a few minutes, his eyes following the path to the vantage point at the top of the cliff. "I know this place." His brows furrowed in apparent confusion. "It's Castle on the Hill ... Remy's castle."

"Yes, isn't it a beautiful view?"

My brother's face grew more serious. "Why'd you paint it?"

"What do you mean?"

His jaw stiffened. "You heard me."

"I was thinking of Remy ... actually of all of us. This was the scene that came to mind, so I painted it." I unclipped the paper from the mounts. "It isn't very good. I'll put it away." I pulled back the canvas tarp in the corner of the room and laid the paper on the stack of paintings.

"You know it's good. Better than good." He looked around the easel. "What's all that?"

"Oh, different paintings. Nothing great." I felt his eyes watching me, and a strange tingle crept along my neck.

"Of what?"

I straightened the tarp until the stack was fully concealed and tried to ignore the question.

"Seems like you're hiding something under there."

I turned around and met Jack's stare. "That's silly. It's just a pile of paintings."

"Then why are they covered up?" He stepped toward the corner of the room, his right leg making a thump on the hardwood floor.

"Why are you so interested?" I stepped in front of him and crossed my arms.

He stopped inches from my face, smelling of hay and dirt. "Just wondering what you've been up to since I've been gone." He forced a smile. His teeth were stained, probably from cigarettes and coffee.

"Painting when I have the time." I swallowed hard and maintained my stance. "I've been helping Papa and Andre keep the farm and the vineyard."

Jack walked to the window and pushed aside the curtain. "How convenient it's been for Andre to take over the family business." He snorted.

"That's ridiculous. You know Papa can't do everything. If it wasn't for them working together, the business would have shut down. It was hard to keep it going during the war."

"How many bottles did they give away to the Nazi sympathizers?" He continued to look out the window. "I always wondered the real reason Andre didn't leave with Remy and me." He turned. "Or was it because of you?"

"Please stop. Let's not—"

"What have you two been doing since I've been gone?"

I started for the door. "That's none of—"

"Sure it is. I should know what's up between my little sister and our *brother.*"

His sarcasm made my stomach lurch. I hurried down the hallway, out the front door, and into the open air. I held my stomach and breathed, trying to still my racing heart.

Twenty

Jack's Fury, 1946

Jack's curt answers and short temper made the dismal winter and late spring even bleaker. We tried to make conversation with him to soften his steel edge, but even Papa was denied access to his son's heart and mind.

"I've asked him to work with me in the cellar." Papa ran his fingers through his thinning hair. "Andre and I need help staking the vineyard, but he wants no part of it."

"Maybe I'll ask him to go with me to deliver these in the southern towns." Andre lifted a crate filled with bottles of cabernet. "I could use the help, and maybe it's time for him to get involved with the family business. Give him some purpose." He hoisted more crates into the truck. "Might give us a chance to talk."

"You can ask, but I don't think he'll go." I continued to mark and date the list of orders as the truck bed sagged.

"Probably not, but I feel like I have to keep giving him chances to come around."

"He's choosing not to be here much." Papa stacked another crate. "I hear he's spending time with a woman in Fountaines."

Andre loaded another box. "I meant, give him chances to come around in how he's acting. How he's treating all of us."

"That too." Papa heaved the last crate, the bottles clanging inside.

"Careful there. Let me get that." Andre took the crate and set it in the truck.

"Thanks." Papa wiped his brow with his shirtsleeve though the temperature was still cool. "Time for a rest." He strode across the lawn, shoulders hunched and pants hanging loosely around his hips.

I glanced at Andre. "I'm worried about him. Are you?"

"He doesn't seem to have his usual energy. But I have to remind myself, I turned twenty-three and that makes him forty-seven."

"That's not old. But you're right. Ever since Jack got home, Papa seems older."

Papa and I ate alone that evening. Andre wouldn't be home until the next day. He was making deliveries to restaurants and a few long-time private customers who were still able to afford the luxury of a home-delivered order of Moreau's vintage. After making stops in Avignon, Nimes, and Arles, Andre would follow the coast to Marseilles. There, he would deliver two crates to Monsieur Lenoir, stay the night at his home, and then continue the trip north through Aix-en-Provence, Pertuis, Apt, Manosque, and back home.

Papa had gone to bed shortly after dinner. After painting most of the evening, I pulled on my gown and crawled into bed. I was almost asleep when shouting came from the edge of the drive. A woman's voice yelled, and then a deeper voice ranted. A car door slammed. Soon the engine's rumble faded in the distance.

I waited in the dark and listened for the front door to open. When it didn't, I figured Jack wanted to sleep in the barn again. Turning on my side, I gathered my blanket to my chin and wondered what nightmares still chased my brother.

It must have been long into the night when I awoke to shuffling in the hallway. By the uneven sound on the floorboards, it had to be Jack, probably coming in the kitchen for something to eat. A cupboard banged. There was silence for a few minutes, then the shuffling resumed and stopped at my open door. A sliver of moonlight cast itself across my bedspread and toward the doorway. I watched my brother through barely opened eyes. He swayed to the side and bumped into the door jamb. He mumbled something and stared at me. I wanted to sit up and call him out, but uneasiness swept over me. Instead, I played possum like a frightened animal. After several minutes, he staggered down the hallway. I tried to calm the gnawing in my stomach. How sad to be fearful of my own brother. *Why does it have to be like this?* There was no answer, so I prayed—for Jack—for God to heal his heart and protect him from the anger that consumed him like a raging fire.

I must have dozed during my prayer because suddenly I sat up in bed and cocked my head toward the doorway. I slipped out of bed and tiptoed down the dark hallway, sliding my hand along the smooth plaster wall. A faint light peeked from under my studio door. I wrapped my hand around the knob, turned it slowly, and pushed the door open enough to peek inside.

Jack hunched in the far corner with his back toward me. The canvas tarp was tossed in a crumpled pile near his feet. I gasped and pushed the door open. He hovered over toppled piles of my canvases and strewn papers, digging through them as a dog retrieves a forgotten bone.

"What are you doing in here?"

He remained huddled over the piles, flipping through and tossing them randomly.

"What are you doing? Leave those alone!" I marched toward him and slapped him on the back. "Answer me!"

He turned to face me, swaying in a circular motion. His eyes were bloodshot and swollen. Then he belched. "I want answers from you, little lady."

"You've been drinking."

"And you're smart." He lifted an empty bottle to his lips. "Time for another." He cursed the bottle and threw it on the floor.

"Get out of here right now."

"I'm not leaving until you tell me the truth."

"About what?" I crossed my arms and stepped back.

"About you and Remy." He grabbed a paper from the floor and held it in my face. "What's this about? Don't you think I know who these people are?"

"They're only people walking down a—"

"Holding hands and in love."

I pushed the painting to the side. "What's wrong with that?"

"You don't get it, do you?" Jack sneered. "I know it's you and Remy. You loved him and now he's dead."

"What's that supposed to mean? Of course I cared about him, but I wasn't in love with him. He was your friend. We all loved him. What does that have to do with him getting killed?"

He kicked at the disheveled pile on the floor, staggered, and then regained his balance. "It has to do with everything." He raised an accusing eye and growled the words. "Everyone you've loved has left us or died."

Pierced through the heart, I stumbled at hearing the same words that relentlessly stalked me each day. I grasped the frame of the easel to steady myself as tears swelled in my eyes. "We all loved them—Mama, Charles … Remy."

"But it's you, Ella. Don't you get it?" He rummaged through the paintings and held a small canvas to my face. "You're a curse to our family."

As if my deepest fear had been unleashed, he snatched handfuls of paintings and held one after another in front of my face. Mama reading on the front porch, her pearls twisted around her fingers. Mama in the garden cutting cobalt delphiniums. Mama and me walking through the twisted and tall poppy fields. Charles swinging on a rope, his feet skimming over the surface of the pond. Charles wrapping his big brother arms around Jack and me, the three of us dwarfed by the hovering sunflowers in the field behind our house.

"By painting lovely scenes, you want to appear innocent." He lowered the paper and glared at me. "But you know the truth. Don't you?" He leaned inches from my face, the stench of his breath nauseating. "You chased Mama away. You let Charles drown in the pond. And I don't believe you. You loved Remy and they killed him."

"And you've gone mad." I tried to hold my ground, but my knees were shaking. I had created those paintings in my best attempt to hold on to the special memories of Mama and Charles, images and details I couldn't bear to lose, now dried and preserved in layers of paint. Now, with papers and canvases being shoved toward my face, they were traitors, tormenting and mocking me for making a ridiculous deal with God.

"Enough." I pushed his arm.

"Ah, but there's more. I've barely touched the pile." He motioned to the disheveled mess of wrinkled paintings. "I suppose you have hundreds more hidden." He tossed the paintings onto the floor. "But I do owe you a compliment." He let out another belch. "You are good, Ella. These are fine paintings. In fact, so good I bet Hitler would have loved to get his hands on them. Apparently, the crazy man stole Europe's finest works." Jack raised a finger to his lips, shifted his eyes side to side, and whispered, "I suggest you hide these better. We don't know if a stray Nazi is still lurking around these parts."

I shook my head and held tighter to the easel. "You're a fool. No one knows why Mama left. I tried to help Charles. I wish I had drowned instead of him." Tears were streaming down my face. "And I already told you I wasn't in love with Remy."

"Then who's in that painting with you?" He motioned to the bent paper protruding from beneath a large canvas.

"Andre." I covered my mouth, ashamed at my own betrayal.

Jack smirked, obviously pleased with his interrogation. He paced the room, walking circles around me as though I were his prey. He paused and whispered in my ear. "You let him drown, Ella. You were chasing a butterfly and didn't even hear him call for help." He lifted the large canvas and propped it on the easel. "See, you even painted the evidence." He jabbed his finger at the image of me running through a field in pursuit of the orange butterfly while Charles swam in the pond. "You may not have painted the final scene, but we all know what happened."

I couldn't speak. How could such a cruel brother share my darkest thoughts and fears? Perhaps I was no better than he, and everything truly was my fault.

"And as for Andre, your lover—"

"Stop it."

"Well, isn't that what you call someone when you're in love?"

"You couldn't possibly know about love. Could you?" I was surprised at my own sarcasm and looked away when he glared at me.

Then he chuckled. "I know about *making* love, that's for sure. If that wench hadn't thrown me out of her car tonight, I'd be having a lot more fun with her right now than with you."

"What's happened to you?" I straightened my stance. "We don't know you any longer."

He mumbled something and I stepped toward him. "What did you say?" My brother looked at me and for a brief moment, I saw him again as a young boy.

The words came in a gravelly voice. "I said ... maybe I don't know myself anymore."

It must have been my last ounce of compassion or a desperate hope, but I reached to embrace Jack. He held me at arms length, then gave me a push.

"As for Andre ... he's the next to go." Jack snatched the watercolor painting from the floor and waved it above his head.

"I don't need to hear this." I started for the door.

"But you'd better." His voice teased, privy to a secret I must know.

I stopped in the doorway though my better sense told me to keep walking. "Are you making a threat?" I spun around in anticipation of the answer.

He held the painting with two hands and tilted it side-to-side, mocking its content. "No. You're the threat. You better end whatever relationship you have with Andre before it's too late. Go away from him if you have to. It's his only chance." With one quick motion, my brother ripped the painting in two, then again and again until ragged pieces fluttered to the floor.

"I hate you!" I stormed from the room and down the hallway, running directly into Papa.

"What's going on?" He grabbed my arms, steadying both of us.

"Jack's drunk and acting like a fool." Papa started for the studio, but I held on to him. "Leave him alone. There's no reasoning with him tonight."

"I'll reason with him all right. No drunk comes stumbling into my house in the middle of the night."

"Papa, please." I held my stance, blocking his way down the hallway. Behind me, the back door slammed as Jack slipped out into the darkness.

Twenty-One

To Paris, 1946

Summer proved to be miserable. The brutal heat and lack of rain stifled the vines and restrained them from reaching their potential. Like the vineyards, I was depleted of life, keeping an uncomfortable distance from Andre while trying to bury my feelings for him deep into the cracked earth that was my heart.

Papa sat on the edge of my bed as I pulled clothes from the closet. "I spoke with Monsieur Lenoir this morning. He confirmed Madame DuBois is sending a woman from her office to meet you at the Gare du Lyon. Your train should arrive in Paris at the nineteenth hour." He refolded a blouse ready for my luggage. "Are you sure about this, Ella?"

I smiled at my father. Strands of gray wove through his hair, even more obvious in his morning stubble. "I'm sure." I set my winter coat next to the same leather case I carried when we traveled from America. "You remember when I was fifteen? Monsieur Lenoir told me I needed to go to Paris for my art. Now that I'm twenty-one, I wonder if I should have gone sooner."

"The war wouldn't have allowed it. It will be hard enough in the city. They say Paris is waking up, but it's still difficult to find enough food. People don't have jobs, and I can't imagine many have extra money to buy art." He secured the latch and slid my heavy case onto the floor.

"Yes, but Madame DuBois promised I'll be able to learn from some of the best artists in Europe. Do you know she's a personal friend of Picasso? Also, Monsieur Lenoir said there's an artist … Monsieur Ma—"

"Matisse. Yes, an older gentleman. Apparently, Madame DuBois is the hub of the art world in Paris. She has always made quite a statement."

"Do you know her?" I waited for his answer as I recounted the money for my first month's rent and tucked it back in my pocketbook.

He pulled a handkerchief from his pocket and wiped his brow. "No."

"You're sweating. Do you feel alright?"

He stuffed the handkerchief back in his pocket, stretched out on my bed, and laid his hand over his chest. "I'm fine. Only heartbroken you're leaving home." He grinned, but I knew my papa's expressions, and he couldn't hide his sadness.

I turned away, not wanting to lose my determination to leave. "To think she's allowing me to rent the back room of her gallery. I'll always be grateful to Monsieur Lenoir for making the arrangements." I peered in the vanity mirror and, for a moment, saw my mother looking back at me. Like her, my light blue eyes contrasted with my long, dark hair. I pulled it away from my high cheekbones and, wrapping it into a low knot, realized I wasn't a young girl any longer. Perhaps it really was time to leave home.

"Apparently, when my friend showed her your painting, she said you have a talent she hasn't seen in years." In the mirror, I saw Papa blot his damp forehead with his shirtsleeve. "For your sake, I hope she's right and can help you succeed, maybe even become famous, because I surely can't." He sat up, his eyes finding mine in the mirror. "I've bought you supplies—"

"And built me a lovely studio." I turned and faced him.

"Yes. But for my sake, Ella—"

"Oh, Papa. I need you to support me in this decision." I sat next to him and leaned my head on his shoulder.

"I do. Completely." He gave me a sideways look. "Well, not entirely. I hope someday soon you'll come back here to live and paint." He stood and looked out the window. "Even though it's nearly winter, what could be more beautiful than Roussillon?"

I approached the window and slipped my arm around my father's waist. We stared out at the landscape, breathing in rhythm, enjoying another moment in our shared passion for Roussillon. When he kissed the top of my head, an odd mixture of excitement, sadness, and guilt washed over me. I would never be able to tell Papa or Andre the other reason I must leave home.

In the kitchen, Andre clanged his cup and saucer. "We'd better go before you miss your train. I'll meet you at the truck." He left, not bothering to catch the front door as it slammed.

"Andre hasn't said a word to me in days. He won't even look at me."

"You haven't spoken to him either." Papa poured himself another cup of coffee. "I wish I knew what's happened between you two." He raised an eyebrow.

I fidgeted with the buttons on my coat, then reached for a hug. "I better get going. I'll try to call you late tonight when I reach the gallery."

He lifted my chin. "Ella, listen to me." He paused and brushed my cheek with the tips of his calloused fingers. "You love Andre."

"Of course I do, Papa. He's been a brother to me since I was young."

Papa shook his head, still holding my chin. "You are *in* love with him."

I felt my face redden.

"And he is in love with you." He pulled me to his chest and held me tightly as my tears soaked into his worn, cotton shirt. "Ella, don't ignore love like I did."

Andre opened the door and a breeze swept in. "Hop in the truck, Ella, or you'll miss the train for sure."

Papa gave me a last squeeze. "I'm sorry I can't take you to the station myself. The new customer from Lyon will be here any time now to tour the cellar."

"I understand." I kissed him on both cheeks, then followed Andre to the truck, climbed in, and pulled the heavy door shut. We rambled down the drive and turned onto the gravel road. I stared out the side window as we drove, going past the all-too-familiar scenes of Roussillon. I wondered if this was how it would feel from now on as I let my life pass me by.

* * * * *

The train whistled and snorted its arrival at the small station. Two tracks ran through Roussillon, one heading south, the other north. I lifted my luggage and stepped onto the platform for passengers heading toward the colder and bleaker wintertime in the north.

I wonder on which platform Mama waited the day she left us? Am I no better than her?

The stout, blue-suited conductor strode along the platform calling passengers to board.

I fumbled deep in my pocket. "My ticket." I tried the other.

"You put it in your pocketbook." Andre gestured toward my purse.

I rummaged a moment, then pulled out the paper. "Thanks. I'm a little nervous."

"I was hoping you had lost it and couldn't go." Andre smiled but his eyes were sad.

"That's the most you've said to me in days." Then I made the mistake of looking into his eyes. "Do you mean that?"

"Of course not, I mean …" His mouth hung open but no other words came out.

I grabbed my bag tightly to my waist. "Madame DuBois is expecting me. I have to go."

He stepped toward me. "It was only a joke, Ella. You have to go for your art. You're too talented to stay here forever. It's time Europe learns about Ella Moreau."

"I'll be lucky if anyone notices me."

Andre slowly raised his hands and placed his palms on the sides of my cheeks. I closed my eyes for a moment and felt my legs weaken. *What am I doing?*

His warm breath whispered in my ear, "You'll be noticed. I have no doubt about that. Just be careful."

Our eyes locked, and we stood silently for what felt like a long time before the conductor's whistle pierced the air and knocked us out of our trance.

"Andre, I need to tell you—" My voice was suffocated by the train's engine.

"Have a safe trip. Let us know how things are working out for you." His voice was flat and his face expressionless as he backed away into the engine's steam as if fading out of my life.

"Of course." I lifted my case and walked toward the steel steps leading to the passenger car and stood in line behind parents who were loading the last of their luggage. Their three young children squirmed with excitement, each holding a small bag.

A set of round, cobalt eyes, framed by dark hair, looked up at me. "I'm going to America." The tiny head bobbed. "To live there forever." Her head continued its motion. "Where are you going?"

Like racing back in time, I stared at the little girl, seeing myself so long ago—the same inquisitive blue eyes and swirling dark hair.

She spun in a circle and then stopped. "Are you going home?"

"I … well, I'm going to Paris."

"You are very pretty." Her delicate pink lips curved upwards.

"Thank you. You are very pretty too."

She cocked her head like a tiny sparrow perched on a windowsill. "Why are you going to Paris?"

I had no answer for her. I could only stare at the petite reminder of myself.

"Aimee. Come along." Her mother gave me a quick smile and took her daughter's hand.

"*Auvoir.*" She waved her other hand and disappeared into the train.

Panic grabbed me and I needed to find Andre. But he was gone, the platform empty except for a skinny man sweeping the cement, with a cigarette dangling from his mouth.

The train snorted and lunged. I surveyed the platform one last time, grabbed hold of my case, and stepped into the train.

Twenty-Two

Madame DuBois' Influence, 1947

The winter was bone-chilling, so cold even the *bourgeoisie* shivered in unheated homes. The food shortage was taking a toll on Madame DuBois' mood. Tonight she was particularly grumpy.

"Imagine hosting a party and not having enough food for the guests." She slipped her chubby feet out of her stilettos and propped them on a velvet-covered stool. "*C'est* sacrilege."

My feet ached from being forced into high shoes for the duration of the party. I kicked them off and slumped into the chair facing the Madame. Her width was equal to her height, and I wondered how her proportions remained the same despite the market stalls and *boulangeries* having little inventory since the war.

"See if you can find me something else to eat. I'm starving." She tilted her head back, unable to fully recline due to the dark, tight bun at the base of her neck.

"*Oui*, Madame." I pushed myself up from the chair, my swollen feet welcoming the coldness of the wooden floor.

"And, Ella, as I told you before, I prefer that you call me Emelia when we are alone and Madame DuBois in the company of others." She shut her purple-shadowed eyes. False eyelashes hovered above her high cheekbones like sleeping spiders.

I tiptoed into the small kitchen near the back of the gallery and opened the pantry. A canister of coffee, a bag of hard biscuits, and a small bowl of apples sat alone on the shelf. As well-known and influential as she was, even Madame DuBois had little.

And I have nothing except a back room in which to sleep. "What was I expecting?" I mumbled. *It was my decision to come here. Remember. I had to leave Andre.* I clutched the pantry door and at the thought of his name, my heart ached.

"Did you find something? My stomach is growling." Emelia's voice was drowsy. Even though food was in short supply, there always seemed an ample amount of alcohol in the homes of the wealthy patrons of the arts. Emelia was particularly fond of Chartreuse and, as usual, tonight she befriended too many servings.

"Coming." I peeled an apple, grabbed a handful of biscuits, and hurried into the office, trying to shake the pity from my mind.

"Sit down and talk with me." Emelia's eyes remained closed. "You've been working hard. Your inventory has increased to a point that it's time for your own show."

"Madame … I mean, Emelia. Do you think I'm ready?" I perched on my chair.

"Of course you are." Her crimson lips curved into a sly grin. "The landscape paintings of the south are the most appealing—fields of sunflowers, poppies, lavender—any subject of that sort. The patrons enjoy being reminded of the beauty of France, especially since it's been depressing in Paris for too long."

"What about the cityscapes? I've loved painting the people strolling in the parks, sitting at cafes, and—"

"They want to escape." She stretched her neck from side to side. Pearl earrings dangled and brushed each shoulder. "That is why you will be successful."

"What do you mean?"

She opened her dark, piercing eyes, propped herself upright, teetered, and then leaned forward. "I mean, my dear, you are not of this world. At least not of Paris." She hesitated as if contemplating which words to speak. "Your art takes people to a place that few get to go."

"Didn't they vacation in the south before the war? I'm sure they've seen beautiful landscapes before."

"Listen to me." Her tone was curt. "Of course these people have traveled. In fact, quite extensively. They have the means and, for most of them, the time to vacation." She rolled her shoulders, her heavy chest lifting and falling. "Understand this." She took my hands in hers and rubbed my fingers with her cold hands.

The diamonds and emeralds sparkled on the ring she wore on her right hand, and I wondered if she had ever been in love. "I'm listening."

"It's my job to provide my clients with pieces of art for their enjoyment. They are a competitive group, each wanting to outdo the others by adding to their collections of paintings by Monsieur Legar, Derain, Utrillo. They even fight over Monsieur Picasso's latest works—the odd sculptures made from garbage." She shook her head and frowned. "I can't understand the attraction to those but, regardless, my point is this …" Emelia released my hands and heaved herself from the chair. She paced and the floorboards squeaked beneath her steps. "You have arrived at the perfect time. There's an opportunity for a new look, a revival of paintings depicting what is beautiful about France. You have that talent."

She stopped behind me and whispered in my ear. "You also have the face. A beautiful face desirable to many, but most importantly, to one of my wealthiest customers."

"I'm not—"

"What? Interested?" She resumed her walk. "First, let's see if your art can prove itself. That's why your first show must occur soon. Monsieur Saillard is determined to see more of your pieces."

"Monsieur Saillard?" My disgust was surely obvious as I recalled the older man who eyed me at the evening's party.

"*Oui.* Jean Saillard has noticed your beauty."

I cringed.

Emelia laughed. "He's interested mostly in your art." She displayed a sly grin. "It's his son, Victor, who is interested in you."

So that's who he was—the handsome young man who smiled at me on several occasions tonight. I noticed him too, very tall, light blue eyes, and … "I don't know who he is." Heat rushed into my face.

"Really?" I felt Emelia's eyes cut through me. "Regardless, I've kept most of your inventory tucked away in the gallery for a reason. I'm holding Monsieur Saillard off until I arrange your debut. That way, I'll stir their competitive nature. If one of the patrons wants your paintings, then so will the others. That, my love, raises your value and my profit." She stopped in front of me and ran a finger through my long hair. "And if the show isn't a success, we may need to resort to your good looks." She plopped into the chair.

"I'd like to believe my paintings are good enough …" My voice quivered. "That my appearance doesn't matter."

Emelia stretched back and propped her feet again. "You have much to learn, my dear." She closed her eyes again. "Never underestimate the power of a woman's beauty."

"Or the power of a God-given talent." I winced at my boldness.

The Madame shot me an unsettling glare. "That too. But God made woman for a reason. Didn't he?" A wide grin stretched across her face, and heavy lids reappeared. I watched her chest rise and fall until a loud snore released from her parted lips.

Twenty-Three

Success and Seduction, 1947

I continued to paint from my memory. Endless hills of cadmium yellow, alizirin red, and olive green, lay alongside fields of lavender hues. The skies danced in a swirling mixture of cerulean and cobalt blue while titanium white clouds meandered by.

Only in the privacy of the small workroom in the rear of Emelia's gallery, I dared to journey home. Once there, I imagined embracing Papa on the porch steps. Later in the evening, when the sky's blues turned to deep purples and shades of dark, Andre and I kissed passionately beneath the twisted olive trees.

"It was a grand success." Emelia beamed from one saggy earlobe to the other. "My strategy was perfect. At one point, Monsieur Saillard and Monsieur Batou were about to come to fists over the large poppy field." She released a boisterous laugh. "I love a good fight when it comes to my art."

"Pardon, but don't you mean *my* art?" I wiped my hands on my paint-covered smock.

"Of course it's your art. But at this stage of your career, without me, it would be impossible to get noticed. I divulged you to influential art buyers, and they would like to believe they discovered you."

I secured the lids to the paints and covered my palette with a damp, linen rag. "I am grateful. You've provided opportunities for me that I never would have had in Roussillon." I embraced her and for a moment, missed my mother. "Emelia, tell me, what does it really mean now that you say I'm *discovered*?"

She stepped away and placed a blank canvas on the easel. "It means your work is now in high demand. You need to paint profusely and take advantage of this window of time to sell your work. If your popularity continues, the prices of your paintings will only increase." She uncovered my palette. "You noticed who was at your debut?" Her back was toward me.

"There were so many people. I recognized several from the parties we've attended. The Hensley's from England, Crisella and Raymond Chambrun, the Americans—"

"Arthur and Phyllis Barclay, prominent New Yorkers. They returned after the war. Lovely woman, she is."

"Yes, I enjoyed speaking with her. She asked if I had ever been to New York. I told her I was born there."

"Your mother was from New York, wasn't she?"

"Yes. We think she lives there. Would the Barclays know her?"

"You don't know for sure?" Emelia looked over her shoulder, eyes wide and forehead creased in her typical questioning facade.

"She left when I was seven." A familiar guilt washed over me and I turned away. "I haven't heard from her since."

A deep line appeared between the Madame's brows and her voice softened. "I'm sorry, Ella. Monsieur Lenoir mentioned something happened with your mother."

I stared at her, the Grand Madame of the Parisian art world, a woman whose influence could either ensure or destroy one's future. However, at this moment she wore a dark veil of sorrow, and I wondered what her past held.

We stood for several moments in silence until Emelia seemed to return from a faraway memory and her usual determination resumed. "Do you know who else was at the exhibit? I'm surprised you didn't notice."

"Tell me." I smiled, happy we'd finished the topic of my mother.

"For one, Monsieur Henri Matisse."

"The older gentleman? He complimented my work but didn't introduce himself."

"He likes to go unnoticed, but everyone knows who he is."

"My father said I might meet Monsieur Matisse."

"Did he?" She raised an eyebrow. "Monsieur Matisse, has been a friend of mine for many years. I wish I could say I was the one who secured his success. His exhibits have been popular for years. Although

111

he would never admit it, his friendships with Rouault, Pissarro, Marquet, and especially, Monsieur Picasso have been essential to his career." She shrugged. "He used to work in his Villa Alesia, drawing and painting magnificent nudes of his Hungarian model, Wilma Javor. Now he prefers the warmer climate of the southern town of Venice and comes to Paris only when his health allows."

"I'd like a chance to speak with him again."

"Perhaps. Your conversation with him would be enlightening. He sees something different in your work. He used the word *spiritual*."

"Spiritual?"

"He said your paintings are created with the hands of God." Emelia turned her hands, palms upward, and studied them as if contemplating Matisse's comment. "I'm not a religious woman, so I can't say for sure, but there is truth to what he says. There's an element to your work as though you're painting for God instead of man." She gathered my hands, turning and studying them in the same manner. "The natural talent you possess makes me wonder if you made a deal with God." She grasped my hands firmly and peered at me. "Did you sacrifice something to have this talent?"

I could only stare at the woman's penetrating eyes as memories flooded my mind and drowned my dreams. My head began to spin and I grasped her arms.

"Here, sit down. You must need a rest."

I steadied myself. "No, I'm fine. Probably a little hungry." I rubbed the shirt that hung over my flat stomach.

"I'll send Philippe to get our lunch." She glanced at her wristwatch. "He was due in the gallery five minutes ago. It's good that Brigitte begins work this week. Since sales are picking up, I decided we could use more help than Philippe is willing to offer. Besides, Brigitte is beautiful. She'll attract businessmen into the gallery as they pass by on their way to work."

Ignoring the remark, I felt obligated to acknowledge all she had done. "I'm happy to help your business. I wouldn't feel right staying here if that wasn't the situation."

"We'll see what the critic from *Le Monde* writes in tomorrow's paper."

"A reporter?" My eyes widened.

"*Oui*. The one and only Richard Tetin attended the exhibit. I made sure he knew of the event. He reviews art exhibits, haute couture shows, and, occasionally, the theater. His opinions can either launch or kill an artist's future."

"What if he didn't like my paintings?"

A mischievous grin was accented by lipstick that bled into small wrinkles above her lips. "I wouldn't be too concerned. I know Richard better than anyone, even his wife." She tapped the stark canvas with red-painted fingernails. "It would be a good idea for you to paint before lunch arrives." Emelia turned and walked though the doorway, her high heels chattering on the floorboards.

"Oh, Ella," she called from the gallery, "the other person you should have noticed was Victor Saillard. Why do you think his father was determined to win the bid for the poppies?"

From the storefront, Emelia couldn't see my face redden. I had noticed Victor on several occasions walking along the Avenue des Champs Elysees and near the Place de la Concorde. Several times a week, I followed the avenue toward the busy city center, navigated through the hoards of cars and bicycles circling around the Obelisque, and finally ventured into the Jardin des Tuileries. With my sketchbook, pencils, and small box of paints, I'd find the perfect bench for capturing the images of the magnificent park—gardens thick with a myriad of flowers, spouting fountains, and watchful statues.

Each time, I found myself entranced by the mothers and children. The women would visit with one another while their children waited in line to receive a brightly-colored toy sailboat from the gray-bearded man who rented the *bateaus*. Wooden sticks in hands, the children directed their boats along the edge of the circular pond. When the boats escaped their captains' control and floated out of reach, the children ran in circles around the edge, anticipating the shore to which the tiny boats would eventually travel. The children would jump and scream with excitement as the boats returned from their adventures, and the mothers continued to smile.

I tried to picture my own mother smiling as she watched me run around the pond in my yellow dress. I wanted her to laugh as I chased my boat while it traveled to imaginary ports. But as hard as I tried to create a memory, I only saw myself chasing after her car as she drove away.

* * * * *

It was a particularly sunny day for Paris, and the park bustled with activity as I completed a sketch of the towering chestnut trees casting shadows on couples, young and old, walking hand in hand along the gravel walkway. Even though Emelia requested, or rather required, provincial landscapes, I snuck away each day to paint miniatures of images and scenes in the city.

"May I sit with you?" I looked up from my pad into the silhouette of a man. The sun shone behind him, darkening his face. "Here, the sun's in your eyes." He stepped to the side of me, his wide smile revealing straight, white teeth.

"Monsieur Saillard."

"Victor, please. Monsieur makes me sound as old as my father. May I?" He motioned to the bench.

"Of course." I gathered my supplies and shifted to the left.

"Beautiful day to paint." He surveyed the people passing by. "May I see your paper?"

"It's just a sketch, nothing very interesting." The pad was pressed against my chest, and I blushed at my lack of confidence.

"All your work is good, Mademoiselle Moreau." His smile remained as though rehearsed to perfection.

"Call me Ella. Mademoiselle makes me sound old as well."

"That would be if you were Madame. Luckily for me, you are still Mademoiselle."

Suddenly, the heat of the sun felt intensified, and I began to collect my supplies. "I'd like to move to the shade."

"Let me help you." He gathered the box of paints, and I followed him across the path, under the canopy of the trees where we found an empty bench. "How is this?"

I nodded and sat. Victor laid the supplies on the ground and then settled next to me, his shoulder touching mine. It was uncomfortable, though oddly inviting to be so close to him.

"The painting of the poppy field is bringing much enjoyment." He looked straight ahead.

"I'm happy your parents wanted it for their home." An older couple settled on a bench across from us.

"It's in my home."

"Yours? But I thought your—"

"Yes, my father did the bidding for me. We knew Monsieur Batou would never want to be outdone by a young man. The price would have been outrageous."

"I'm not sure if that's a compliment or not." I focused on the older man holding his wife's hand, neither of them speaking, but enjoying being quiet together.

"That's not what I meant, really. Forgive me." He turned and looked at my profile.

I glanced at him, and then looked straight ahead, cautious not to look directly into his blue eyes. He was handsome, with a strong jaw and brown hair filled with streaks of blond.

"Forgiven."

"Good. Now may I see your sketchbook?"

"Why?"

"Because I'm fascinated by your talent. I want to see how your mind works, and these sketches show your first thoughts before you go to a canvas or sheet of Arches."

"Are you an artist?"

"No, only one who appreciates fine art."

I handed him my sketchbook, studying his expressions as he turned the pages. When he reached the last page, I swallowed hard. "What do you think?"

He hesitated, rubbing his clean-shaven chin. "I think you are incredible." He leaned closer. "I want to learn more about you, and not just as the artist."

"And you are not a bit shy, are you?"

"No, but I prefer *confident*." He stood and stretched his arms above his head. "But I do have a question about your art."

"Go ahead."

"Why are people in your sketches and paintings of Paris, but never in your paintings of Provence?" He tilted his head, obviously waiting for my answer. "People do exist in the south, don't they?"

"Of course people live in the south of France." I scoffed at his question. "My family lives in Roussillon."

"Then why don't you put them in the paintings?"

I straightened my shoulders and looked away. "No reason."

"I'm not the artist, but it seems to me that you intentionally keep them out?"

"That's ridiculous. The paintings are only landscapes. The people don't matter."

"But they do in your scenes of Paris?" He flipped through the pages of my book. "See. The people make the scenes come alive."

"Then perhaps you should ask Madame DuBois if you could

purchase a painting from my Parisian collection." I pulled the pad away and stuffed it into my bag.

Victor sat down, this time near the opposite end of the bench. "I didn't intend for our first meeting to go this way."

"I didn't know we had planned to *meet*."

"Touché. You aren't as shy as I thought you might be. Besides, I've seen you in the park for several months. Today, I finally got the courage to speak to you."

"I thought you were *confident*." He frowned and I regretted my sarcasm. "I'm sorry. That wasn't necessary."

"No offense taken." He scooted closer. "I am confident in most matters, but I admit, there is something about you that unnerves me."

"Again, I'm not sure that is a compliment or an insult."

He chuckled. "A compliment. A beautiful and talented woman unnerves any man."

Victor Saillard successfully unnerved me. We remained silent, seated on the bench. In my mind, I pictured my paintings of the south, especially Roussillon and our home. I tried to place Papa, Mama, Charles, Andre, and even Jack in the settings, but I couldn't see them clearly. My memories, the people I loved from my past, were slowly sailing away like the toy boats drifting out of arm's reach. And as the sounds, sights, and smells of Paris intensified and awakened my senses, the tiny boats drifted farther away until finally out of sight.

I feared they would never return to where I waited on the shore.

Twenty-Four

Marie Observes from America, 1951

Twenty years had passed since I left France with the intention of never looking back—cutting all strings so I would feel no remorse for leaving my husband and children. But for the last four years, I couldn't deny the constant tug of one string—one common thread keeping me attached. My daughter, Ella.

"Charlotte," I called for what seemed the tenth time.

"Yes, Miss Marie." The resonating voice echoed from the stairwell that led to the basement. "I'm comin' up, haulin' more linens." The stout woman appeared on the landing. Her black eyes, round like an owl's, sat above fat, dark cheeks. "What you been hollerin' about?"

"Where did you put the scissors? I've looked all through the kitchen and desk drawers."

Charlotte plopped the basket to the floor and set her hands on her wide hips. "They're probably under that stack of newspapers and magazines you've been choppin' to bits." As she wagged a finger at the mound of clippings on the dining room table, the loose skin under her arm swayed rhythmically. Everything Charlotte did and said had a sort of beat, the intonation in her voice and the syncopated movements of her ample body.

I shuffled through newsprint articles and magazines spread across the table. "Aha. So that's where you hid them." Pointing the scissors at Charlotte, I smiled at the woman who bathed, fed, and sang to me when I was a child. Now, her job consisted of doing the same for my mother, except for the singing. Ever since Father died ten years ago, Mother's life went in reverse. For the last year, she'd been shriveled in her bed like a baby, depending on Charlotte to meet her basic needs.

Charlotte nodded her head toward the stack of papers. "Why don't you go see her?" She folded the cream-colored sheets, perfectly matching corner to corner, finally reducing the fabric to a neat square as though it were new from the department store. "You've been collectin' those articles and pictures for nearly five years, but you've never talked with or seen her. Mmm, mmm, what a shame." She shook her head, giving me the same, disappointed look I had received from her as a child when I misbehaved.

I pulled a worn article from the pile and scanned to the bottom. Though it could have been recited from memory, I reread the caption aloud. "In attendance at her premiere exhibit across the Channel, artist Mademoiselle Ella Moreau made a stunning debut with her collection of watercolors and oils depicting the beauty of Provence. Escorting her were Monsieur Victor Saillard and Madame Emelia DuBois. The exhibit continues at the Victoria and Albert Museum in London, England, May 17 – June 2."

"What year was that?" Charlotte made her way to the table and shuffled her broad hand through a pile.

"Last year, 1950." I shooed her hand. "I had these in order until now."

She continued moving the papers. "That man, Victor. Ain't he still showin' up in the latest news with Miss Ella?"

"Charlotte, you're making a mess." I grabbed her hand.

"Here it is." She snatched an article and held it above her head.

"What are you doing? Put that back." I reached for her arm but she stepped away.

"Not 'til you listen to me, Miss Marie." She pursed her lips.

I slumped back in the chair, knowing that when Charlotte had something on her mind to say, it was best to listen. "Go ahead."

She took a few steps, paused as if gathering her thoughts, and then continued to walk around the table. "Long time ago you came runnin' back home, all the way across the—"

"I know my pathetic story. I'm the awful mother who ran away from her husband and—" I stopped myself as Charlotte narrowed her eyes at me. I breathed deeply, readying myself for a rehearsal of my own tragedy.

"That's right. You ran away." She spread her arms apart. "But after all these years …" she glanced from one hand to the other as if they were two sides of the ocean, "you still runnin'." She waved one hand, then the other. "And chasin' after somethin' I'm not so sure about."

"That was a long time ago." I rubbed the spot on my temple that was beginning to throb.

"Well, I know somethin'."

"And what would that be?"

"You still want to be a part of what you left. At first, I believed you came back 'cause you thought your dream was waitin' for you here. You know you could have been a professional— singin' and playin' the piano for crowds all over Manhattan. The Lord gifted you since you was a child."

"I was never that good."

"Oh, Lordy." Charlotte untied her apron, lifted it over her head, and swatted it against the sofa. "Enough of your self-pity. You could have been somebody. You could have used the talent you was given to be happy and please the Lord at the same time."

"I *am* happy." I winced at my obvious lie.

Charlotte rolled her eyes. "You're a miserable woman, Miss Marie."

"That's not true." I stood and faced her. "Don't ever talk to me like that."

"Then why do you spend so much time readin' the newspapers and magazines? You're followin' your daughter's life, and that boyfriend of hers, like you have none of your own."

My jaw tightened. I wanted to scream that she was wrong—that she didn't know me as well as she thought. But her eyes looked straight through me, all the way to my heart.

My shoulders sagged with the weight of the truth. "You're right, Charlotte. I can't remember being happy. Well, maybe a few times." I counted with my fingers. "First, when I finally got back home and saw a whole new life ahead of me. Then, when Father bought me the new piano and I intended to play again." I paused and raised another finger. "When Mimi Sulzburger invited me to join her and her high society friends at the Metropolitan Club, I thought I was happy. That was my best chance to be a part of the group."

"You don't want any part of those women." Charlotte raised an eyebrow. "Do you?"

"Don't worry. We have money, but not that kind." I smiled and raised a fourth finger. "When I first fell for Theodore Hudson I thought

I was in love and happy."

"That poor man. He still loves you."

"He's not the least bit poor. He has more than enough wealth."

"You know what kind of poor I'm talkin' about. Broken-hearted, that's what I mean. You were only in love with his money. I always knew you didn't love him."

"I was confused." My fingers resumed rubbing both temples as I tried to avoid the eyes of my old nanny who knew me inside and out. "Was it that obvious?"

"No."

"Then how did you know?"

"Because you never stopped lovin' Henri." She patted her heart.

"That's ridiculous! I stopped loving him when he had ..."

Charlotte came closer. "Had what?"

I lowered my head, feeling bathed in a grotesque pool of disgrace, guilt, anger, and sadness, that had been slightly diluted with the passing of time.

Charlotte's voice was a whisper. "It's fine to tell me now." Her hand touched my shoulder. "It was a long time ago."

I raised my head and looked into the only eyes I could trust. And from a dark place, locked inside me for over twenty years, I released the words. "Henri had an affair. He was in love with another woman."

She held my shoulder. "Did he say such a thing?"

"He told me he made a horrible mistake. There was a woman in the city when he went there for work." A familiar nausea returned. "Promised it would never happen again. Said he loved me and wouldn't let anything ruin our family."

"Did he love her, child?"

Charlotte's words stung like a furious wasp. "He swore he didn't, but I didn't know what to believe." I slid Charlotte's hand from my shoulder and stood. "Anyway, you're right. It was a long time ago and that life is over." I started for the kitchen. "It must be time for you to make Mother's lunch."

"Marie." Her firm voice caught me in mid-step. Even when I was a child, Charlotte never called me by only my first name. "I'm talkin' to you now as my best friend."

I turned. As thousands of times before, I watched Charlotte slip her apron over her head and fasten the ties around her waist. Her eyes were moist.

"What he did was wrong, so wrong that it broke the Lord's heart over and over." She pulled a tissue from her apron pocket and wiped her eyes. "But what you did made him cry too."

"You don't understand. He pulled me away from home—my parents, you, my dream to be a musician, and then, when Henri told me what happened, I didn't know who I was any longer." I clutched a handful of hair, a habit I started as a child when tears were about to erupt.

"Come sit down." The large woman fluffed the sofa pillow.

"It's crazy, but I wondered if somehow it was my fault." I paced around the table, trying to make sense of the uninvited conversation about my life. "He asked me to forgive him, but I didn't know if I could ever trust him again. Of course, I didn't want to leave the children." Now the tears flowed. I didn't care that a trail of mascara was surely streaking toward my quivering lips. "They were so young, beautiful Charles, silly Jack, and Ella ... my little shadow." I stopped and grabbed Charlotte's hands—my only life preserver in a stormy sea. Holding me afloat, she squeezed my hands.

"Marie ..." For once, my wise counselor was speechless.

"Charlotte ..." My voice cracked. I wanted to plead with her for an excuse—wanted her to grant permission for the decision I had made. "All I could do was run away."

She pulled me into her arms and held me as we cried together, our bodies heaving in two-time rhythm.

* * * * *

Charlotte changed Mother's nightgown and tucked her in for the night. I kissed my mother's forehead and ran my hand along her bony arm. With bluish skin draped over hallow cheekbones, she looked like a skeleton. From a decade ago, I wouldn't have recognized her. As I stood at her bedside, I realized I had never really known her. I watched for a few minutes until she fell asleep, then followed Charlotte to the doorway and silently pulled the door shut.

"Been a long day, Miss Marie. Do you need anythin' before I go to bed?"

I followed Charlotte down the stairs as she rocked back and forth, navigating each step carefully. "I'm fine. I'll catch up on the news for awhile." I settled into my reading chair and opened *The New York Times.* After scanning the first pages, I flipped to the arts section, always looking for mentions of Ella Moreau.

Charlotte closed the heavy drapes, putting the house to rest as she had done for years. "Searchin' for Ella. Mmm, mmm."

"You'd do the same if she were your daughter."

"If she was mine, I'd jump on a plane and go see her tonight."

"Would you, now?" I peered over my reading glasses. "Ever since overhearing the couple at the restaurant talking about attending Ella's debut exhibition in Paris, I've followed her career. Do you know that couple was enticed enough by her paintings that they bought an entire series and had the pieces freighted back to New York? They made a wise investment back in 1947. I wish I had some of her pieces." I raised the paper and continued to read.

"You talk like an admirer instead of her mother." Charlotte placed an article in front of my face.

I set the *Times* across my lap and took the article. I had clipped it from *Le Monde* after making my weekly stop at the international magazine stand a few days ago. It featured a photograph of Ella in a long evening gown. She was wearing a strand of pearls.

"Those were my pearls. I left them behind for her."

"She's a beautiful woman. Looks like you, take away twenty years." Charlotte leaned over the back of the chair.

I pinched her arm. "I still have my looks."

"Sure do. Mr. Hudson thinks so."

"I don't want anything to do with him. No man for that matter."

"Honey, you aren't gettin' any younger." She pinched me back. "But now I understand why you never married again. Even though you couldn't."

"I could have married if I chose."

"No. You never let poor Henri go free. You've got to divorce one before you can have another. At least, that's what civilized folk do."

"Charlotte, please. We trampled that grass enough this morning. After all these years, I'm not going to hunt down Henri to ask for a divorce. He's moved on with his life, and I'm the last person in the world he'd want to see."

The woman maneuvered her ample body in front of my chair and crossed her arms. Her wide eyes locked with mine. "When do you plan to see your children?"

"I can't simply show up after all these years? Besides, I—"

"You should give it some good thought, Miss Marie. I know you better than anyone, except maybe your father, but he can't help you now."

"I don't need help, Charlotte. Not that kind of help. I need you to take care of Mother and the house. That's all." I started up from the chair, but Charlotte held her position.

She leaned over and placed her wrinkled hand on mine. Her crooked, callused, and dark fingers rubbed my transparent skin. "Look at me, child."

"I'm not a child any longer." I started to pull away, but she held my hand firmly.

"No, you're not, but ..." She peered at me with eyes that seemed to have been on earth for a thousand years. A sheen of milky-white glaze had begun to cover their depths.

I breathed and held her hand. "I'm listening—again."

"Now, I ain't goin' to be around forever and neither is your mother. I'd say her time is gettin' close."

"Don't talk like that."

"It's the truth. Do you expect us to go on forever?"

"Well, at least you." I winked at her, hoping to chase away any possibility of tears.

"Oh, Lord, don't keep me here forever." She rolled her eyes. "Now seriously, the Lord has some unfinished business with you, and you've got some with him."

"You know I'm not a religious woman."

"It ain't religion I'm talkin' about." Her voice was stern. "It's faith and forgiveness that you need to be thinkin' about."

* * * * *

The next morning, Charlotte and I found Mother had silently slipped away in the night, like a cat that sneaked out the back door and strayed from home. I tried to cry—felt obligated to grieve the death of my mother, but I realized I'd lost her years ago when she didn't believe in my dream—when she didn't believe in me. I'll always remember when, shortly after I returned to America, Father surprised me with a new piano, hoping I would pursue a chance to perform. Mother commented that it was an awkward piece of furniture she didn't need in her home. I don't think she needed me either. I never quite fit into her life.

* * * * *

That week, Charlotte organized and prepared food for the small reception to be held at the house. The guests would include a small number of remaining friends of my parents, a few of my father's past business associates, and a handful of long-time neighbors. The only child of Franklin and Elizabeth Evans, I would be the sole family member in attendance. An uncle lived across the country in California, but regretted it was too far to travel at his advanced age.

Charlotte lifted the phone, wedging the handle between her cheek and shoulder as her hands continued to knead the dough. "Evan's residence. Mmm, hmm. I'll get her for you." She handed me the phone, the receiver smeared with a sticky mixture of flour and butter.

I scrunched my face in disgust and delicately put the receiver to my mouth. "Hello. Yes, this is Marie Evans." I listened to the man reintroduce himself as Richard Hensley, an old friend of my father from the New York National Bank and Trust and the executor of my parents' estate. "Yes, you're correct. My legal name is Moreau." I caught Charlotte raising an eyebrow. "Do you plan to come to the house for the reception following Mother's funeral this Friday?" I nodded at his acceptance and then listened as he explained the primary reason for his call.

As he spoke, I stretched the phone cord around the corner of the kitchen, out of Charlotte's view, but not her earshot. When he finished, I thanked him for the information, then slid my back down the wall and slumped onto the linoleum floor. Holding the phone to my chest, I was frozen until the disconnect tone sounded and I jerked.

Charlotte peeked around the corner and looked down at me. "What are you doin'?" Flour dotted her forehead and the tip of her nose. She looked like a clown, but I was in no mood to laugh. "What's wrong?"

I pushed myself from the floor. "Everything's fine, just fine." I dropped the phone and marched through the kitchen and down the long hallway toward the front door. Swinging it open, and as fast as my fifty-two-year-old body would move, I hurried down the walkway, onto the sidewalk, and ran.

It didn't matter that it was pouring rain and the stone slabs were slippery. I ran as drops mixed with my tears. Nobody would know I was crying—it was only the rain streaming down my face.

Twenty-Five

Ella—Deceit, 1951

The doorbell chimed in the gallery. I had locked the door while Philippe and Brigitte were running errands for Emelia while she was north in Lille for the day. I didn't want to speak with or entertain any customers today. So I ignored the arrivals of purposeful buyers, as well as window shoppers along the Champs Elysees who decided to venture into the gallery to have a closer look at paintings by many of Paris' well-known artists.

Yesterday's phone conversation with Andre left me with a daunting realization that Papa was getting worse. I knew my denial of his heart condition wouldn't suffice any longer. As Andre's voice lingered in my mind, an unwelcomed emptiness filled the room. Since I had moved to Paris, I tried to metamorphose from a provincial to a city girl, but despite immersing myself in the Parisian art and night scene, I desperately missed home.

* * * * *

"I'll only be gone a month." I pressed my clothes deeper into the suitcase, hoping the latches would secure this time.

"But you're canceling one of your biggest shows." Victor stepped behind me and slid his arms around my waist. "Besides, what do you expect me to do without you?" He tried to kiss my neck, but I skirted around the end of the bed.

"You'll be fine. You're never without entertainment."

"Is there an edge to that statement? I'd say you occupy yourself the same way."

"My time is spent painting. You know that." I kept my back to him.

"Maybe that's the problem."

"Problem?" I turned and frowned at him before checking the closet for the third time.

"Ella, we've talked about this." Victor sat on the bed, swung his legs up, reclined, and crossed his arms behind his head. "You're always serious. Why don't you have more fun?"

"I do have fun. But I don't have leisure time like you." I closed the closet door and sat on the edge of the bed. "Emelia is right. My work must take priority while there's still a demand. You never know when my paintings won't be popular and no one will buy them."

After five successful years in Paris, I could easily afford to move to a flat in the trendy Marais district, or even across the Seine near the Jardin du Luxembourg where I often drew sketches of people strolling and children playing. Instead, I continued to occupy the small bedroom and kitchenette in the back of Emelia's gallery and paint in the adjoining studio. Now, the walls were closing in, and I needed Roussillon—home. I needed Papa. I needed—

"She may be right about meeting the demand, but your paintings will always be purchased. Art lovers never seem to tire of the same old landscapes."

"Same old landscapes?" I jumped from the bed, but Victor grabbed my hand and pulled me next to him. "What's that supposed to mean?" I rolled over, my back toward him.

He pressed himself against me. "It means you have a life here. You don't have to keep living in your past." He burrowed his mouth into my hair. "You have me." He kissed my shoulder, moving his way up my neck. "I want you, Ella."

His whispers sent a tingle down my back. He rolled me over, and I slipped my arm around his waist. Looking into blue eyes that continually captivated me, I ran my fingers through Victor's tousled hair and along his clean-shaven skin.

He kissed my fingers and then held my bare ring finger. "I've been patient, but I need your answer before you leave for the train tonight." His face grew serious. "I need to know if you want to be my wife. I won't ask you again."

And as had happened so many times before, he kissed me passionately, and my hesitation to resist his touch melted away.

* * * * *

"We have plenty of time, Philippe. Don't drive like a madman." I patted the thin man on his shoulder. He gave me a sideways, nervous smile. Ever since I met Philippe at the gallery, he flitted around the paintings, clients, and the Madame as though he were a bird released from its cage, not knowing where to land.

"In fact, the train doesn't leave until eight o'clock, and I don't want to wait long at the station." I pointed out the window to the Pont St. Michel, spanning the iridescent Seine River. Behind it loomed the 295-foot spire and flying buttresses of the Cathedrale Notre Dame de Paris, poised for centuries on the Ile de La Cite. "Let's go over to the Latin Quarter. I want to have a quick meal before the long ride home. I know the perfect café."

"Can't you eat on the train?" Philippe drummed his fingers on the steering wheel. "What if the train leaves early?"

"You know the trains leave only at the appointed time, or later." I smiled at him. Then I turned and smiled to myself, mentally rehearsing my answer for Victor.

Philippe turned onto the rue de Turenne and then left on the charming Place du Marche Ste-Catherine, dotted with several small bistros and cafes. "This one." I tapped on the car window. He pulled the car alongside the sidewalk which was always bustling with Parisians and tourists. "This may sound rude, but do you mind giving me a few minutes in there alone?"

My friend's thin lips puckered in disgust. "You're up to something and I don't want to know. Just make it quick because if we miss the train, the Madame will not let me drive you back a second time to the station."

I kissed Philippe on his pale cheek and slipped out the car door. "Give me fifteen minutes."

"No, I'll be back in ten, and have a *mousse au chocolat* for me." He forced a smile and then pulled away into the stream of cars, scooters, and bicycles.

Facing the crooked brick building, I caught myself in the window's reflection. I smoothed my hair, gave myself a nod, and stepped into the dimly-lit café. The sun was setting and candles adorned each table as ladies chatted, men laughed, and couples whispered over flower-filled vases.

I scanned the crowded tables, knowing Victor would occupy a spot before the night progressed. As was his habit, he began the evening at a popular café, and next moved on to an expensive restaurant. Later, when the City of Lights remained illuminated, he made his way to one of the finer cabarets until the early morning hours called him back to his apartment.

Throughout the afternoon, I had rehearsed my acceptance of Victor's proposal and began to construct a scenario of how my life would appear as Madame Ella Saillard. In my mind, I completed the final dress rehearsal.

The head of a perky waitress popped up from behind the counter. "*Bonsoir*. There's a short wait for a table tonight."

"*Merci*, but I'm meeting someone." My mouth was dry and my heart pounded. Then I heard his laughter, turned, and saw him seated in the back corner. With arms wrapped around Victor's neck and a low-cut blouse predominately in his face, a young woman giggled as he bounced her up and down on his lap.

My jaw dropped as my purse slipped from my hand and thumped onto the floor. I imagined all the people in the café turning and staring at me. Then their silence turned to cruel laughter for my foolishness for thinking I could be loved. Like an animal caught in headlights and unable to move, I watched as Victor took the woman's long hair in his hand and gathered it away from her pretty face. His laughter stopped and was replaced by the same focused stare I knew so well. He gathered her closer and kissed her poised, red lips.

I wanted to run out the front door but, instead, lifted my purse from the floor and made my way through the cramped tables to the rear of the café. Each step seemed to be in slow motion as my eyes locked on Victor's intimate display.

"Excuse me." I stood behind the woman.

Victor's eyes met mine. "Ella." He pushed the woman to the side and slid her off his lap. She stood, looking back and forth between red-faced Victor and me.

"Victor." I crossed my arms, willing myself to maintain composure.

"I thought you were gone." He pushed his chair against the wall and stood.

"Obviously." As I glared at him, a hatred I didn't know existed rose in my chest. I felt sick but was resolved to speak. "I came to give you an answer before leaving—just like you asked." My head tilted toward the woman. "My answer is probably quite obvious now."

The woman's lower lip pushed forward in a pathetic pout as she slumped into the chair. "Who is this, Victor?"

"A long-time girlfriend," I answered for him. "He asked me to become his wife, but apparently that would have been foolish." I turned my eyes to Victor.

He averted my stare and shook his head. "Let me explain. It's not what it looks like."

"Victor?" The woman's lower lip extended even further until she reminded me of a fish.

I nodded at the woman. "Well, good luck to both of you."

"Ella, this is ridiculous. We were just having some fun. I would never—" He stepped toward me and I backed away.

"As I was saying, best of luck to—never mind, I don't need to know your name. And Victor ..."

For a moment he appeared genuinely heartbroken, but his humility quickly vanished. "It probably wouldn't have worked anyway." His smug response made my stomach wrench.

"Then we agree." I spun around and tried to navigate my way through the jutting chairs, keeping my head down and zig-zagging through the sea of leather loafers and black stilettos.

I shoved the glass-plated door and spilled onto the sidewalk. Heading in the direction of the river, I jogged to the corner to look for Philippe's car. As I waited, smiling people sat around intimate, outdoor tables at the adjoining bistros. They poured wine from bottles and lifted their glasses in orchestrated movements. I wanted to imagine them raising their glasses as a toast for my courage to end my relationship with a traitor. But in my heart I was resolved—if they knew what had just transpired, they would merely raise their glasses as a farewell to a foolish and unlovable girl.

Twenty-Six

Madame DuBois' Fury, 1951

I awoke with drool on my satin pillowcase and, for a brief moment, I thought it had been a cruel nightmare. Perhaps Ella hadn't really left Paris and my profits would only continue to increase. Instead, my stilettos pinched my toes unmercifully as I clicked toward the gallery in the dreary weather, which reminded me of my new reality.

"*Bon matin*, Madame DuBois. You look beautiful as usual. Mademoiselle Brigitte has your fresh *café au lait* in your office, and I have—"

"Philippe." My body ached from the few hours of sleep and the many glasses of wine I had consumed last night.

"Yes, Madame?" Philippe's thin body jumped to my attention.

"Don't patronize me. I don't look beautiful as usual. I'm wearing a dress that's been worn twice this month already and I ... I had to fix my own hair."

"But it looks fabulous." Philippe raised both hands with animated excitement.

"You need to polish my shoes today." I winced at the pain shooting into my left big toe. "And try to stretch them."

"Yes, Madame."

"Stop nodding your head like that. It might pop off."

The double doors leading to my office opened. "*Bon matin*, Madame DuBois. You look lovely today." For a moment, I considered screaming at my stylish assistant, but decided I didn't have the strength.

"You have fresh coffee on your desk and a bouquet of delphiniums, lilies, and—"

"I will not enjoy the flowers. Not today or any other day until that ungrateful, spoiled provincial artist gets herself back to Paris and begins painting again." Tiny beads of sweat surfaced along my smoothed hairline. "And by the way, I've already had enough coffee to last for weeks."

"Pardon, Madame." She wasn't the brightest from my choice of applicants, but her looks and flirtations continued to attract the wealthy male clients to the gallery.

"What is it now, Brigitte?"

"Mademoiselle Ella Moreau called this morning."

"Why didn't you tell me?"

"You just arrived, Madame."

"Indeed. What did she say? Is she returning promptly?"

"Well ..." Brigitte said, "not exactly."

"Philippe, clean up the studio. Get new paints and canvases—large canvases. She needs to paint big. We need bigger pieces and those mean bigger profits for me. Oh, and that means a job for the two of you."

"Madame, I think—"

"Get busy, Philippe. I didn't discover her, bring her to Paris, and spend all my time just to have her return to that godforsaken hill town to play in the poppies and stare at sunsets. She's supposed to be painting them. Do something besides standing there staring at me."

"She isn't coming back." Philippe ran his slender fingers through coiffed hair, a nervous habit he repeated several times a day. "At least not right now."

"Repeat that. No, don't. I may want to hurt you." Taking a deep breath, I walked to the window and looked onto the Champs d'Elysees.

"Madame. What should we do?" Philippe joined me at the window.

"Do you see the people out there going about their business?" I tapped my long fingernails on the glass. "There's a new optimism all across Europe. France is revived from years at war and has figured out how to use its resources again. Surely, I will not lose mine." My heavy breath fogged the glass and blurred my vision of the world outside. "Have you spoken with Victor? Surely he can get her back here."

"He won't speak of her. Apparently, it's ended between them."

I eyed Philippe, wondering if he knew more than he had shared with me the evening he returned from taking Ella to the train station. He was noticeably shaken when he returned and informed me the love birds had an argument in a café.

"What did she tell you before she got on the train?" I continued to breathe on the glass.

"She could hardly speak. That's why I waited with her until she was on the train. She couldn't stop crying. She did say her father needed her, and she never should have left home. She said she betrayed God, but I'm not sure what she meant." Philippe wiped the fog with his shirtsleeve.

"I can only imagine what Jean Saillard and his wife are saying. They were counting on Victor marrying Ella. Not that they need her money—only her fame. What did she say on the phone?"

Again, Philippe ran his fingers through his hair. "She said her father is getting worse and needs her. She doesn't know when she will return."

I had an urge to yank a handful of his wavy locks and toss them on the floor. Instead, I took a deep breath and tried to calm myself. "He needs her? Well, guess who needs her more."

"We do." He circled his arms in the air as if conducting an orchestra.

"Me. The art world. My buyers. Do you know I've had clients in America demanding her work? People are getting tired of waiting for her next series. My accounts are dwindling. And don't assume you have jobs any longer."

"Should I get her on the phone?" Philippe scurried to my desk and lifted the receiver. "Tell her how desperately we, uh, the clients need her?"

"No, the problem is her sick father. Until he dies, I believe our little problem won't go away. Don't you agree?"

Brigitte stared at the floor as Philippe turned toward the window, creating his own fog.

I settled into my chair and smiled, as devilish thoughts filled my mind. "Brigitte, clear my calendar next week. We're going to vacation in the south."

Twenty-Seven

Ella—Return to Roussillon, 1951

"Pardon, Mademoiselle Moreau."

I raised my head from the same page of the magazine I had tried to read three stops ago.

The young porter balanced a tray of beverages on his palm. "May I offer you something to drink?"

His adeptness to maintain such balance was amazing. Strange to live a life in which the ground is in constant motion beneath your feet. "No, thank you."

"I'll be back through if you change your mind." He smiled and stepped toward the seat ahead of me.

"Monsieur?"

The porter looked over his shoulder.

"I have a question. Do you like always moving?"

"Pardon, *moi*?" He passed the tray to his other hand as if it were a magic trick.

"Just curious … does it ever bother you when you think everything is always in motion? When nothing stays still?"

"I don't understand, Mademoiselle. Are you sure I can't get you—"

"No. I'm fine." *Even though my life is spiraling out of control.*

The ride to Roussillon droned on like a bad movie. My time in Paris replayed across my mind—artistic success and financial benefits I never imagined were punctuated by the false sense of loving a man I never really knew. Even worse, the plot was complicated by trying to convince myself I could love him. As the train pulled into the small station in Roussillon, I wondered if the culminating scenes would have any redeeming elements. Would the series of tragedies and losses that made up my life continue to roll, frame by frame?

* * * * *

I stepped from the train and saw Andre standing near the lamppost. As if my life had been rewound five years, he waited on the platform, hands pushed into his jean pockets, shirtsleeves rolled to his elbows. His face and arms were dark, an immediate reminder of how provincial people live in tandem with the sun, unlike the pale complexions of those in the north. At the sight of him, excitement swept over me that I hadn't felt in a long time. I flipped my hair behind my shoulder and approached him, acutely aware of a lingering sadness tiptoeing beside me—knowing time had been wasted and, perhaps, what I had lost.

"Andre." I set my case on the cement and hugged him.

"Good to see you, Ella." He gave me a quick hug in return. "How was your trip?"

"I tried to sleep, but no luck."

"You look tired. You can get a good night's rest at home."

He doesn't need to know my eyes are swollen from confiding in Philippe about Victor's escapades. Throughout the train ride home, the other passengers didn't seem to notice tears streaming down my face as I talked with God and watched the scenery rush past my window.

Andre lifted my case. We walked across the empty platform and down the stairs to the parking lot. The air smelled of fresh rain, and I concentrated on sidestepping around the puddles and deep tire marks in the lot.

"Looks like the rains have been heavy." My heels sank in the oozing, red mud.

"Good thing. The vines are off to a good start this season." Andre strode through the muck, his work boots accustomed to the rich earth.

"Wasn't Papa able to come?" The hem of my dress dipped into the murky water.

"Here, let me help you." He took my hand as we made our way to the truck. I slid onto the passenger seat and pulled the door shut. Andre hopped in, started the engine, and pulled onto the road that would take me home.

"Papa's not feeling well tonight. He sent me to pick you up." His eyes focused on the road as his hands tightly gripped the wheel.

And you didn't want to come for me? "What's wrong with him?"

Andre shot me a sideways glance. "I told you he wasn't doing well. When I called yesterday, I said he was spending a lot of time sleeping."

"I understand. But what's going on with him tonight. Is he worse?" My stomach churned as guilt surged. I shouldn't have stayed away so long.

He cleared his throat. "Doctor Levin said his heart is wearing out, and there's nothing anyone can do. He takes a handful of pills each day. Apparently, your grandfather had a weak heart as well."

"Maybe we should take him to another doctor in Paris. I know many—"

"He trusts Dr. Levin."

"I wasn't suggesting that he didn't. I know Dr. Levin's a good doctor. He's taken care of our family—"

"For years."

I sighed. "You're right, for years." I looked out into the darkness and remembered fragments of my feverish dream. So long ago. Another lifetime.

We drove home, silent most of the way. This wasn't the homecoming I imagined, but then, what exactly did I expect? Even though it was only a three-hour train ride from Paris, I had been away from Roussillon almost five years. Papa and I spoke on the phone on occasional Sunday evenings. Even then, after we talked about his wine business and my recent art exhibits, I was usually preoccupied with joining Victor for dinner or returning to my paintings.

Several months ago, Papa had told me he saw Jack in a neighboring town and considered asking him to help with the vineyard since the business was growing and he wasn't able to do as much himself. He added that Andre, though committed to the business, was spending extra time with a nice young lady from Nice. I forced myself to comment, matter-of-factly, that it was good for Andre to find a woman and be happy. Now, the memory of our conversation awakened the same sickness I had felt that evening. My hand shook as I held the phone to my mouth, and Papa and I both knew it was a lie. Besides allowing myself to become caught in the far-reaching tendrils of Madame DuBois—her Parisian world of art and wealth—I was never able to tell Papa the real reason I couldn't return home.

I looked at Andre's shadowed profile. Although his features were always handsome and defined, he clearly wore the face of a man. Any hints of boyhood long since gone.

"Thank you for taking care of Papa."

"Of course, he's my father too."

"I know. I just wanted to thank you anyway." My hands nervously smoothed my dress, feeling the damp hem. What was I thinking to arrive home dressed up as though parading down the Champs Elysees or shopping at my favorite boutiques on the Boulevard Saint Michel? I had worn this same dress to impress Victor when I accepted his proposal. *Victor.* The thought of him holding the other woman, laughing, kissing her in front of others …

I was glad it was dark in the truck so Andre couldn't see me blush from embarrassment at being such a fool. "Do you think he'll still be awake?"

"Most likely. He's missed you an awful lot." Andre turned the truck onto the final road leading to the vineyard, the muffled sound of the paved road turning to the familiar crushing of gravel. "It's been hard for him to have you gone so long."

"I've missed him terribly." I hesitated, forming the words in my mind. "And I've missed you as well."

The truck stopped in front of the porch, and Andre turned off the ignition. It was silent in the country except for the distant bark of our old farm dog, probably making his way from the back field to welcome the familiar truck home. Unlike illuminated Paris, the sky was black and speckled with stars. I had forgotten the stars. A single light came on in the kitchen.

"He must be awake." I opened the door and started to get out.

"Ella." Andre's voice was low. "I've missed you too." The soft beam of light lit his face enough for me to see his eyes were moist.

"Andre, I—"

He looked past me. "He's up. No keeping that man in bed." Andre slid out of the truck and shut his door.

I sat for a moment, wondering what I was going to say to him next. But I knew what I felt. Being away from Andre for all that time had only made me love him more. It wasn't supposed to work out this way. *Now what do I do?*

"Well, are you going to sit there waiting for a red carpet?" Papa called from the porch.

"Absolutely not." I smiled at the figure standing framed between the porch posts. "I'm going to march straight through this mud, high-heels and all." I stepped onto the soft ground as heels sank deep into the mud. "To heck with these." I pulled off my shoes, tossed them over my shoulder, and ran up the steps into my papa's open arms.

* * * * *

Over a bottle of wine and a small platter of my favorite cheeses, Papa and Andre shared about the vineyard and the surge of business since the country had recovered from the war. I told them about my recent exhibition on the Left Bank of the Seine. What we didn't talk about was just as evident—Papa's health, Victor, and the woman from Nice.

My father pushed himself from the table and stretched his arms above his head. "Well, it's late and I'm getting up early tomorrow."

"Me too." Andre corked the bottle. "Remember, I'm doing the southern rounds the next few days."

"You're leaving already? But I just got here." I wiped my mouth with a napkin to conceal my disappointment.

Andre extended his arms, a common gesture he and Papa had shared for as long as I could remember. "Ella, you're on duty to keep him from working too hard. Make sure he's taking his medicine too."

"I don't need to be reminded. They're lined up in that silly pillbox you organized." Papa pointed to the cupboard.

"Just watching out for you." Andre stood. "I'll be back in a few days. There are good paying customers in the coastal towns. St. Topaz, Cannes, Nice—"

I flinched at the word and hoped no one noticed. "I'll take good care of him." I carried the empty platter to the sink, opened the faucet, and looked at my faint reflection in the dark window. For a moment, I saw myself as the same, scared little girl who once lived here.

"Papa, I'll come in and kiss you goodnight before I go to sleep. Andre, if I don't see you in the morning, have a safe trip." I busied my hands rewashing the clean platter.

"Good night, Ella. Glad to have you home for a while." I couldn't miss Andre's broad shoulders reflected in the window as he walked out of the kitchen.

* * * * *

I awoke the next morning to the sound of the truck starting and then driving away. Papa was in the kitchen when I went for a cup of coffee.

"You look good this morning. How are you feeling?" I tightened the robe's sash around my waist.

"Was I not looking good last night?" He smiled, his silver, morning stubble highlighted on his tan skin.

"You're always handsome, just ornery." I patted his back, glad to be with him instead of only hearing his voice over the phone.

"Things go pretty well in the morning after a good night's rest. By noon, I'm ready for a nap. After that, it's up again until I'm worn out by evening." He rubbed his stubble. "To be honest, things are not what they used to be, but the Lord keeps me going. He still wants me around for some reason."

"Don't talk like that." I refilled our coffee cups.

"What? The Lord having a plan?"

"No, the part about not being around."

"Still here." He chuckled. "I may have a bad heart, but it's still pumping."

I hugged my papa and rested my head on his chest. "You have the best heart ever."

He squeezed me back. "And how's your heart, Miss Ella? I'm more concerned about yours than mine."

I raised my head and looked into his brown eyes, accentuated with thick, long eyelashes that should have been reserved for a girl.

"It's fine, everything is ..." Knowing I could no longer hide the truth from him, I breathed deeply, gathering the courage to invite him into my private world of fear and sadness.

"The truth is ... I'm a mess."

With my face buried in Papa's shirt, I sobbed like that little girl, scared and confused in the middle of the road so many years ago. He wrapped his arms around me and let me cry. I cried for Mama, for Charles, for Jack, for Andre, and for Papa's failing health. But mostly, my tears were for myself for believing I could control God, demanding that he protect me from loving others for fear of losing them—especially Andre.

My part of the deal was to paint for him—to resolve myself to that task. It was my penance for loving too much in the past. And though painting was as natural to me as breathing, I would spend the rest of my life with paints and brushes, instead of loving. God would allow me to glimpse into my past and venture into dreams of an unattainable future, one where love was allowed only through my secret paintings. They remained in my studio, hidden beneath a tarp and several years of dust.

When I had exhausted what felt like all the tears one person could cry, Papa took my hand and led me to the front porch where we settled into chairs to let the early autumn sun bathe our faces. We talked for hours, sharing most everything that had gone unsaid over the twenty years since Mama had walked away. Andre arrived. Charles died. Jack left, returned, and then left again. I told Papa about the dreadful night in my studio with Jack and my deal with God.

The painful details of my last evening in Paris tumbled out, followed by my deep feelings for Andre. I confided to my father that I had probably loved Andre since the day he arrived at the farmhouse, along with my fear that our lives had taken us too far apart.

"You realize Andre doesn't understand any of this."

"Yes, but I wouldn't know where to start."

"Like you're doing now." Papa faced me. "By being honest."

I rubbed my eyes, avoiding his look. "Is she pretty?"

"Who?"

"The woman in Nice. You know who I'm talking about."

"Jeanette? Yes, she's very pretty. She owns a successful restaurant with her parents on the boardwalk. He met her there a few years ago."

"Then he doesn't see her often?"

Papa raised an eyebrow to my question, calling me on my jealousy. "They manage to get together often for living in separate towns." He patted his thighs with his broad hands. "I think he really likes her. Even mentioned getting married."

His words shot through my heart like a bullet. "I didn't know they were serious. I assumed—"

He sat forward in defense of his son. "You haven't made any attempt to talk to or see him in five years. Did you assume he had no life of his own? That yours would go on and his would stay the same as when you left?"

"That's not fair. Of course he's allowed to fall in love." The words burned my tongue. "Any woman would be lucky—"

"That could have been you." Papa grabbed my arm and looked in my eyes. "It's probably too late though." He let go of my arm. It dropped onto my lap like a lifeless appendage belonging to a woman with a broken heart.

We didn't talk again for some time. I don't think either one of us ever imagined my first morning home would have drummed up so many truths and emotions. As we sat in silence, I tried to make sense of Papa's news in light of my confession to him that I was deeply in love with Andre. What, if anything, would I say to the man who was a second brother to me, yet with the thought of him, an overwhelming passion was unleashed.

"I had a chance to marry," I blurted out, and then felt embarrassed for my childish tone. "Victor proposed to me several times, but I kept telling him I wasn't ready."

"I'm sure you never told him the real reason."

"No, I couldn't. I didn't want to believe it myself. For a long time, I tried to love Victor, to really love him."

"But you couldn't?"

"We had fun together. He took me places, introduced me to all his friends, treated me well …" I pictured Victor holding the young woman's hair and kissing her pretty face. "Until he cheated on me." I shook my head, admitting my stupidity for wanting to believe that was the only time he was unfaithful.

"What he did was wrong. I understand, believe me." Papa leaned his head back and closed his eyes. "But if I understand all you've shared with me—the real reason you left in the first place and why you haven't come home in five years—you betrayed Victor too."

I nodded, relieved to finally concede my own sin. "You're right. I thought I could love him by being part of his life and becoming someone I'm not. I'm an artist—"

"An excellent one," Papa added, still with eyes closed like a faithful, hunting dog preparing to nap in the sun.

"By God's grace."

"And plenty of hard work." His breathing was interrupted by a few brief snores.

Papa rested peacefully and for the first time in many years, I felt that someday I would be able to sleep as he did. I had released a torrent of fears from my past, exposing them to the light and stripping them of their dark and unsettling presence.

"Papa, there's something else." I had tried to ignore a growing uneasiness over the last month, but it rose to the surface like an awakening sea monster, rearing its ugly head. "I thought I could learn to love Victor by being intimate with him. I think I'm pregnant."

Papa's snoring was rhythmic and his hand twitched. I was relieved he didn't hear me whisper my last secret. I ran my hand over my stomach, wondering if it were true and, if so, how I would tell Victor—and what I would say to Andre.

Twenty-Eight

Painting Over Demons, 1951

I laid a blanket over Papa as he napped in the shade. Securing my hair with a barrette, I stepped into the house and headed down the hallway to my studio. My hand rested on the doorknob for too long. Before, I would have burst into the room, anxious to choose a favorite brush and unleash the myriad colors of paint onto a palette. I turned the knob, nudged the door open, and entered. The sun had made its way around the side of the house and cast a long-reaching beam across the oak floor. The light touched my sandaled feet as if it expected me in the studio at this appointed time.

A sunlit path led me to a small table in front of the window. I bent over a jar filled with fresh lavender sprigs, shut my eyes, and breathed in the calming scent. I straightened, turned in a full circle, and surveyed the room. Everything had remained the same, and yet the feeling was completely different. My life was comprised of two different worlds, and I stood with one foot in each—incongruent, foreign to the other.

My paint-stained easel waited silently in the center of the room. A blank canvas loomed on its rim, and I felt small in comparison. I approached it as though it were the altar in Sainte Chapelle, one of the magnificent churches in Paris that beckoned me when the guilt for ignoring God became too great, and I longed to be in his presence. But instead of a gilded and ornately-carved altar, bathed in hues from the famous stained glass windows, I stood in front of a stark canvas. I stared for a long time, mesmerized by its vast emptiness. A Scripture echoed in my mind, *Be still and know that I am God.* Those were the simple words Papa recited from his Bible as he wept when Mama left.

A waft of lavender carried by a light breeze returned me to my surroundings. Next to the easel, a supply table was prepared, offering a bouquet of brushes arranged in a glass jar. My eyes followed the path of paint tubes lined up in immaculate order alongside the clean palette. I scanned the familiar names—yellow ochre, cadmium yellow, burnt and raw sienna, viridian, alizarin crimson, cadmium red, ultramarine blue, cobalt blue, and cerulean blue. Reading the names was like music inside my head.

Out of habit I lifted a brush from the crowded jar and eyed the specks of colors, remnants of my past paintings. I stroked the soft, sable bristles, closed my eyes, and thought of my latest series on display in the Exhibition de les Artistes on the Left Bank in Paris. But now I needed to leave that world.

I was back in Roussillon—home.

"God, we need to talk."

* * * * *

It was late afternoon when I cleaned my brushes and returned them to the jar. I had talked, prayed, and listened to God as I painted—something I hadn't done in my studio in Paris. But here it felt natural. Surely the Lord had brought me home for reasons besides Papa's health. I ran my fingers gently across the painting, wishing I could touch Andre's skin instead of the damp pigments mixed together in varying tones to bring him to life. His eyes were created from earthy browns and warm greens. Now they stared back—convicting me to be honest. When he returned home, I would tell him everything. And after, I resolved to trust God with the rest.

Outside the open window, the sound of the truck announced Andre's arrival. I pushed the curtain to the side and watched him park the truck next to the barn. *He's supposed to be gone a few days. Why is he back?* Papa greeted him and with folded arms on the truck door, the men talked through the rolled down window for several minutes. Then he gestured toward my studio.

I slipped away from the window, organized the paints, and then tossed a sheet over the easel to conceal the canvas.

"Do you wear your robe when you paint in Paris?"

I jumped at the sound of his voice.

"Only when I've been out late the night before." Immediately, I regretted my remark. "What are you doing home? I thought you'd be gone a few days."

Andre leaned against the windowsill, resting his chin in his hand. "I decided to come home early. Is that all right?"

"Of course, it's your home too." An awkward silence fell between us. "I'm going to get dressed now."

"Good idea. But this time, put on jeans and decent shoes."

"And why is it your business what I wear?"

"Because you and I are going on a long walk."

You can't tell me what to do, I wanted to say.

But then a gentle nudging gave me the right word. "Fine."

* * * * *

We walked along the overgrown path, winding our way through the fields leading to the pond. Long ago, the route was clearly defined, trodden by my brothers' bare feet and mine. Now the golden grasses of autumn infringed, but we gently pushed them aside, the passageway to the water forever etched in our minds. We crested the hill above the pond and stopped. The water was still and peaceful, no longer the ominous depths that had taken Charles' life.

I pushed my hair out of my face. "I haven't been here since ... You?"

"A few times. I'd look for Charles in the tree, getting ready to launch himself from the swing." Andre smiled and shook his head. "He was the bravest of us all." He tugged a long blade of grass and twisted it around his finger. "Thinking of him still hurts."

"Me too. It never goes away." I stepped down the path toward the bank. The water lapped against the edge, inviting us into its coolness as it had hundreds of times before. Although many years had passed since Charles drowned, I knew I'd never accept the invitation.

"I wonder how life would have been different if he were still here." Andre stood beside me looking into the water. "He loved the vineyard. We would have been working the business along with your father."

"Papa mentioned Jack coming home to help."

Andre picked up a stone and skimmed it across the pond. "Three skips. Not too bad."

"What happened?" I asked.

"Papa gave him plenty of chances. He saw him a few times. Jack wasn't doing very well. No money and living with a girl from up north."

"He was different when he came home from the war." I picked up a stone and tossed it in.

"No skips."

"I wasn't trying." I threw another, this time three skips. "Where is he now?"

"Probably living with that girl, doing odd jobs when he can get them. He drinks too much. It was planned for him to help oversee the vineyards. He showed up drunk, yelled and cursed at the other workers, and passed out under an olive tree. After that, he was told he wasn't welcome until he could get his life straightened out."

"Papa didn't share all of that. He only said Jack needed to be on his own, and being part of the family business wasn't working out for him."

"No lie in that." Andre stepped back on the path that led around the pond. "Besides, I'm sure he still hates me, and I don't have good feelings for him either." He snapped a low-lying branch and tossed it into the grass. "It's better this way. I just wish Charles were still around."

A butterfly flitted beside the path, stopped at a periwinkle orchid, and then moved on to another. I thought it was odd seeing a butterfly after the long days of August, and its presence urged me to begin my confession.

Andre walked ahead on the narrow path. With a deep breath, I forced the words I had been rehearsing. "There's so much to tell you."

"Go ahead." He kept walking, his broad shoulders accentuated by his narrow hips.

"Will you stop and listen to me? Please?"

He stopped and ran his fingers through his hair, a gesture he did when it was time for deep thought. He probably wondered where our discussion would take us. He turned and looked at me. "And I have much to tell you. Will you listen?"

I nodded.

"It's best we keep walking." He spoke with determination, so I followed him along the path, over the ridge, and into the open field. The poppies were long since dried, their twisted stems leaning over, preparing to become part of the earth until their arrival next spring.

We talked about how I chased the butterfly on my last trip to the pond with Charles. Andre listened as I shared my consuming guilt for allowing Charles to drown at the expense of following the creature away from the pond, intent on pursuing something beautiful.

We sat on the wooden footbridge, rickety after many years of rain and the swelling of the creek that wove behind our property. Our feet dangled over the edge, now touching the gently flowing water that we couldn't quite reach when we were young. I told him about my argument with Jack—about believing his lies that I had chased Mama away and let our brother die.

Andre listened, a sadness etched in his face that he wore for both of us. "I know where to go next." He stood and offered his hand. I accepted, and we headed for the red rocks and steep path leading to Remy's Castle. At the top, we settled next to each other on a slab of rock, smoothed for centuries by rain and wind. We sat looking over our kingdom laid out below us like a feast—fields of ripe grapes, late summer vegetables, and orchards heavy with fruit.

"I was convinced it was necessary to leave." I paused, trying to make sense of the last several years. "I believed that by loving you, something awful would happen. You'd eventually go away too."

"Jack told you that?"

"He did, but I believed it before he even said it. That's why I made those paintings." My logic sounded ridiculous. "I thought I could capture the wonderful memories and dreams about you, Mama, and Charles. In those paintings I could love all of you and nothing bad would happen. Andre …" I touched his arm. "It's safe for me in the paintings."

He remained still, eyes focused in the distance. Then he turned and held my face in his hands. My body shook, not from the cool breeze, but from his touch and the intensity of his eyes.

"Can you be safe with me, Ella?"

I opened my mouth, but couldn't speak. Andre needed an answer as much as I needed to be truthful.

"Can you ever love me?" His eyes pleaded for my answer. "Outside of a painting?"

A whisper rose from my core. "I *do* love you. I always have." I leaned toward him, touching his face with mine. I kissed his cheek and then moved slowly to his lips, where we finally found one another, over and over, on top of the world—our Roussillon.

* * * * *

The sun was setting as we navigated down the loose rocks below the cliffs. Andre held my hand and I felt like a young girl again. When the ground flattened, I stopped and sat on a large rock. "You listened to me. Before it's pitch dark, I need to listen to you."

He leaned against the rock and seemed to gather his thoughts for too long. "I've been seeing another woman for a while. She's from—"

"Nice. I know. Papa told me a little."

He laughed. "Well then, he's made this easier for me."

"Go on. I'm listening." I tucked my legs to my chest, preparing for what he had to say.

"She's a wonderful person. Very smart, loving—"

"And beautiful."

"Yes, she's beautiful." He paced, hands pushed into his pockets in another of his customary thinking positions. "I left this morning to see her again. We try to see each other on weekends, but it's been hard with Papa getting worse. I haven't wanted to leave him alone. When you came home, I figured it was a good time to visit her." Andre stopped and furrowed his brow. "Besides, I couldn't be around you. It was hard enough getting you at the station."

I rested my head on my knees and braced for the answer. "Do you love her?"

"I don't know." He began to pace again. "No, that's not fair. I do love her. I've even thought about asking her to marry me."

I held my breath and in my mind, begged the lurking fear to pass by.

"But, Ella, it's all changing now that you're home. That's why I came back early. It wasn't right for me to be with Jeanette when I'm thinking about you. I don't know when you're going back to your life in Paris and, for that matter, that boyfriend of yours."

"Victor?"

"The man in the photos with you. I've seen enough of him to know."

"He's not my boyfriend any longer."

Andre stopped and stared at me. "Why not?"

"Because he doesn't love me."

"Do you love him?"

I shook my head. "No, not really. Whatever we had is over."

"Are you going back?"

"I don't know what to do. I'm not planning to go back to Paris anytime soon. Papa needs me." I slid off the rock. "And you."

He didn't answer, but took my hand as we walked home in the light of the moon. Papa was asleep. We kissed him on opposite cheeks and tiptoed into the kitchen. Sitting on the porch, wrapped in a blanket, we watched the stars. It was nice to talk about small things—my paintings and favorite new meals from Paris, and his plans for an addition to the wine cellar. We could have said nothing at all. I was utterly content being together at this precise time and place.

But soon, I would not be able to ignore the swelling of my stomach and the tenderness in my breasts.

Twenty-Nine

Madame DuBois' Persuasion, 1951

A month passed and the three of us settled into a rhythm, much like a finely-tuned string quartet, minus one musician. Each morning I painted in the privacy of my studio until it was time for Papa to rest. Then I joined Andre and the remaining seasonal workers to prepare the vineyards for next year and organize the inventory in the cellar.

Andre and I were enjoying coffee on the porch when a shiny black car pulled up the drive and stopped near the house. The back window rolled down, revealing the clownish face of Emelia DuBois.

"The great Ella Moreau!" The Parisian accent drenched the words in sarcasm. The door swung open and the woman struggled to emerge. She was finally pushed from behind by a thin arm sporting a gold cuff link. The Madame regained her balance on the loose gravel and rolled across the drive like a brightly-colored beach ball.

"I didn't know you ever awoke so early. Or perhaps you never went to bed. I remember the Paris nightlife all too well." I stood on the top step wearing my dirty leather work boots and canvas pants that once hung loosely from my waist. Papa didn't feel well this morning and, against his protests, I had ushered him back to bed.

"Fond memories for you, I'm sure." Emelia enunciated each word with blood-red lips. "I've come all this way to see you. You've been missed. Everyone wants to know about you, so I enlisted myself on this trek into the unruly south to see if you've survived."

"Here's living proof that I've survived these harsh elements." I stretched my arms and leaned my face toward the sunny blue sky.

"What is it they want to know?"

"Oh, you remember Philippe? He decided to join me on this adventure. Besides, we all needed a vacation."

"*Bonjour*, Ella. You look stunning. The sunshine has served you well. Are you going to introduce us to *him*?"

"This is Andre. He's been with our family forever."

Andre sat in a chair and propped his feet on the ledge. "Welcome. And you are …?"

"Philippe." He placed his hand on Emelia's shoulder.

"I'm sure you know who I am." Emelia brushed Philippe's hand away.

"Of course, the famous Madame DuBois." Andre stood and approached Emelia. He took her hand and kissed it above the fingers laden with gold and bejeweled rings.

Emelia eyed me wickedly. "Charming."

A smiling face peered out the limousine window and Brigitte, thinner than a stick, stepped from the car.

"Brigitte, it's good to see you. I'm surprised you're still with these vipers." I stepped from the porch and offered the expected kisses on both sides of their cheeks. "So tell us, why are you here?" I looked between them and then focused on Emelia. "I'm sure there are many people missing your presence back in the city."

"They'll survive for a day." She winked at me with a thickly-lined eye.

"Andre and I were about to unlock the cellar. Come with me. I'll show you the fruits of the family business."

Emelia teetered as she walked, shifting her weight to the balls of her feet as she tried unsuccessfully to keep her pointy heels from sinking in the dirt and moist grass. I laughed as she yanked the red shoes from her plump feet and threw them at Philippe, who was trailing behind.

"Ah, the reason we're here is you, my dear Ella. We've come to rescue you. You are the hidden gem. You are the diamond in the rough, so to speak."

I stopped and turned. "No, I'm—"

"Let me finish." Dark eyes looked me up and down, lips curling with disgust at my worn pants and work boots. "However, the difference is you have already been discovered. You can't hide your uniqueness and talent, your value to the art world, any longer. Everyone wants you. We've come to bring you home. We've come to take you from this languid hideaway back to the excitement of Paris. That's where you and your artistic talent were meant to be."

"When I left Paris over a month ago, I had every intention of going back. But things have changed. It wasn't right then, and it isn't now. Besides, my father—"

"How is he? Such a good man. Stubborn, but, ah, so handsome, so—"

"You've never even met him." I exchanged glances with Andre. He shrugged.

"Oh, well … perhaps not." Emelia smoothed her slick hair in a nervous gesture.

Andre stepped forward. "He's not doing well."

"I'm sorry. I didn't know."

I shook my head at the absurdity of our conversation. "You knew. Brigitte surely filled you in on our phone conversation."

"True, she did mention something about that. But, Ella, we haven't talked. You haven't returned my calls or letters. How would I have known if he's—"

He's inside." I motioned to the farmhouse. "He's only fifty-nine, but has the heart of an old man."

"How awful. And you're taking care of him all by yourself?"

"Andre and I take care of him when he lets us."

"You must be exhausted. No wonder you're unable to paint." Emelia edged herself nearly face-to-face with me, but her short, shoeless stature forced her to look up. She squinted in the sun and wrinkles spread across her face like an ancient road map.

"There's really not much to say, but it wouldn't be hospitable not to invite you to stay for lunch." I skirted around the woman's mass and marched toward the farmhouse. Andre walked with her as Philippe and Brigitte trotted behind.

I cut a baguette and made sandwiches for our guests. A plate filled with cheeses, freshly picked apples, and a pitcher of lemon water was brought to the table. Andre excused himself to work outside, leaving an uncomfortable foursome to sit around the small table.

"It appears you're quite busy. Have you found time to paint?" Emelia asked as she cut thick slices of cheese.

"Not really. It takes a lot of work to keep the farm and vineyard, especially with my father unable to do his share."

"I see." The woman maneuvered her words around a mouthful.

"Besides, I'm really not that good after all." I took a bite of my sandwich and tried to conceal a smile. It was quite satisfying to toy with the great Madame DuBois.

"That's ridiculous. I discovered you and made you one of the most desirable artists in Europe." She sliced into the cheese with vigor unnecessary for a brie.

"Maybe I fooled myself all along. We were all deceived—the patrons, the art critics, you, Philippe, and even Brigitte." I watched Philippe and Brigitte peck nervously at their food. "I wanted to paint things that mattered, but in the famous words of Victor Saillard, they were just the same old landscapes."

"That's why you haven't come back." Philippe wagged a skinny finger. "You're not over your fight with Victor at the café."

"First of all, it wasn't a fight. Besides, I handled the situation quite well."

"Until you fell apart in the car on the way to the station." He smirked like a spoiled child.

"I was entitled to some emotion after that big surprise, don't you agree?" I wanted to exchange the same look, but decided to keep my head. "I'm not painting because I'm needed here for other reasons." My mouth dried as the half lie slipped out. I poured a glass of water.

Brigitte folded her thin arms on the table and smiled. "Ella, your paintings have always mattered. They're all beautiful. If only I could have your—"

"Talent? Is that what you were going to say, Brigitte? I, as well as the world, realize how talented our friend Ella Moreau truly is. Such a shame she won't share it any longer." Emelia's face was deepening from shades of pink to red, and bits of cheese and bread stuck in her white teeth. "Is it really true you don't paint? Your brushes are dried on the shelves? You don't wish to share your talent with the rest of the world ever again?"

I felt cornered, realizing how quickly my *benefactor* put me on the defense. "Not your world. I don't wish to share my gift with the world of Madame DuBois."

She leaned across the table as far as her ample chest would allow. Her red nails clawed at the tablecloth. "Is that why you have paint under your nails? Is that why there is a streak of cerulean on the back of your arm?"

A conglomeration of expensive floral scents emanated from her perfumed skin. I locked eyes with her as her jowls tightened like a predator about to make its lethal bite.

She grabbed my hand with a relentless grip. "Do not try to tell me you were painting the side of your barn. Do you know why I know this? I know this because the barn is rouge. It is red—as red as your face at this very moment."

A low, raspy voice came from the doorway across from the kitchen. "She paints in the mornings and late at night."

"Papa." I pushed away from the table and our visitor's hypnotic trance. "When did you wake up?"

"Ella, Madame DuBois, and whoever you two others are, give me a moment to get properly dressed, and then we will all talk." By the stern tone of Papa's voice, even Madame Emelia DuBois, the premiere patron of the Parisian art world, did not argue.

We sat in silence like naughty children waiting to be reprimanded. Papa entered the kitchen, looking refreshed after sleeping all morning. He wore a pressed shirt and clean jeans.

Emelia rose from the table and walked toward him. "Henri, you look good."

"Not so sure about that, but I'll take the compliment." As Papa sized her up, I blinked several times, confused about their odd exchange. "And you look … good. Different."

"I'll take that as a compliment too. The years have been good to me in some ways, but not others." Emelia wrapped her arms around Papa and gave him a kiss on both cheeks.

I shoved my chair away from the table, stood, and looked from one to the other in disbelief. "Do you know each other?"

Emelia laughed out loud and looked as though she had won a prize. "We knew each other a long time ago, but I see he's never mentioned that to you."

Papa shifted his weight and ran his fingers through his hair. "I suppose this is called serendipitous that we meet again under such unusual circumstances."

Emelia rolled her lips into a coy smile. "I'd call it destiny, wouldn't you, Henri?" She placed her hand on Papa's waist and turned toward the table where Philippe and Brigitte sat looking as confused as me. "Henri, meet Philippe and Brigitte. They work for me at my gallery in Paris. We make quite a team, don't we?" She winked at her assistants.

"Pleasure to meet you." Papa brushed Emelia's hand from his waist.

"Why don't you two visit Andre outside. I'm sure he would be happy to give you a tour of the vineyard and cellar. You can enjoy a bottle of wine when you're finished."

Philippe and Brigitte excused themselves, probably happy to miss the rest of the discussion. Papa and Emelia settled at the table.

"Aren't you going to join us?" Emelia patted the tablecloth.

"I'll stand."

Papa poured himself a glass of water and then poked at the lemon that bobbed to the surface. "It's true, Ella." He submerged the lemon again. "Emelia and I knew each other a long time ago. We met each other in Marseilles when I worked in the city." He looked at me with an odd sadness. "Do you remember when I would go to work and be gone most of the week?"

I nodded and remembered the day Papa was on his way home and found me in the middle of the road. "You were friends?"

Emelia lifted her glass to her lips. "More than *friends*." She sipped the wine and then set her red, lipstick-marked glass on the table.

"What's that supposed to mean?" I glared at her.

Papa rested his arms on the table. "It means I made a big mistake."

"Why, thank you, Henri, I didn't know you considered—"

"Enough, Emelia." Papa cut her sarcasm short. He grimaced as though what he was about to say caused physical pain. "I was unfaithful to your mother. I had an affair." He shook his head as if trying to erase the past. "It was a long time ago. I told your mother everything, but she—"

Emelia chuckled. "No wonder she left."

Papa ignored her and continued. "She didn't believe me when I told her I wasn't in love and it would never happen again."

Emelia rubbed her hands together. "Henri, you are cruel. To sit in front of me and say our times together meant nothing." She turned a ring around her forefinger. "You gave this to me. Don't you remember?"

"Papa, how could you?" I looked at him and then back at the sapphire stone perched on a platinum band.

"I was stupid." Papa's face grew red. "I gave that to you because I felt guilty that you were falling in love with me. Don't you remember? I gave you that ring and said I never wanted to see you again because I was in love with my wife and didn't want to ruin my family."

"How could I forget?" Emelia's eyes filled with tears. "I was deeply in love with you."

This surreal exchange was like a dream—the reality of Papa and Madame DuBois twisting and contorting into grotesque shapes. I looked at the hunched figure of my once-strong and perfect father. I thought of Emelia's flirtations and late nights in Paris. Now I understood the sadness she tried to conceal behind layers of make-up and her boisterous laugh.

"You knew he was married." I directed an accusing stare at her. "But that didn't matter to you. Did you know he had three children at home?"

"It was just as much my fault." Papa held his head in his hands and rubbed his temples. "I loved your mother so much. But she wasn't happy with me for bringing the family to France. She was angry. It was wrong, but—"

"But what?" At this point I needed to hear the entire story.

"I wanted to be happy. The job in Marseille was good, providing plenty of money to improve the vineyard. I could work in the city a few years, then be on the farm full-time and work the family business like my father and uncle did."

"What did that have to do with Emelia?"

"She made me laugh." Papa raised his head and looked at her. "And I was able to make her happy. I couldn't even get your mother to smile toward the end."

Mama's beautiful face and smile were fading from my mind. "When did she find out about the two of you?"

"I told Henri he needed to tell Marie about us, or that would be the end." Black streaks ran from the corners of Emelia's eyes. "My goal was never to be just a mistress." She blotted her eyes. "That's what love does to you."

"Your mother was informed soon after it was over, but I think she had a sense something was going on all along."

"I heard you fighting one night." I whispered the words as if I were eavesdropping again.

Papa cocked his head. "And ..."

"The next morning she left." Stunned by this revelation, I leaned back and felt the same numbness that occupied my body the day we buried Charles. My father's mouth turned downward as if the tips of his gray mustache bore weights.

"You sent me to live in Paris with your mistress. Did Monsieur Lenoir know about this?"

"No. He had only good intentions when he suggested you live with

Emelia. We both knew it was the only opportunity for you to become a professional artist."

"Can't agree more." Emelia pulled lipstick from her purse. "Ah, such a funny little man. He knew nothing about us. He was always too in love with his wife and his work to notice."

"And you …" I shook my head. "I trusted you not only with my art, but as a friend."

"And I've done an excellent job making you successful." She swiped the lipstick and then rubbed her lips together. "Although, maybe I haven't been the best friend. I never shared the little secret between your father and me." She made a loud smack with her lips. "And best friends do share their secrets, don't they dear?"

Her attitude made me nauseous. "You know what's crazy? All these years I've blamed myself for Mama leaving."

"Ella." Papa reached for me. "I am so sorry." Tears ran down his wrinkled face as though navigating a bumpy road. He took my hand. "Please forgive me."

I wriggled my hand from his and walked out of the kitchen, down the hallway, and into my studio. Once safely inside, I locked the door and slumped to the floor. Instinctively, my fingers grabbed a brush, wanting to create a picture of the Papa I loved. Instead, I threw the brush across the room as images formed in my mind of someone I no longer knew.

Thirty

Paris Calls, 1951

That evening, long after the shiny black car pulled out of the drive and headed north, I told Andre what happened. He had already noticed an uneasiness between me and my father that never existed before.

Now, the three of us sat on the front porch, each wrapped in a blanket. This was our usual way to complete the day, but tonight the silence hovering over us brought a chill that wasn't from the late September air.

"I've decided to go back to Paris for a while." I pulled the blanket closer. "There's a series that needs to be completed in Madame DuBois' gallery. The exhibit was cancelled before coming home this summer." Papa and Andre's silence urged me to continue. "It wouldn't be right to leave those pieces unfinished. Besides, it's time to get more involved managing my own work. I'll be looking for another studio."

"In Paris?" Andre's voice rose in surprise. "I thought you weren't going back."

"She changed her mind because of me, Andre. Not you," Papa said.

"Ella told me what happened. I'm glad you were honest. It must have been hard."

"He should have told me a long time ago." I wanted to lash out at Andre for being kind to Papa.

My father cleared his throat, as he often did now before speaking. "You're right. I thought it could remain a secret forever, especially when Marie left, but it was like poison inside me all these years. I asked for your mother's forgiveness and hoped we could reconcile. When she wouldn't forgive me, I pushed that sin out of my mind. It's eaten me alive ever since."

Andre rubbed my shoulder and then turned toward Papa. "What were you supposed to do if Marie wouldn't forgive you?"

"Go straight to the Lord and ask Him to forgive me. Even trying to ignore what I did, it was a cancer in my heart and soul." Papa coughed. "I need to thank you, Ella, for listening to all that today. I never wanted to take those lies to the grave. It hurts to know you've carried that guilt since you were a little girl. No one should have to do that. Your mother loved you."

Pictures of Mama flipped through my mind like an old scrapbook. The photos were yellowed and faded, but I forced myself to see her holding my hand and smiling at me. There were pictures of Papa too—but those were crisp and focused. He had been in my life all along, and I knew I could never abandon or stop loving him.

"Thank you for telling me the truth. I promise I'll come home soon."

* * * * *

For the third time, Andre stood on the platform. We held one another close before we kissed a final time. I boarded the train and assured him I'd call when arriving at the gallery, even though it would be late. I settled into my seat and watched him wave to me as the train rolled into motion once again.

My plan was in place. As if nothing had changed with Emelia, I would complete the paintings stacked along the wall in my studio in preparation for the exhibit at the Musee Marmottan. The paintings would be on display through November, in the same 19th century mansion where an impressive collection of Monet's landscapes graced the elegant rooms.

Meanwhile, I would find another gallery to represent my work and return to Roussillon before the New Year to resume painting in the country. By now, I was established as a talented and sought-after artist. I could paint away from the city and return on occasion. The only flaw in my plan was the slight bulge under my loose, cotton dress. I would have to make an appointment with Dr. Vancil within the week.

* * * * *

I arrived at the gallery expecting to see only the dim glow from the light above the storefront. Instead, the entire building was illuminated and filled with people. I watched them through the window as they shuffled, shoulder-to-shoulder, dressed in fancy attire, and drinking champagne—their long-stemmed glasses a necessary fashion accessory.

The door opened and I was met by Brigitte's dazzling smile. "Ella, we're so happy you're back. Now the party can begin."

"Party? What's this about?" I peeked inside the doorway and was met by the sounds of laughter and talking layered over a song by Georges Brassens.

"It's for you. We found out your train would come in tonight, so we helped Madame DuBois throw a party. Here, come in." Brigitte took my bag in one hand and my arm with the other. She led me into the life I had hoped to escape.

"Ella Moreau, I knew we would see you soon. Paris is smiling now that she has you home." I exchanged kisses with Richard Tetin, the art critic from Le Monde. He had been very kind to me in his weekly column, and I needed to maintain his confidence if I was to venture on my own in the temperamental—and often vicious—art world.

"Good to see you, Richard. And how is your wife? Is she here also?" I couldn't help but mention her, wondering if he was with Emelia tonight.

Ella, remember your plan. Be civil to Emelia.

"No, unfortunately, she's not feeling very—" Richard submerged the rest of his words in his glass.

"Tell her hello, and I hope she's feeling better soon." I turned toward the tapping on my shoulder. "Philippe. *Bonsoir*. How are you?"

"*Bonsoir*, Ella. We are glad you didn't miss the train or change your mind."

I gave him a quizzical look, though I knew Philippe had an uncanny way of finding things out. "How did you know I decided to return?"

"Your handsome friend, Andre, told me. I called your house earlier this evening, and he said you were coming home for a while."

"He didn't say I was coming *home*. Home would be Roussillon."

"I stand corrected. He said you had decided to return to Paris for a short time." Philippe pursed his thin lips. "Is that true, Mademoiselle Moreau?"

For a moment I wondered how much longer it would take for Emelia to siphon any remaining compassion and self-worth from the young man. "I believe that's true, Philippe. I have unfinished business here."

He breathed deeply, as though a weight had lifted from his narrow shoulders. "Well then, welcome home ... I mean back. I'll let Madame know you've arrived. She's in your studio showing a client your new series."

"But they aren't finished." I grabbed Philippe's wrist. "She knows I don't—"

"Ella." He squeezed my hand, as mine dug into his cufflink. "This client can see *anything* at *anytime* he wants." Philippe's lower jaw jutted forward. "Don't ruin this." He released his grip, and then whispered in my ear. "You may want to know, someone else is here to see you."

He didn't try to conceal the smirk that spread across his face, making him look like a caricature.

"Who might that be?"

He poised his lower lip beneath his front teeth and silently mouthed the word. "Victor." Then he spun around and made his way through the crowd.

I glanced around the gallery and recognized many faces, returning a wave and smile when eyes met mine. There were several guests I had never met, and I wondered what plan Emelia had concocted while I'd been away.

My wrinkled cotton dress and flat shoes made me feel even more out of place as I pushed myself further into the mingling bodies toward my studio. After exchanging kisses on cheeks, accepting compliments for my work, and anticipation for my upcoming exhibit, I reached the rear of the gallery where the door was closed leading to my studio.

I can't believe she has the nerve to show someone—

"Ella." The voice made me jump. I had cautiously scanned the crowd looking for Victor—and perhaps the girl from the café—but now he had found me. I turned to find him standing with arms outstretched as though I should fall into his embrace.

"Victor." I stepped back, avoiding his touch.

"Not even a proper greeting?" His face was flush, his usually neat hair disheveled. He leaned to kiss me, but I raised my hand, feigning to push the hair from my face.

He frowned like a spoiled child. "You're still angry with me."

"No, I just don't want anything to do with you." I reached for the doorknob to the studio.

"You shouldn't barge in there." His words were slurred.

"You still drink too much. And why not? It's my studio."

"Actually, it belongs to Madame DuBois and she lets you use it."

Not wanting any more exchange with Victor, I turned the knob and pushed the door open. I slipped inside and was met by Emelia's prominent backside next to a tall man wearing a suit. They stood in front of the easel, apparently in a concentrated discussion.

I considered eavesdropping, but it seemed childish, and I had no intention of being outwitted in Emelia's game. "*Bonsoir.*"

They both turned. A jack-o-lantern smile spread across Emelia's face. "Ella. I didn't know you had arrived." She waddled toward me.

"I thought Philippe told you I was here."

"He may have tried. I told him no one was to interrupt Mister Hudson and me if the door was closed." Emelia blushed. "Forgive me, Theodore. That didn't sound proper."

"I understand." The man, probably in his early sixties, had dark hair laced with silver streaks that mimicked his pinstripe suit. He stepped forward and offered his hand. "Mademoiselle Moreau. I'm Theodore Hudson. It's a pleasure to meet the woman behind these magnificent paintings."

"It's nice to meet you."

"Mr. Hudson is from America. He has come from New York to see your work."

"That's a long way to come to see unfinished pieces." I exchanged a look with Emelia, assuring her I wasn't pleased with having my pieces shown without my permission.

"I'm interested in more than viewing your work. There's a woman in New York who's interested in you. She's an old friend of mine, and I'm helping her acquire some European artists. She's particularly fond of your talent and style."

"Is she acquiring for her private collection?"

"A few pieces, perhaps, but her primary interest is to represent you in the States."

"May I ask who this woman is?"

Mr. Hudson glanced at Emelia. "I'd rather not disclose her name until we've finalized the agreement."

"The agreement? I'm afraid I don't understand what's going on."

Emelia lifted a bottle of Chartreuse from the small table and refilled the champagne glasses. "Would you like to join us in a toast?"

"A toast? To what?" I swallowed hard, realizing Emelia still had a clenched grip on my life and future.

She lifted her glass. "To the demand for your art spreading across the Atlantic to the United States, where patrons with hefty bank accounts will pay tremendous amounts for European, especially well-known,

French artists."

"It's a winning situation for all of us." Mr. Hudson lifted his glass. "Madame DuBois loans my friend and me your new series. That is, when it's completed, and the exhibit at the Musee Marmottan has closed." The man approached the easel and ran his hand over an outline of a barn encircled by the first layer of a field of lavender. "Your work will be available in the finest art gallery in New York, and Madame DuBois, your new American representatives, and of course, you, will share the profits."

I leaned against the wall and tried to follow the deviation from my plan. "It sounds like an exciting opportunity." My legs felt shaky. "But I need to think about it."

"You don't need to think about anything. I've already told Mr. Hudson the series will be air freighted to him after the exhibit. The only thing left to do is agree on how the profits will be divided."

My head was spinning. "And what if I choose not to finish the paintings?"

"We've discussed that," Mr. Hudson said as he held his glass to the light and swirled the Chartreuse, eyeing its unique green color.

"First of all, dear, you *will* finish the series," Emelia said. "You are too tied to your paintings to leave them undone. You are a part of them." She stroked the painting as she would a Persian cat resting on a windowsill. "And they are a part of you." She stepped toward the distinguished man and slipped her arm inside his. "But if I'm wrong, which I rarely am, then I've promised Theodore he has access to several of your completed pieces hanging in the gallery."

I nodded and my head pounded at the movement. "I'm not feeling very well. You'll have to excuse me from the rest of the evening."

"What a shame. You must have arrived only a short time ago." Emelia moved aside as I opened the door leading to my small bedroom next to the studio.

"Good night, Mademoiselle Moreau. I'm sure we'll be talking again soon." Mr. Hudson smiled, his straight white teeth a perfect complement to his thin, red paisley tie.

* * * * *

I awoke the next morning to the phone ringing. My head still ached as I lifted the receiver.

"*Bonjour.*"

"*Bon matin.*" The voice on the other end sounded concerned.

"Andre?" I pushed myself up on my elbow. "I'm so sorry. I forgot to call you when I got here. It's just that there was—"

"I was a little worried and wanted to make sure you're all right."

"I'm fine. Just tired and have a headache. Emelia threw one of her big parties. It was a complete surprise." I fell back on my pillow.

"Your head hurts? Sounds like you had too much to drink last night." His tone was sarcastic, and I mentally kicked myself for forgetting to call him as I had promised.

"Not at all. Not one drink." Victor's sloppy appearance and slurred speech came to mind. "Emelia had a visitor from New York. I'll tell you all about it later, but how's Papa?"

Andre's tone softened. "He's worried about you being away again and had a restless night. He's sleeping now."

"He doesn't need to worry. I'll be on my way home as soon as things are settled here."

We were quiet for a long moment and then Andre spoke. "Ella, you need to let me know when you finish whatever it is you need to do ..." He paused and so did my breathing. "If you want to be back here with me."

With the receiver close to my ear, I listened to him continue.

"I need to decide what to say to Jeanette. I don't want to say something to her I may regret later."

"What do you mean?"

"I mean ..." Silence suspended between us. "I love you and want to be with you forever. You mustn't wait any longer to let me know if you feel the same. I can't do it."

My throat tightened. "Andre ..." I pulled the pillow into my chest and imagined holding him, erasing the distance between us. "I love you and, yes, that means forever." It was silent again as we hung onto each other through an intangible space.

"That's all I needed to know. I'll call you in the next few days and let you know how Papa is feeling."

"Goodbye. Kiss him for me."

"How about a hug?" He laughed. "Good-bye, Ella"

"Andre, I—"

"Yes?"

"I love you." I squeezed the phone until my hand ached. "I just had to tell you again."

"I love you too. We'll talk soon."

After the call I held on tightly to my pillow and must have dozed off because when I awoke, the sound of muffled voices filled the gallery.

* * * * *

Later that week, I spoke with Papa and Andre on the phone and told them about Theodore Hudson and his deal with Emelia. After discussing my intention to find another gallery and studio, we decided the opportunity to make a presence in America with Emelia's influence couldn't be missed. Mr. Hudson appeared to have the money and connections needed to broaden my exposure outside of Europe. It would be best to go along with their plan, at least for now.

I set myself to the rigorous task of completing the series in time for it to be on display in October. Painting early in the mornings until cleaning my brushes late at night, I completed canvas after canvas of what I believed to be some of my best work. Perhaps my wandering thoughts of Andre and a renewed peace with God brought life to the landscapes I had visited before. In my heart, I was painting for His glory again—not the high society of Paris or under the scrutiny of Victor Saillard and Emelia DuBois.

But at the end of each day, exhaustion overtook my body, and I slept deeply throughout the night. At the end of my third week in Paris, I took the metro to the office of Dr. Vancil near the Hopital-de-St. Louis.

* * * * *

There is no color. Why would anyone come here to get better? The door pushed open, interrupting my thoughts as I sat on the edge of the examination table.

"*Bonjour*, Mademoiselle Moreau." Dr. Vancil lifted a clipboard from the table and thumbed through the pages. The doctor had treated me a few times during my previous time in Paris for a bout with pneumonia. On occasion, he and his wife attended an exhibit or stopped in the gallery. He always inquired about my health and complimented my recent paintings. The short man walked toward the window and pushed aside the colorless, vinyl drape. "My nurse recorded the results from your test." He turned toward me with an unreadable expression. "You're pregnant."

I nodded, accepting what I had known instinctively, but wanted to deny for the last couple of months.

"After the exam we'll have a better idea of how far along you are. Do you have an idea?"

My mind swirled with images of the last time I was with Victor—the day he proposed a final time, later to be caught with another woman. I cringed. *It could have been then, but who am I trying to fool? I was with him many times before.* "I don't know."

Dr. Vancil estimated ten weeks with a due date sometime in late April or early May. Just in time for the poppies to bloom.

"Will the father be around to help?" Deep creases ran along the doctor's kind face.

"No, but I'll be fine." I tugged my shirt over my pants. "I'm going back to Roussillon to be with my father and ..."

The doctor looked at me over his wire-rimmed glasses.

"At least that was my plan." I chuckled for the stupidity in thinking I could run back into Andre's life—that he would accept me even though I was pregnant with another man's child.

"For the best care during your pregnancy and a safe delivery, you might consider staying in Paris. The provincial towns don't have the modern medical facilities."

"Why would there be any difficulties?"

"Most likely not. You're young and healthy. But remember, we talked when you were in the hospital last winter about the fact you had rheumatic fever as a child. We'll need to keep a watch on your heart and the stress it can be under during pregnancy." He ran his fingers through his remaining tuft of gray hair. "I want to see you back here in a month. Promise me?"

"I'll try." I thanked him and left the building.

When I finally collapsed on my bed, I wasn't able to recall my return ride on the metro across town. After crawling under the covers, I cried—for Papa when I would tell him the news. For the baby, knowing I'd never be married to the father. But mostly, I cried for myself and Andre, and the brutal truth that we had lost and then found each other's love again. How ignorant to believe we could be together.

My curse to never have true love had returned.

Thirty-One

Emelia tracked my progress for the exhibit like an expectant mother, giddy with anticipation for my watercolors and oils to occupy the same room as some of Monet's greatest works. She spoke often with Theodore Hudson, assuring him that she and I were upholding our end of the deal. The series would receive high accolades in France and soon be on its way to New York for the American debut of Ella Moreau. As Emelia inventoried the paintings and commented on their beauty, she must have been silently calculating her profits and fantasizing about her impending notoriety in America.

Once the pieces were matted and framed, Emelia oversaw Philippe and Brigitte prepare each painting for delivery to the museum. When the last one was wrapped, she beamed with a pride that only a new mother could display. I ran my hand over my stomach and imagined the tiny baby inside was only a dream.

Now that the series was complete, there was nothing to occupy my time and thoughts. I arranged to have coffee with Victor the next day.

The morning rush had cleared the café as I waited at an outdoor table. I had asked him to meet me at nine, but even for morning coffee, Victor was fashionably late.

"*Bon matin*, Ella. Why are you outside?" Victor stood above me.

Just as before when meeting him in the Jardin des Tulleries, I squinted into the sun and saw his silhouette. "The fresh air. Before long, it will be too dreary to be outside."

"All right then. Can I join you?"

"Of course. I invited you, remember?"

He gestured for a coffee and then sat next to me. Le Chat Café was tucked away on the Rue De Ponthieu where we could look across the street and see the row of majestic trees lining the Avenue des Champs Elysees. In the past, we had met at the café for a much-needed coffee after a late night out with friends. This morning, a cup of *café noir* was a necessity since I was unable to sleep as I rehearsed what to say to Victor.

"How have you been?" He lit a cigarette and offered one to me. As so many other things lately, the smoke made me nauseous.

I shook my head and fanned away the smoke. "I've been busy. The series is finished for the exhibit at the Marmottan and Emelia is happy."

"And if she's happy, then everyone is happy." Victor chuckled. "I heard a rumor that you'll soon be famous in America."

"Who said that?"

"Philippe. He told me it was a secret, but I think half of Paris knows by now." His cigarette dangled from the side of his mouth as he laughed aloud.

"That's ridiculous. I have an opportunity to be represented in New York starting the first of the year, but that doesn't mean my work will sell, or even be liked." I sipped my coffee and made a mental reminder to ask Emelia the name of Mr. Hudson's American associate.

The waiter set Victor's cup and saucer on the table with a gentle clank—one of the subtle, though consistent, sounds in the daily life of a Parisian I would miss if I left the city.

"So, tell me why I'm here." He lifted his cup. "Should I be so lucky that you want to work things out?" He grinned.

I pulled my coat tighter, aware of the slight widening of my waist. I decided to ignore his second remark and get to the point. "I need to talk with you about—"

"Brigitte." His cup clanged hard on the saucer. "I knew she wouldn't be able to keep her mouth shut. I had no intention of being with her again. But every time I saw her at a party, I swear she seduced me. Both of us had too much to drink that night."

My mouth hung open at Victor's uninvited confession.

"It was wrong, especially at your homecoming party." He looked at me with rehearsed puppy dog eyes. "Emelia told us you didn't feel well and had excused yourself early. I had planned on asking for your forgiveness that night, but after you left the party, as they say, the night took on a life of its own."

I blinked a few times to focus my thoughts, rolled my shoulders back, and sat up tall. "I asked you here to tell you I'm pregnant."

"And?" His face was expressionless.

"And you're the father."

"Are you sure?" He raised an eyebrow. "Could it be someone else?"

I slammed my fists on the table, unprepared for an inquisition. "No, it's not someone else. You're the only possibility."

"What about the man living with you in the country?" His tone was flippant.

"That man …" I lowered my voice as the waiter glanced at our table … "is my brother."

"Your *brother*? That's not what Brigitte and Philippe say."

"He's like a brother. *You* are the father. I have never been with another man."

Victor sat back and crossed one leg over the other. "I'm flattered." His manner was smug and his conceit sickened me. How could I have imagined having feelings for him?

"That's not a compliment. You needed to know before I return to Roussillon. I'm not coming back—ever."

He raised his finger and ordered another coffee, not even bothering to ask if I'd like one. Until his second cup arrived, we silently watched the people pass by.

"Who will help you?" His voice was soft.

"My father and—" I tucked my chin into my scarf. "I'll be fine."

"I hear he's not doing well."

"How do you know that?"

"Brigitte fills me in."

"I can see why you like her. She's beautiful."

His eyes followed a shapely woman as she strutted in front of our table.

"Like the woman in the café that night," I added.

"Ella." He took my hand. "It's my weakness. I love women."

I jerked my hand away, not sure what I had expected from him. "Then you want nothing to do with the baby?"

He looked confused, as though the thought had never occurred to him. "I'm in no position to—" He tapped a cigarette from its case. "No, I don't want to be a father."

I grabbed the cigarette from his hand and broke it in half.

"Why did you do that?" His lower lip protruded like a spoiled child.

"Because the smell makes me sick." I flicked the crumpled pieces at his pressed shirt. "I wanted to be honest with you. Even though we'll never be together, I thought you would at least want to know you have a child."

He brushed the loose tobacco from his shirtsleeve and then tapped another cigarette from the case. "There are probably others."

"You're heartless." I pulled some money from my purse to pay for the coffee.

He held up his hand. "I'll get it. That's the least I can do."

Trying to maintain the slightest dignity, I threw the money on the table.

"Say hello to your friend in the country." He made a contrived wave. "Maybe he'll be a good father."

Everything inside me wanted to spit in his face. Instead, I spun around and forced a smile at the waiter who graciously opened the wrought-iron gate for me. As though I were a lost child, I set my eyes on the Arc de Triomphe, sitting predominately at the end of the Avenue. I had walked the same sidewalk hundreds of times, but now required a landmark on which to focus, a guide to lead me back to the studio as quickly as possible. I had to hurry to catch the afternoon train to Roussillon.

* * * * *

I rushed through the gallery, avoiding a conversation with the well-dressed couple poised with Brigitte in front of one of my pieces.

Brigitte excused herself and followed me to the door. "Where are you going with your bag?" She looked childish as she forced an unbecoming pout.

"I'm in a hurry, Brigitte. Tell Madame DuBois my father is worse. I'm going home."

"She'll be upset. What about the opening of the exhibit this weekend?"

"She can handle it. I'll call soon." I pulled the door open and the familiar bell chimed.

"Oh, wait. A piece of mail came for you today. It's from New York." Brigitte disappeared into Emelia's office and returned with a letter. "Maybe it's from the American."

"Wouldn't that be obvious?" Immediately, I felt ashamed for my snide remark. But Brigitte's wide-eyes and puzzled expression only accentuated the fact that she was lacking in everything except beauty.

I took the letter and eyed the return address. No name, only a street address. I stuffed it in my purse and hurried to the metro station.

Thirty-Two

I settled in my seat as the train lunged forward, slipping off my shoes and tucking my feet onto the empty adjoining cushion. The train pulled out of the station and took me away from Paris and the people I needed to leave. The faces of Victor, Emelia, Brigitte, and Philippe mixed into a blurred image as the train sped past buildings and finally broke into the open countryside. My breathing calmed until I wondered how to explain my surprise return home.

"*Bonjour*, Mademoiselle Moreau. It's nice to have you aboard again." I turned my attention from the window to the same young porter.

"*Bonjour*. It's wonderful to be aboard. And this time I would like a beverage—*au chocolat chaud, s'il vous plait*."

"Perfect choice for a chilly first day of November. I'll be back right away."

The letter from New York lay in my open bag. I took it out and examined it again. *Strange there is no name. Must be someone important, or very private.*

I slipped my finger beneath the seal and pulled the letter from the envelope. As I unfolded the top portion and read the greeting, I gasped. As the bottom half slowly unfolded, my eyes blinked in disbelief and read the neatly written signature—*Mama*.

10th October, 1951
My Dearest Daughter Ella,
May this letter find you well. Your hands may be trembling

at the surprise of hearing from me after all this time. It's been
twenty years since I last saw you in your pink dress.

I celebrated my fifty-third birthday in September. Shocking
to me, really. It's hard to believe you will be twenty-eight in
March. But the point of my letter—well, we've all grown older
and so much time has passed.

Thinking about that reality, I've decided to plan a trip to
France in the New Year. Ella, I wish to see you more than I
can express in a letter. This may all come as a shock, but I
hope you see things as an adult now, and will have it in your
heart to meet with me. So much has happened in both of our
lives, and the thought of letting more time pass would be a
shame. A small article in a newspaper mentioned you are an
artist and may have some paintings in New York. Is that true?
It would be grand as I remember all the wonderful pictures
you drew for me.

Lastly, I plan to write your brothers and would appreciate
it if you would provide me their addresses. I'll make my
arrangements when you respond, and pray that I hear from
you soon.

Yours,
Mama

P.S. How is your father?

With shaking hands, I folded the letter, slid it into the envelope, and
tucked it deep into my bag. My chest tightened. For a moment I was
unable to breathe. The terrifying panic of slipping under water rushed
back to my mind. *Charles!* I wanted to scream for him to save me, but
he was gone—just as Mama was gone.

No, she's not.

Outside the window, the landscape raced by, whisking me back
in time for the last twenty years—Papa, Jack, and Remy—his parents
Auguste and Eloise—Monsieurs Duval and Lenoir—the lady with the
burgundy peonies—and Charles.

*She doesn't even know her own son is dead. She doesn't know I love a
man named Andre and am going to have another man's child.*

Demanding the past to disappear, I balled my hand into a fist and slammed it against the window. Tears filled my eyes and the passing scene blurred.

"Mademoiselle? Are you all right?" I turned toward the porter who, this time, shifted the tray awkwardly between palms. "Your hot chocolate."

I took the cup, handed him a few coins, and nodded, letting the tears run down my face.

"If I can get you anything …" He turned and walked away.

* * * * *

Freeing my mind from its torment, I dozed until the train slowed into the station. My drink was cold. I pushed my messy hair out of my face, lifted my bag, and stepped back into the world of Roussillon.

I hadn't thought how to get home upon arriving in Roussillon and didn't want to call Papa or Andre. There were few taxi drivers in the small town and, most likely, they were taking the typical late afternoon nap. Wanting to arrive before dusk, I pushed the strap onto my shoulder and headed down the winding road leading toward the vineyard.

Besides, the walk will give me time to think about things. God knows I need that.

I arrived in time to see Andre step out of the cellar. He froze and shook his head as if shaking off a dream. He walked toward me in long strides, and then broke into a run.

"Ella. What in the world?" He stopped a few steps in front of me.

"Hi." The strap slipped off my shoulder and the bag plopped in the dirt. "I'm home."

We wrapped our arms around one another and held on tightly. Although we stood at the end of the vineyard bordering the road, I felt as though we stood precariously near the precipice of our world. Any slight movement or mistake would send us tumbling over the edge and into the unknown below.

He lifted my chin. "I can't believe you're really here. Why didn't you call?"

"It was a last-minute decision. Sorry to surprise you like this."

"Sorry? No, I'm so happy you're home." He kissed the top of my head. "I'm curious, but that can wait. Let's find Papa." Andre lifted my bag, and we strolled toward the house, holding hands as if I had been here all along.

Thirty-Three

Secret, 1951

After dinner, Andre and I joined Papa in the front room. It was time to disclose the letter from Mama. After reading it three times, Papa passed the letter to Andre. The aged man placed his glasses on the arm of his chair and stretched his legs. "Never thought I'd see the day."

Andre finished reading the letter and tossed it on the coffee table. "That Marie would come back?"

"She was always full of surprises, but this is her biggest yet." Papa snorted. "I'm having a hard time understanding if she's sincere."

Tired from my long walk, I lay on the sofa to ease the ache in my back. "I agree. Why would she write after so many years?"

"Maybe she means what she says about getting older and having regrets." Andre propped his feet on the step stool. "People think about those things as they get older."

"Well, I'm old and not at all sure I would think about prancing back after leaving my children like she did. I've got to sleep on this one." Papa grunted and pushed himself from the chair. "*Bonsoir.*"

"*Bonsoir*, Papa." I blew him a kiss.

"Tomorrow when I'm fresh, you can tell me why you came home unannounced. I couldn't be happier, but I know you. Something's up." He steadied himself along the wall as he walked to his bedroom.

Andre came to the sofa. "And we'll talk tomorrow night. I'm leaving early to make a delivery to the coast and should be back before dark."

Panic rolled over me. "You're going to Nice, aren't you?"

"One of my stops is there, but it's not what you're thinking."

I looked away and regretted my jealousy.

"Jeanette and I talked." He scooted the stool closer and sat.

I pushed myself up and our knees touched. "What did you tell her?" I imagined the woman whom I had never met. In my mind, she wept over the loss of a wonderful man she loved and who loved her back. Strange to be sad for her, but I knew how much she had lost.

"We talked about a lot of things." He dropped his head. "We discussed the difficulty in being together when we're committed to our family businesses in separate towns. She wants to stay in Nice. I have the vineyard here."

"Then it's a matter of distance and work."

"That was part of it when we discussed getting married." He looked up from beneath furrowed brows. "But I told her about us. Don't you understand? I ended any future with Jeanette because I love you." He ran his fingers through his thick, dark hair. "She's a beautiful person and I broke her heart. I'll always feel awful about that." Andre held my hands and fixed his eyes on mine. "I wouldn't have been able to do that unless I believed we have our own future."

I held his hands as though clinging from a rocky ledge—tragedy waiting to swallow me if I let go. I studied his face, no longer the determined, yet fearful boy who arrived on our drive years ago, or the handsome teenager who made me privately blush when he tossed his shirt aside in the vineyard on a hot summer's day. He was a man with a physical appeal that caused my heart to race. But most importantly, he had become a man of integrity with a gracious and loving heart. He was a gift from God.

Tell him now, Ella. You love him too much not to be honest.

I lowered my voice to barely above a whisper. "I want to believe that too, and to have a future more than anything in the world, but there's something you have to know." I forced myself to look at him.

"Andre, I'm pregnant."

Like watching him in slow motion, he stood, all the while staring at me with wide eyes. Then, he recoiled, wrapped his arms around his chest, and stumbled over the stool.

"Andre, please don't hate me." I slid off the sofa onto my knees, willing to beg for his forgiveness. "I don't love him."

He avoided my eyes. "Victor?"

"Yes."

He paced the room like an animal caught in a trap. "How could you do this?" He slammed his fist into the wall, knocking a yellowed photograph off-kilter.

"You'll wake Papa."

"I don't care." He grabbed a pillow and gave it a jab.

My tears fell. "I'm so sorry. Can you ever forgive me?"

He shoved his hands into his pockets and hung his head. "I was a fool to think you could go off to the city and nothing like this would happen." He jerked his head up as if reminded of something important. "How far are you? I thought we resolved things when you came home. Did you do this after you said you loved me?" His eyes filled with tears. "You told me you've always loved me."

"No. This happened before I came home. I meant everything I said to you that night. You have to believe me." I inched toward him on my knees.

"Why didn't you tell me?" Andre wiped his tears on his shirtsleeve.

I slumped onto my hands and knees. My hair hung around my face, but I was too ashamed to push it away. "I didn't know I was pregnant. You must believe me."

He was silent as I listened to his footsteps pace the wooden floor. "I don't know what to believe. Nothing seems real anymore."

His footsteps left the room, keys jangled, and the door slammed.

* * * * *

The morning came quickly as if it sensed the urgency for me to tell Papa everything I had shared with Andre the night before. I rolled over and gazed out the window.

Lord, before the day begins, I'm sorry for everything. I need your forgiveness.

My eyes squeezed shut as I silently prayed Andre would forgive me as well.

I willed myself out of bed and pulled on a cream-colored sweater and my worn jeans, noticeably tighter now. It felt good to wear my country clothes. By now, Andre was on his way to the coastal towns, and Papa was probably in the kitchen with his coffee and newspaper.

"*Bon matin*, Papa. How did you sleep?" I pulled the largest cup from the cabinet.

"Good. I'm feeling better now that you're home. Ready for a full day." He closed the paper and folded it in half, a morning habit since I was young. "Andre must have gotten up early. His truck is gone." He rose from his chair.

"Papa." I sipped the black coffee and realized I forgot to add cream. "Last night you said you wanted to know why I came home without calling first."

He rested his hands on the back of the chair, waiting for me to continue.

"Well …" I added more than a splash of cream, and my coffee spilled on the counter.

"You seem jittery this morning." He raised an inquiring eyebrow.

I grabbed the dishcloth off the hook and wiped the counter. "Probably tired. It's been a long month getting ready for the exhibit. But the series is finished. I wish you could see it. The watercolors are some of my best."

Papa cleared his throat as he always did when he expected an explanation from one of his children.

I faced him and swallowed hard. "Papa, I'm home for several reasons. One, I finished my work for the exhibit and kept my end of the deal for Mr. Hudson and Emelia. Painting that many pieces in a short time was exhausting and it was time to rest." I took another sip, contemplating my remaining list. "I wanted to see how you're doing and help around here."

Papa leaned against the wall and crossed his arms as if he had all the time in the world for me to explain myself.

"And of course, you know I've missed Andre. He's surely told you how we feel about one another."

"It's pretty obvious without him having to say a word." Papa grinned and then resumed his serious demeanor.

Looking out the window, I remembered the day Jack limped up the drive. That day seemed long ago. So much had happened. "Papa, the main reason I came home is—"

"You're pregnant." His big arms wrapped around me from behind.

I spun around. "How—"

"I could tell the moment I saw you. You looked just like your mother when she told me she was pregnant with Charles—a certain glow that you've been blessed with." He glanced at my stomach. "Not to mention you're not as thin as the last time you were home."

"Is it that obvious?"

"A bit. You look good, Ella." He refreshed his coffee and then circled the table and straightened each chair. "I can't condone what happened for you to get pregnant. And to be honest, I'm surprised Andre was able to keep the secret."

My cup jerked and a brown stain dripped down my sweater. Again, I grabbed for the dishcloth. Disgusted with myself, I balled it up and threw it into the sink. "It wasn't Andre." I avoided Papa's stare. "Andre wouldn't have allowed this to happen. He's too good of a man."

"Then who—"

"Victor Saillard. The man I dated in Paris. The one I thought I might marry."

"Thought you might marry?" My father's voice boomed. "It seems like you got the order of things mixed up."

My voice tried to match his volume. "Don't you think I realize that? But I told you I didn't love Victor. I thought I did and that's why this happened." I lowered my head, ashamed at my naïveté.

"But you love Andre?"

"More than I ever imagined possible."

"Have you told him?"

"We talked last night." I recalled the shock and the deep pain carved into his face. "He said he'd be gone early in the morning and didn't know when he'd be back."

Papa held the back of a chair and tipped it back and forth as if pacing his deep thoughts with the thumping of the chair legs. "He has thinking to do. He loves you, Ella, but you can only break a person's heart so many times."

"I know, Papa."

I know.

Thirty-Four

Ponder & Pardon, 1952

Papa and I had exchanged a few gifts Christmas morning. I flipped the calendar to the New Year, then added extra blankets to our beds in the coldest months of the year. We braced ourselves for the windy, damp weather of March.

Nearly eight months pregnant now, each uncomfortable change in my body was accentuated by my longing for Andre. The two men in my life talked on the phone often, but Andre and I spoke only on occasion to confirm I was progressing well and to check on Papa's health. He was staying with a friend in Toulon on the coast of the Mediterranean while the vineyard was dormant. I hoped he wasn't making frequent trips east along the coast to Nice, but I couldn't blame him if he had changed his mind about Jeanette.

"What are you going to say to her?" Papa peered over my shoulder at a piece of paper on the kitchen table. "I know your mother. It's driving her crazy because you haven't written back."

"I don't know what to say. How do you respond to a mother you can hardly remember." I tapped the pen on the table.

"Do you really not remember her?"

"Some things perfectly, but there are so many holes—like moths got into my memory." I scooted my chair closer to the table, but my protruding belly kept me at arm's length. "I'm going to tell her about Charles and Jack. She deserves to know what's happened to them."

He nodded, confirming the reality of those tragedies.

"And I'm telling her she's not welcome until after summer. We don't need her showing up when I'm delivering a baby or trying to figure out how to be a new mother."

"You'll do great." Papa patted me on the back. "You're going to be a wonderful mother." He grabbed the keys to the truck, pulled on his coat, and started for the door. "I'm heading to town for supplies. The vines will be waking up soon. We need to be ready for them."

"Make sure you have someone load the truck. I'll help you put things away.""

Absolutely not." Papa laughed. "We make a fine pair, don't we?"

I closed my eyes and wished Andre would come back. We needed him. Then I opened the pen and focused on the quietness of the room and the blank paper awaiting my thoughts.

Anger and sadness mixed with a curiosity of who my mother had become.

8th March, 1952

Mama,

Trembling hands can't begin to describe my reaction when I received your letter. It's taken me months to write back to you because I haven't known what to say. Many thoughts have come to me, several of which would be inappropriate to say to my mother.

Allow me to clarify your memory. My dress was yellow, not pink, the day you left—the one you said made my hair look pretty. Although I wish I couldn't, I remember every sad detail of that day, especially your eyes and red lips reflected in the car mirror. You saw me but didn't stop.

There is no easy way to tell you this, but Charles is dead. He drowned in the pond when he was nineteen. It was 1939 and nobody knew where you were to tell you. Shortly after, Jack went to war. When it ended, he came home but wasn't the same. Papa won't let him come home unless he gets his life in order.

As an afterthought, you asked about Papa. His heart isn't well. He spends more time sleeping, but runs a successful vineyard and has a clear mind and strong opinions.

If you're still planning to come to France, you need to know I no longer live in Paris, but have moved home to Roussillon. I realize that may affect your decision to see me. And, yes, I became an artist, but am taking an extended leave from my work and don't know when or if I'll be back in Paris. If you decide to come, it would be best if you came after the harvest when we're not as busy.

Finally, Mama, please tell me your purpose in coming back after all these years. You mentioned that you would pray I responded to your letter quickly. Are you really a praying woman?

Regards,
Ella

I sealed the letter quickly before changing my mind and tearing it to bits. By responding, I would probably hear from Mama again. Returning to the past was inevitable. Since March weather was unpredictable, I lifted my heavy coat from the hook and walked to the post office.

* * * * *

On my way home, the rain started slowly and then unleashed as though the clouds were ripped open. I secured my coat the best I could and tucked my chin into the collar. My eyes squinted against the pelting drops as my hair matted against my face.

A car slowed and the window rolled down. "Can I give you—"

"Andre," I gasped.

"Ella?" He pushed the door open. "Get in. Hurry."

I stepped over the mud and climbed in. As the rain pounded the car, we stared at each other as if we were both from another world.

"What are—"

"You doing here?" I finished his question.

"I'm coming home … to take care of things here." He looked me over, stopping at my enormous belly. "Including you."

I smiled, imagining how I looked soaked through and waddling like a duck in the rain. "How long are you planning—"

"A long time." He leaned toward me and held my face in his hands as raindrops and tears trickled down my cheeks.

"I'm so glad you're home."

Thirty-Five

Matrimony & Motherhood, 1952

March was preparing to leave as April approached with a handful of brilliant orange poppies making their debut in the fields.

"I would like to take you to the top of the world at Remy's Castle." Andre ran his hand over my hard stomach. "But the field will have to do since you wouldn't make it up the hill in your state."

We walked along a narrow path through the twisted poppy stems. Some buds stood erect waiting for the sun to command them to open, while others drooped in sleep.

He continued walking, then stopped beneath a grove of pale-green olive trees. "I had a lot of time to think while away. About you and me. And the baby." He leaned against a crooked trunk. "I prayed more than ever—kept asking the Lord over and over to tell me what to do. Then I waited. That's why it took so long. Every day I wanted to race back home, but promised myself—and God—I wouldn't return until sure what he was calling me to do."

"Do you know?" Nervously, I plucked a thin, silvery leaf and smoothed it between my fingers, then ran my hand along the rough bark, ready to brace myself against the sturdy tree.

He took my hands and turned me toward him. "Yes. I know exactly what the Lord wants." He pulled me closer. "I also know what I want." His smile spoke directly to my heart and made it skip a beat. "Ella, will you marry me? Will you be with me forever?"

There was no doubt, no uncertainty in that smile or in his eyes. His expression was like a flawless painting, his features pieced together as a masterpiece—peaceful.

My heart rejoiced. *Lord, I am awed by your ability to mend such tremendous pain and piece together brokenness so your plan will prevail. You are truly good and almighty.*

"I will." My lips quivered. "I want to be with you forever too." We held one another under the shade of the olive trees for a long time, safe within each other's arms. Andre kissed me, sealing an oath to never be apart again.

We walked home along the same path, making plans for our small wedding to be held before the baby would be born. We wanted the child to enter the world with parents united and deeply in love.

* * * * *

In early May, Papa gave me to Andre in the old stone church. We stood in front of the beaming faces of Auguste and Eloise Patin, a small group of other neighbors, and Monsieur Lenoir, who came from Marseilles for the day.

"Papa, I love you so much." I kissed each cheek, damp with tears of joy, then turned toward Andre. The pastor joined our hands as I gazed at my future husband, handsome in his borrowed suit and tie. Eloise had sewn a lovely cream dress for me and, despite my awkward shape, I felt beautiful.

After the private ceremony, we stood on the church steps, looking over the fields of poppies and hints of lavender spread before us like a banquet. For that moment, we were a king and queen. I kissed my husband again, and then again, as we began our life anew.

We agreed our honeymoon would consist of walks in the sweet-smelling vineyards and dangling our feet in the coolness of the pond. The baby was due soon and we needed to be close to home and minutes from Dr. Levin's clinic in town.

* * * * *

It was wise not to venture from home because the day after our wedding, the baby was ready to be born.

"Papa!" I shouted his name as we rested in chairs on the porch. He roused from his nap.

"What's wrong?" He shook his head, trying to throw off his deep sleep.

"Get Andre. We need to go to the clinic." I held my stomach and tried to breathe deeply. The contractions had started in the morning and then stopped. Now they had returned, powerful and frequent.

Papa pounced from his chair like I hadn't seen him move in years. "Get Andre up here," he called to a young worker tying up the vines that dangled at the end of a row. "And hurry." He pointed to my chair. "You stay here. I'll pull the truck around."

Despite the growing pain, I grinned at Papa's newfound agility. "I won't move an inch."

Andre bounded onto the porch, breathing hard and sweating. "What should I do?"

I laughed before another contraction made me wince. "Help me get in the truck."

The three of us sped down the dirt road, marking our haste with a plume of dust. As we screeched into the parking lot, Papa yelled out the window to announce our arrival. He must have expected Dr. Levin to hear us through the brick walls of the building.

Andre helped me into the waiting room. Quickly, after seeing what must have been the predictable look on my face, a heavy-set nurse put me in a wheelchair and hurried me down the hallway to the delivery room. She helped me into bed and I lay back on the crisp pillow. The pain was unbearable and I cried out, scaring myself—and Andre too, by the startled expression on his face.

The doctor scurried in and offered a brief hello. "You sure like to keep things exciting. It's a good thing Andre is a fast driver."

Andre rubbed his head. "As fast as that old truck can go."

"She'll be fine. You can wait in the room down the hallway," the nurse said.

Andre glanced at me and then the nurse. "I'm not leaving her."

"Monsieur Donato, it's best that you join your—"

"Let him stay," Dr. Levin said. "He's going to be a father soon. He can pay me back for all the times I took care of the Moreau children when they were young." He gestured to Andre to blot my head with a cool towel. "Are you ready for this?"

Before Andre could answer the doctor, I moaned in pain.

Andre smoothed the hair away from my face. "We're ready."

It seemed surreal. I was experiencing every part of my body at the same moment. Each nerve and capillary stood at attention as my body declared war against the pain. At the same time, it affirmed a treaty with each pang, working in tandem to complete the intended task. Then it was over, my body triumphant at last. The nurse laid our daughter on my chest.

Andre stood over me, his eyes wide and wet with tears. "She's beautiful." He kissed my forehead and I wept.

"Well done." The seasoned doctor stood on the other side of the bed. "You have a healthy baby—such a blessing." He beamed as though he was genuinely awed each time he participated in the miracle of helping a child into the world. "Did you decide on a name?"

Now Andre beamed. "Now that we know the baby's a girl, her name is Aimee Columbina Donato. Aimee means loved and Columbina was my mother's name. It means little dove. She's our loved little dove."

"Beautiful. Very Italian." Dr. Levin winked at me. "I'm going to get Henri. He's going to be a proud grandfather."

* * * * *

During the weeks and months that followed, Papa held Aimee while I sneaked away for a nap after being up several times in the night. Andre oversaw the vineyard throughout the summer and into its busiest season as the workers prepared for the harvest. Each day he found numerous times to stop by the house to cuddle his daughter and give us both kisses.

"I'll take her now, Papa." I pulled my hair into a knot after an afternoon slumber.

He held on tightly to his granddaughter. "But you just went to sleep."

"I did not." I set my hands on my hips in mock disgust. "She's going to think you're her mother if you hold her all day."

"She smiles at me." Papa lifted the tiny bundle close to his face and displayed an ear-to-ear grin. "You're my loved little dove, aren't you?"

"I have to feed her before I'm miserable." The familiar tingling sensation stirred in my breasts. "And she's hungry."

Papa reluctantly passed the baby. "All right, but she's growing like a weed."

I settled into a chair on the porch and nursed my child. Our world was perfect. I couldn't have been happier, except for the letter I was about to share with Papa. It had arrived yesterday, reminding me of Mama's impending return.

27th August, 1952
Dear Ella,
Thank you for finally writing back to me—I wasn't sure if you would. I am shocked and devastated by the news of Charles and Jack. I realize you didn't want to share more details in

a letter, but I want to know what really happened to both of them. I'm sorry you couldn't find me when Charles died. That makes me feel horrible.

Also, thank you for correcting my mistaken detail of our last day together. You were always beautiful in your yellow dress. I mentioned before that I am getting older and my memory presents challenges at times.

It's a shame that housework and taking care of Papa are keeping you from painting. For your sake, I hope you resume your work soon. I distinctly remember how much you loved your artwork as a little girl. One of my clearest memories is watching you carry a wrinkled pad of paper and a blue, wire-handled tin box everywhere you went. It swung back and forth in your hand as you followed me around the kitchen and garden. I can still hear it—a clanging as if you were a calf. I always knew where you were.

As I'm sure you know, New York is known as one of the art capitals of the world. A friend of mine mentioned he'd recently seen some of your work on display in a gallery here. Is it true? I haven't had time to make a visit to that side of town. New York City is very big. I would love to see your paintings when I'm in France. To that point, I arrive in Paris on the fourteenth of September and plan to spend a few days in the city. I'll travel by train to Roussillon toward the end of the week. Don't worry about meeting me at the station. I'll take a taxi to the house since I'm not sure of my exact arrival.

I can only imagine what your father thinks of me resurfacing. Please let him know that I, too, am still sound of mind and have aged well. By the way, I noticed you didn't sign a sentimental closure. I understand and appreciate your honesty. Perhaps being transparent is an artist's trait.

My love,
Mama

P.S. No, I'm not a praying woman. You're right; too much has happened over all these long years.

Thirty-Six

Red Hills Calling, 1952

We tucked our baby into bed and crossed our fingers she would sleep through most of the night. Papa was asleep and snoring loudly as we tiptoed down the hallway, ready to relax on the front porch in the cool September air.

"Amazing, isn't it?" Andre asked. We stood huddled together, and he covered my shoulders with his jacket. It smelled like the earth—a mix of fallen leaves and autumn's ripe grapes. "I never tire of watching the vineyard change from season to season and dawn to dusk."

"It's beautiful." I shivered and pulled his jacket closer. "So peaceful, but sometimes I wonder …" I tried to push the memory away as I had done so many times before.

"What do you wonder?" Andre gently rubbed my neck, sending another shiver through me—but it wasn't from the cool evening air.

"Nothing, really."

"Tell me." He kneaded my tight muscles.

"When I opened Mama's last letter, fear escaped from the envelope and crept into my heart. When I think of her coming back, I see her out there in the vineyards. She's confused and trying to get out—but she's lost."

"Ella, so many years have passed. I know it's hard to believe, but her letter seemed sincere." The last ray of sunlight slanted across his tan jaw and onto his lips. At that moment, I wanted him to pull me into his arms and kiss away my fear. Instead, I took a step backward and steadied myself against the stone wall.

"I don't know what to believe. Why would she come back now?"

"She's getting older?"

"She's in her fifties and that's not old."

"Maybe she really is sorry. Maybe she wants to make things right after all these years."

I spun around. "Who says I want to be a part of that?" My own voice shocked me. "I'm sorry. You're only trying to help."

"It's all right. This is hard. Her letters took us all by surprise."

"You've been helping me since you first came here. Way back when I was a little girl, little and scared to death." I sat down and rested my chin on my knees.

He sat by me and we tilted our heads back to look at the veil of stars. "We've helped each other, Ella. You've been a part of me from the beginning, more than I ever realized." His voice was hoarse. "Do you know what happened, with your mother I mean? Something seemed wrong even before she found out about the other woman."

The stars drew me in. I felt dizzy in their vastness and pulled my knees tighter to my chest. "I remember the day when I knew she wasn't happy."

With my head against his shoulder, my mind drifted once again into the past. "I loved to walk between the rows of grapevines, tucked away from everyone. The leaves would wave at me in the breeze, and I'd pluck the largest one to fan my face. The curly vines tickled me. They'd wrap my hair in their spiraled fingers like they wanted me to play, and I'd breathe in the ripe scent of the fat clusters. But on one particular day I had squeezed a handful of grapes and the red juice dripped between my fingers and glided down my arm. I licked the back of my hand—it was delicious. Then, jumping from shadow to shadow, I hopped over the thin slices of sunshine lying across the dirt. It's strange, but the bees provided the music to the rhythm of my childhood dance." I paused and frowned at my husband. "Then I came to the end of a row."

I sat up and peered toward the vineyard. "Andre, did you hear that?"

He cocked an ear toward the field. "There's nothing out there. Maybe a rabbit." He settled back next to me and held my hand.

I shivered and he moved closer.

"You're cold. Time to go in."

"No. I can't leave her out here."

"She isn't there, Ella. She's on the other side of the ocean."

"But not my memory of her."

"Tell me what you saw."

I breathed deeply and allowed the past to return. "I had started down the next row when I saw her. She was crumpled in the dirt between the walls of vines, not moving. Her hair was tangled. And I can't forget the sound. Frenzied bees circled her head. I called to her, but she only lifted a dirty hand to swipe the bees away. I ran to her and knelt in the dirt. 'Mama, what's happened?' I freed a strand of her hair from the grip of the vine and shooed the bees away with my leaf. She looked at me with swollen eyes. Her tears had left paths on her satin skin."

I rubbed my forehead, but the image remained. "She stared at me for a long time. Then, just like it was any other day, she said, 'I'm fine. Everything is just fine.' She stood and brushed the dirt off her dress, flattening the wrinkles with the palms of her hands and pulling her hair into a twist. She pinned it with her favorite tortoise clip."

"Did she say anything else?"

"No, nothing. We walked holding hands through the long tunnel of grapevines toward the house. She looked straight ahead like she was determined to reach the light at the end of the row. After that, I didn't think I'd ever go back into the vineyard."

"I don't know what to say."

"At that moment, something changed in my beautiful world." I searched my husband's eyes, wishing the memory was only a dream and needing him to understand how drastically that event determined much of my life.

I leaned my head back and breathed again. I had done it—relived the past and allowed myself to admit that Mama was vulnerable. She wasn't the perfect mother, wife, or person I had perceived her to be when I was young. And even though I had seen her cry on occasion, time had let me turn her to a woman made of stone—a person with no feeling or emotion, no heart.

"When we came to France, our vineyards and the countryside were God's perfect beauty. Mama seemed a natural part of it. Somehow, almost innately, I knew God had brought me to Roussillon to use my art to glorify His creation—my way of praising Him. But for her, she couldn't see it. She only saw what was missing—her stolen beauty, her lost potential, and the hope for a future of her own. When Papa took her away from America and brought her across the ocean, Mama withered like a spent garden."

Andre squeezed my hand, but remained silent.

Now, a sadness for Mama that I had never allowed, washed over me like an ocean. It was encompassing, yet welcoming in an odd sort of way. I had held back the waters for so many years. Perhaps acknowledging the past would quench my thirst and provide new life.

Warm lips brushed my cheek, met my lips, and ushered the past away for the moment.

Thirty-Seven

Mama's Return, 1952

"She may show up today." Papa coughed and spread the newspaper across the kitchen table.

"Maybe you should get back to bed. I heard you get up several times last night." I refilled his coffee cup and set it on the table.

"I'm not going to be lying down like a dead dog when she comes waltzing in here after more than twenty years." He chuckled and winked at me. There was a new light in his eyes. "Maybe I'll crawl up on the barn and paint it pink. That would show her all the fun she's missed not being with us."

"Has it been fun?"

"Sometimes. Yes, I would say so. I have plenty of good memories."

"Me too."

"Maybe a better word is blessed. Yes, we've been blessed." The pages of the newspaper continued to flip. He smoothed the center crease with his weathered hand. "Look at these articles—Vietnam, now fighting in Tunisia. There's so much sadness and death." He adjusted his glasses on the tip of his nose and studied a photograph of a wounded soldier. "The Lord has blessed us despite our losses.

I tore a piece of fresh baguette and sliced some Gruyere. "Andre's going to take the day off and be with Aimee. It's been a while, but I'm ready to begin painting again."

He took off his glasses and laid them on the table. "That's a fine idea. It makes me happy to know you're painting."

I nodded and rubbed his hunched back. "Do you need anything before I go to the studio?"

"I do." He reached for my hand and stroked it with his thumb like he had done hundreds of times before. "Pray for God's hand to be in this day. That somehow we understand what his purpose is in having your mother return. I believe God's in this. I'm just not sure how."

"I'll pray. That's what I seem to do best when in my studio."

"You paint pretty well too." He smiled then coughed several times.

"Go back to bed, Papa."

"I told you, I'm no dead dog, at least not yet."

"You're a stubborn old dog."

"Get painting and praying, young lady."

My precious father winked, put on his glasses, and retreated into the day's news.

* * * * *

It was well past morning when I emerged from the studio. Even though I tried to pray, my mind was restless and unfocused. Papa's loud snoring reached my ears. It concerned me that he chose to go back to bed after putting up such a fuss.

Even before the dog barked on the front porch, my gut told me she had arrived. Taking a deep breath, I cautiously opened the door. A taxi driver unloaded her suitcase while she rummaged through her purse. She said something and pointed to the house. That's when she looked over his shoulder and saw me.

I couldn't breathe. We stared at each other. Separating us was the screen door, the barking dog, a taxi driver, and twenty years.

Mama started for the porch, holding her head high as she ascended the steps. The dog was barking wildly now, and I shushed him from behind the screen. The closer she came, the more my heart raced. On a rare occasion over the years, I had imagined her coming home and how happy I'd be to see her. Now, I was numb, not knowing what to feel or think. She stopped inches from the screen and our eyes met. I could smell her rose perfume.

"Friendly dog you have." She forced a smile and looked very nervous.

"He doesn't know you." My hands pushed deeper into the pockets of my smock.

"Can you do me a small favor and pay the driver? I seem to have lost my wallet."

"I'll be back in a minute." Without thinking, I closed the door and rushed to the bedroom. Outside the window, my mother yelled at the taxi driver in broken French.

Steadying myself against the dresser, I saw myself in the mirror. My skin was pale as if I'd seen a ghost. Perhaps I had. "You can do this. It's Mama." I grabbed money from my purse and stepped onto the same porch where I had waited for her many years ago.

The driver carefully flipped through the money and smiled a wide, coffee-stained grin. "*Merci*, Madame." He hopped into the taxi and sped off.

"Thank you." Mama stood behind me.

"*De rein.*"

"You'll need to speak English with me. It's been a while."

I faced her. "Don't you have friends in Paris? In your letter, you mentioned you'd be staying in the city before you took the train here?"

"This is certainly not the welcome I imagined." She stepped toward me, but I took a step backwards. "Ella, I've come a *long* way to see you."

"And you've been gone a *long* time."

"Touché. But now I'm here, hoping we can make the best of it." She reached, suggesting an awkward embrace.

I looked at her hands. Her nails were painted a deep red and sparkling in the sun was the same diamond wedding ring I had admired as a child. "Why are you wearing that?"

"The ring? I've never taken it off." She cupped her hands and held them over her chest.

"You're not married to Papa any longer."

"We never divorced."

"I'd say being gone twenty years qualifies."

"That's between your father and me."

"You appear out of nowhere. No money. Expect me to pay for your taxi, then tell me you're still married." I clenched my teeth. "You must be crazy."

"Perhaps a little, but I'm still your mother." She lifted her suitcase and headed across the porch, head held high.

"And what a mother you've been," I yelled, feeling like I had been reduced to nothing.

My mother spun around and smiled. "Oh good, now we're getting somewhere." She opened the screen door and came face-to-face with Papa.

"Henri."

"Marie."

Thirty-Eight

Madame DuBois and Jack's Conspiracy, 1952

I closed the front door to my gallery, shutting out the sounds of the bustling Parisian boulevard, and twisted the lock an hour before closing time. My headache was ruthless, and I couldn't attribute it to too much drinking the night before. According to my ledger, Ella Moreau hadn't produced any paintings in almost a year, and my drop in sales was proof. Her gallery inventory was sparse, and the American dealers were desperate for more pieces. Ella's popularity was soaring in New York, and her value continued to climb.

"Madame DuBois," Brigitte said, peeking her head into my office. "There's a gentleman insistent on seeing you."

I rubbed my temples. "Tell him we're closed."

"I did, but he won't go away."

"Who is he?"

"I don't know. Should I ask?"

If only she had as much common sense as she has good looks. "That would be helpful, Brigitte, especially if he is a buyer."

"Not by the looks of him, but I'll ask his name." She disappeared before I could tell her not to bother.

For heaven's sake, now I have to hobnob with a despondent stranger.

I turned and watched the people outside my window, busy about their day up and down the street. Brigitte's urgent footsteps sounded on the hardwood floor before her face reappeared.

"Madame DuBois?"

"Well, who is it?"

"He says he's Ella's brother, Jack Moreau."

I spun around, now intrigued. "Invite him in." Ella had mentioned her brother only once or twice, and if I recalled, he had returned disturbed from the war. *I wonder why he's here.*

Brigitte scurried into the gallery. She returned with a young man limping behind her.

"Madame DuBois, this is Jack Moreau." Brigitte stepped aside as Jack entered my office.

The man stopped in front of my desk and extended his hand. "It's a pleasure to meet you, Madame DuBois."

I walked around my desk. "Ella's brother, eh?" I eyed him, noting the creases on his shirtsleeves and unblemished leather shoes—newly purchased. The knot on his striped tie was loose. He was clearly a man who didn't typically dress up. I offered my hand in spite of my misgivings. "It's a pleasure to meet you also. Ella mentioned she has brothers."

"She has …" The man looked away and mumbled. He did not continue and an uncomfortable pause lingered in the room.

"Would you like to sit down?" I gestured to the velvet-covered high back. "Brigitte, please bring us something to drink." Jack lowered himself into the chair, accommodating a knee that apparently wouldn't bend. "What would you like? Wine? Brandy?"

"Do you have vodka, on ice?" He leaned back, obviously relieved to sit.

"Of course, only the best."

"Then we will become great friends." He smirked and I raised an eyebrow in return.

Brigitte returned with our drinks as I studied Jack Moreau. He couldn't be much older than Ella, perhaps in his early thirties, although his skin was weathered and his eyes tired—not taut and clear as a man in his prime should be.

"So, tell me why I have the pleasure of meeting you." I crossed my arms on my desk, one of my favorite business postures.

He took a long drink like a man who enjoys his liquor. "I'm here to do some business with you regarding my very talented and accomplished little sister."

I raised both eyebrows this time and was reminded of the throbbing in my forehead. "Really? And what might that business be?" I stood and walked near the window. "Monsieur Moreau, I must tell you I find it very odd that your sister's career has become a family business."

"What do you mean?" He tipped his glass, emptying the contents. "Another vodka?"

"Absolutely." He held out his glass toward Brigitte.

"If Ella has decided to have you and your mother represent her, I need to know."

"My *mother*?" Jack lurched forward and slammed his fists on the arms of the chair. "She left over twenty years ago. No one even knows where she is or what happened to her. Why in the—" He settled back into the chair and breathed deeply. "Why would you bring her up? She has nothing to do with why I'm here."

Well, well … isn't this interesting? I ran my finger around the rim of my glass, calculating my position in this family feud. "I assumed you were following up with me on her behalf." I walked behind his chair, stalking my prey and enjoying the game. "After all, she met with me earlier this week."

He jumped from his chair with agility reserved only for someone who had been scared to death before. "What?" He glared at me over the back of the purple chair. "She's here?"

"Well, she's not *here*." I looked around the room in a mock search. "She mentioned taking a train south to …" I tapped my temple as if to think. "Roussillon. Yes, that's where she was traveling."

"What's her business with you?"

"My business matters are private. I don't share them with just anyone."

"I'm Ella's brother, and I have a right to know why our mother was here." The young man was seething like a wild dog.

Brigitte glanced at me, nervously twisting her long hair around her finger. I patted the top of the chair. "Monsieur Moreau. Jack. Sit down and let's talk. This week has been full of surprises for all of us." I returned to my desk and folded my hands, another of my favorite gestures to keep the discussion moving. "It's best if you tell me why you came to see me. And then, if necessary, I'll share with you about your mother's visit. Deal?"

Jack peered over his raised glass and nodded. "Is it true Ella has stopped painting?"

"Remember our deal? You're supposed to be giving me answers." I winked. "But sadly, it's true. She hasn't produced any new pieces in nearly a year. Buyers are requesting her work, but there are few paintings left. The last series she painted, beautiful watercolors and oils, was sent to New York. Every piece has sold."

Jack twirled his drink, ice cubes clinking as if he had an important announcement. "There are more paintings."

I forced myself to remain calm and appear ambivalent. "And where would those be?"

"In her studio in Roussillon."

"Ah, yes. She was painting a bit when I visited her a year ago. It was before she returned to Paris and completed the series for the exhibit at the Marmottan. She said the pieces were smaller sketches and a few canvases—nothing of interest to the public."

Jack chuckled. "There's a pile up to here." He raised his hand to his shoulder. "She hides them under a tarp. They're for her eyes only."

"Except you've seen them?"

He nodded. "Not that I'm an expert, but I think those paintings are her best—better than anything you've hung in your gallery or sold in New York."

Jack stretched his arms and then crossed them behind his head. "Can you imagine what those are worth, especially since she may be finished painting?"

I took a full swallow and emptied my drink. "How do you know she won't paint again?"

"For one, she's had a baby."

"A baby?" *The surprises never end.*

"I heard it's a girl."

"You *heard*?" I shot a questioning look. "Haven't you seen your sister?"

He examined his shoe. "We don't talk anymore. I'm not exactly welcome there."

"Why not?"

"My father got fooled into thinking Andre is some sort of saint—that he could never do anything wrong." He leaned forward as if to strengthen his case. "Maybe my father didn't believe I'd ever come home from the war." He paused as though he had bounced back in time to a horrible place. "When I came home, Papa had already given the vineyard and the entire family business over to that false brother of mine. Rumor has it that Papa's getting weaker and can hardly work." He sat back and folded his hands, obviously finished presenting his case.

Henri was so handsome and strong. If only I could go back in time—

perhaps it could have worked out differently for us. I shook myself unwillingly out of my past.

"Who is the father?"

"Of who?"

"The baby, of course."

The agitated man squeezed his hands, turning his knuckles white. An eerie frown appeared on his face. "Andre. My beloved brother, Andre."

I was jittery, but unsure if it was from being unnerved by this odd man or excited at the prospect of unearthing Ella's hidden treasure. I rose from my chair and paced the room while trying to maintain my composure. "Let me understand this. You don't speak with your sister or anyone in your family, but you have personally seen a stash of what you consider Ella's best paintings." I stopped behind his chair, relishing the power of an interrogation.

He nodded, so I continued.

"You and your mother have not seen nor spoken to one another in twenty years and you had no idea she was here. Am I right?"

"Yes."

I halted in front of him, squared my shoulders, and crossed my arms. "Then tell me, Jack Moreau, what is your plan?"

Using both hands on the arms of the chair, he pushed himself to a stand. He should have towered above me, but with his crooked leg, he was reduced to only a few inches taller. "It might be bold, but I will be honest. I have little to my name—no future, no money, and no family. I've received the raw end of everything in my life."

He stepped closer and my seasoned instincts told me to be frightened of this man. I stepped back. "Brigitte?" I glanced around the room. *That harlot, she slipped out. I'll fire her in the morning ... if I see another day.* "Would you like another drink?"

Jack grabbed my arm. I considered screaming, but assumed no one would hear. *Pacify him. Ask him about his ingenious plan.* Slowly, I moved his hand off my arm and walked back to my desk, aware that my twenty-two pistol was tucked inside my drawer. He sat again, appearing to relax. I opened my drawer slightly, and slipped my hand inside.

"I feel horrible for you, sir. No one deserves to have such a hard life." I shook my head, trying to seem sincere. "Tell me the rest."

"Fine, but you must tell me about my mother and why she was here."

"Agreed."

"I'm going to pay an unexpected visit home." A wicked grin spread across his face. "But no one will be there." He cracked his knuckles and my skin crawled. "I'm going to take the paintings, every one of them." He smiled as if making a simple statement that he was stopping by a friend's home on a Sunday afternoon to pick up a basket of vegetables or a plate of pastries.

My hand wrapped around the pistol. Its steel was cold, and I made a mental note to thank Philippe for convincing me to have this around in case of trouble. "You plan to steal your sister's paintings?"

"I don't look at it that way. I deserve some of the family profits." He cracked his knuckles again and grinned.

"How am I involved?"

"Good, you're actually listening. I take the paintings and get them to you the same day. You have your buyers ready and make the sales." He clapped his hands as if that were the end of the matter. "Done. The paintings are sold, the money in your hands—which you promptly pay me half of the profits. I disappear and we all live happily ever after."

"Simple as that?"

"Yes, simple as that. I should have thought of it sooner but now the timing is perfect since her demand is high, and there are few paintings to be found."

I slipped my hand out and slid the drawer closed. "Interesting idea. It could actually work. Of course, it would permanently end my business relationship with Ella if she chose to paint again. She would never forgive me for selling her work without her knowledge." I rubbed my temple out of habit and realized my headache had subsided. "She would have to think I was under the impression she had the paintings delivered to me to sell for her—not that they were stolen." I gave Jack a stern look. "You can't get caught and, if you do, I had no knowledge of any of this." This time I cracked my knuckles. "I have people who take care of me." I circled my glass with my pointer finger. "And anyone else who isn't on my side. I'm sure you understand."

He smirked and nodded. "Then I can count on you?"

"The biggest complication is your mother." I poured myself another drink. "As it turns out, she has been financed for the last year by a wealthy New Yorker, Mr. Theodore Hudson. We've wondered who he works with to represent Ella's art in the States. He would never say, so we assumed it was someone famous who needed to remain anonymous. As long as the paintings were selling and I received my portion of the profits, we didn't need to know." I twisted the rings on my fingers. "Who would ever believe it was her own mother?" *And if only Marie Moreau knew who I was and how I fit into her past.*

"She's my mother as well. We have much in common."

I shook my head at the absurdity of the evening. "Your mother told me she came to France hoping to make amends with Ella after all these years. But she and I know her real purpose is to smooth things over and try to convince Ella to sell more paintings in New York."

Jack cleared his throat and spit in his glass. "Leave it to our mother to return as unexpectedly as she left."

"You realize the problem with your plan, don't you?"

He nodded. "My mother could get to the paintings first."

Thirty-Nine

Secrets Revealed, 1952

Always a gentleman, Papa held the door for Mama. My body remained frozen on the porch, unable to syncopate with my wildly beating heart. I took a breath, gathered my wits, and followed her into the house.

She strolled about the front room, lightly running her hand along the top of the sofa and stopping to look at a collection of photographs on the end table. She lifted the tarnished frame with the picture of her three young children—arms wrapped around each other's waists as we sat on the bare back of our mare. She lingered there and a pensive smile appeared. She carefully replaced the frame on the table. My eyes tracked her movements. She was still lovely with dark hair and a graceful neck accentuated by a strand of pearls. She wore a slim-fitting dress and high heels, though she seemed shorter than I remembered. But I was only seven then, a tiny girl when she left. Her appearance showed time had passed—hints of veins beneath transparent and wrinkled skin. But her skin remained ivory, unlike Papa's weathered and sun-scarred skin. He and I were silent—mesmerized by the apparition that floated around the room as if looking for her home.

Mama lifted a book from the shelf and thumbed through the pages. "I never read this one. Maybe someday." She set it down.

I bit my fingernail. "Where do you plan to stay?"

Papa shot me a warning look.

"What? She can't stay—"

"I'm staying near the market square. I've already rented a room."

She walked along the hallway toward the rear of the house, casually viewing a few paintings on the walls.

"How long are you staying?" I called after her.

She stopped and faced me. "None of these are your paintings. Why not?"

I chewed another nail, a habit I had just acquired since my mother arrived. "No reason. We like them. They're pretty. Right, Papa?"

"Not as pretty as yours." Papa winked at me.

Mama's ivory skin blushed pink. "I'd love to see your work." She glanced up and down the hall. "You do have some at home, don't you?"

"Not really. My paintings are in galleries in Paris and New York. You mentioned a friend of yours saw the pieces in New York."

"I did, didn't I?" She sauntered past us and entered the kitchen. "What a shame there are none here." For being away from the house for twenty years, she acted as though she owned it.

I followed her. "You didn't answer me. How long are you staying?"

Her slender fingers lifted a glass from the cupboard. "That's not a very nice way to speak to a guest."

"You're not acting like one." My heart pounded again.

"Who else would like a glass of water?" She poured the pitcher.

"Pour one for Ella and for me. This conversation needs something to help it run more smoothly." Papa raised his index finger. "Better yet, I'll go to the cellar and gather some bottles of wine." He made his way out of the kitchen door slower than usual.

This is too much for his heart. I should have told her never to come back.

Later, an empty bottle sat on the kitchen table. Mama droned on about how she initially lived on her own when she returned to New York and was preparing to pursue singing and playing the piano again. When her father became ill, she set aside her dreams of performing and moved in with her parents to provide help along with the family's long-time maid, Charlotte.

"Charlotte. Such a dear woman." Papa chuckled and scratched his head. "She had a wit about her that no one could match. How is she?"

"She's better than ever." Mama pursed her lips in disgust.

Papa and I glanced at each other.

"Don't get me wrong. I love that woman." She took a long drink. "But apparently, my mother loved her more than she loved her own daughter."

"A mother's love certainly is fickle, isn't it?" I raised my glass in a mock toast.

She bowed her head and ignored my gesture. "After my father died—"

"I'm sorry to hear that, Marie. I know you were close to him." Papa rubbed his chin.

"Yes, I was." She drifted for a moment, perhaps visiting her father in a pleasant memory. "Everything went to Mother. She was sick for a long time, and when she passed last year ..."

"What happened?" I encouraged her to finish.

"She left the money, the house, everything, to Charlotte." My mother, appearing older than her years, slumped back in her chair and shook her head as if still in disbelief over her loss.

Papa cleared his throat, I assumed partly from his worsening congestion and to allow the awkwardness to settle that hung in the room like a cloud of dust. "I'm sorry. Quite a surprise."

Mama nodded and inspected the empty bottle.

"What did Charlotte think? I'm sure she had no idea your mother planned to leave her the estate." Papa opened the other bottle and refilled her glass.

"No, Charlotte never knew. She even offered to split some things with me, but after the shock wore off, I declined. She wanted me to stay in the house, but I needed to leave. I found a small apartment in the city, and she helps me out when things get tight."

"Why did grandmother do that to you?" My feelings were a sour mixture of pity for my mother and skepticism as to why she had returned.

Mama's eyes filled with tears, but she tried to blink them away. "Because I wasn't a good daughter to her. I guess I didn't love her enough." Tears escaped and ran down her cheeks. "She never forgave me for loving my father more than her."

I glanced at Papa and a fierce love swelled inside me. I would do anything to protect him from harm—even from Mama. Any pity quickly subsided.

"Why did you never marry?"

"I almost did a few years ago. It didn't work out, but we're seeing each other again. We make a pretty good pair." Nonchalantly, she held her glass to the light streaming in from the window. "I could ask Henri the same question." She raised her penciled brows at Papa.

The front door opened before Papa could respond. Andre walked into the kitchen holding Aimee. She wore a woolen hat and her tiny nose was pink from the cool air.

"*Mon bebe.*" I reached for her. Andre placed her in my arms, and I kissed her rosy cheek. "This is my wonderful husband, Andre, and our beautiful daughter, Aimee."

Mama knocked her glass, spilling red wine across the table. "Oh my. I'm sorry." She stood and noticeably swayed. "I had no idea." She grabbed a dishtowel and blotted the tablecloth. "Why didn't you tell me I'm a grandmother?"

"There's a lot you don't know." I took Andre's hand and squeezed it. "We've known one another for many years."

"It's nice to finally meet you," Andre said.

Mama continued to blot the table, then stopped and tossed the cloth on the counter. "It's wonderful to meet you, Andre ..."

"Donato."

"Monsieur Donato. Then you are from this area?"

"I guess you could say that."

Mama directed her attention to me. "And you are now Ella Donato. Is that how your paintings will be signed?"

"I haven't thought about it. Why are you so interested in how I'll sign my work?"

"Oh, I don't know. Just curious."

Andre and I exchanged quizzical glances.

My daughter giggled as I bounced her on my hip. "How is my little girl? Did you have fun today?" I never tired of watching her changing expressions. "Aimee Columbina. Her name means loved little dove."

Mama stood behind me. She leaned over and I smelled her fading rose perfume.

"My God, she's absolutely beautiful." She pushed closer, her chest resting on my shoulder. I shuddered, realizing this was the first time my mother had touched me since I was a child. "She looks like you, Ella."

Mama hovered over my shoulder for a long time staring at her granddaughter. Two strangers brought together for what purpose? Would we ever know each other beyond this point in time?

Papa excused himself from the table. "Marie, I don't mean to be rude, but I need to take a catnap. The wine made me sleepy."

My father had enjoyed wine his entire life and I had never seen him forced to bed because of it. Andre and I exchanged the same concerned look.

"Papa, I'll check on you soon."

"No need for that." He half-waved at Mama. "I assume you're in town for a bit. We'll have time to catch up. Why don't you come for dinner tomorrow night?"

"I'd like that, Henri. We have plenty to share with each other."

"It's time for Aimee's nap. I may take one too." I gave an exaggerated yawn.

Mama understood my intention. "Yes, it's been a long day for me as well. Trains always made me sleepy. Andre, would it be possible for you to take me to the market square? My apartment is an easy walk from there."

"I'd be happy to drive you to where you're staying." He took his keys off the hook. "I'll put your bag in the car. That must be yours sitting near the front door." Andre winked at me.

Mama had surely hoped to stay with us, but I wasn't ready for that. I hardly knew the woman. After all, Papa was my biggest concern. She would have to take care of herself.

* * * * *

The next day I pushed the stroller around the perimeter of the market, taking in the delicious sights, sounds, and smells of autumn in southern France. Aimee seemed to enjoy the market and its shops—especially the busy *boulangerie* and *patisserie*. I hoped she would grow to love Roussillon as much as me. We entered the *charcuterie* and she squealed at the sight of the pigs, chickens, and turkeys hanging from the overhead hooks. For her, they dangled like the mobile above her bassinet.

"*Salut*, Ella and Aimee." A large man leaned across the counter. His sleeves were rolled above his elbows, displaying his massive forearms.

"*Salut*, Louis. How are you?"

"Perfect in every way." He beamed in his usual manner.

"You've been saying that for years, so it must be true."

"*Oui*, I cannot lie." He blew a kiss to my daughter who remained infatuated with the plucked and limp birds. "What can I get for you? Having a guest for dinner tonight?"

My brow shot up in surprise. "There is nothing secret or sacred in this town, is there? How did you know?" I pointed to a large chicken. Louis released it from its upside down perch and wrapped it in brown paper as though it were a baby.

"Marie stopped in earlier. She bought a sausage to take tonight." The butcher smoothed his white mustache. "I hadn't seen her in over twenty years, but I would have recognized her anywhere—still a beautiful woman. How's Henri doing with her coming back?"

"I'm worried about him. He's not feeling well and my mother isn't helping the situation."

"If there's anything I can—"

"*Merci.* I know you and Papa have been friends since you were boys." I paid for our dinner's main course and bundled Aimee before beginning our walk home. "Stop by and visit with your friend. He'd love to see you."

"I'll do that, real soon."

"*Au revoir.*"

I pushed the stroller onto the cobbled street and bumped along toward home. Aimee fell asleep in her stroller once the road became paved and then turned to hard-packed dirt.

Careful not to wake her while balancing the bag of poultry, I headed into the kitchen and slipped the package into the refrigerator. Aimee could sleep a while longer in her bassinet so I would have time to start dinner before Mama arrived and Andre and Papa returned from helping the Patins replace their fence. Papa was trying to do too much. He especially sought ways to support Auguste and Eloise. The Patins were older now and didn't have their strong son to help them.

I stepped into the hallway and quietly closed the bedroom door. At the end of the hall, my studio door stood ajar. The wind could have blown it open, but the window was closed when I finished painting this morning. I had awoken before sunrise, kissed Andre on his forehead, and disappeared into the solitude of my studio. Praying and painting—the best method to confront my conflicted heart over seeing my mother again. Maybe someone had gone in after me.

Before going into the studio to check the window, I heard a muffled voice, confirming someone was inside. I inched the door open enough to see inside. Mama sat on the floor with her back against the wall. She held her knees tightly to her chest with one hand. In the other was the small watercolor painting I had completed this morning. Like a baby, she rocked back and forth ... and wept.

"How could you love me after what I did?" She spoke to herself between sobs. "You were never allowed these moments. I took them away, but you imagined them still."

My eyes moved from piece to piece scattered on the floor in front of her. Paintings depicting fragments of what I could remember of my life with Mama before she left, lay alongside painted images I conjured in my dreams of what could have been.

Her hand traveled slowly across a poppy-filled canvas. "You don't know how often I imagined holding your tiny hand as we walked through a field just like this."

As tears trickled down her cheeks, she lifted the newly-painted paper and studied it. "Oh, Ella, you didn't erase me from your life even as the years should have done." She placed her hand over her heart. "Is this what forgiveness is like?"

I watched her, breathless and astonished. Like a butterfly about to emerge from her chrysalis, this was her opportunity to prove she had changed and become new. Realizing tears of my own, I saw the painting she held—the piece that had demanded to be painted this morning—Mama, Aimee, and me with our faces toward the sun, surrounded by sunflowers—paying the same respect as we gazed heavenward to our Creator.

She set the painting on the floor and pushed herself to her knees. I stepped back into the shadows. A few moments later, I heard shuffling and leaned forward again. Grabbing at the piles of paintings, she seemed panicked as though she had lost a priceless jewel in the sand. *What is she doing?* I placed my hand on the door, ready to shove it open and catch her in whatever act she was committing. But her shoulders slumped and she held a watercolor limply at her side.

"I can't do this. I have to tell her the truth. Getting my daughter back is worth more than her paintings." She bent over and began straightening the papers and stacking the canvases in the corner of the room.

I slid into the room and closed the door.

Mama spun around, eyes wide. "You scared me."

"What are you doing in here?" I leaned against the door, intent on getting answers.

"I came early to help with dinner. This used to be the pantry and I came in to get—"

"Hasn't been for years. It's rather obvious what it's used for now, don't you think?"

She ran her fingers under her eyes in an attempt to remove the smudged mascara.

"You were crying?"

204

"Sorry. I got emotional being in my old house."

She finished putting the paintings where they were found, and gently concealed them with the tarp. "They're beautiful, Ella. I shouldn't have looked at them without your permission, but after I saw the watercolor on the easel, I had to see more."

My lips remained silent.

"I had no idea how talented you are."

I waited to see if she would share more.

Mama stepped toward me and extended her hand. "Ella, I can't lie to you anymore."

Aimee's awakening cry pierced the air. As I turned to open the door, Mama's hand was still reaching for mine. I stepped toward her and touched the tips of her fingers.

"No more secrets, Mama."

She nodded and wiped again at the mascara.

* * * * *

I fed Aimee and Andre put her down for the night. We all gathered in the front room to hear Mama's story, knowing dinner would be delayed until well into the darkness of the evening.

After a few moments, Andre interrupted. "Wasn't it difficult for you to follow Ella's career all those years and not talk with her?" He was trying to piece the events together as well as Papa and myself. "Buying those European magazines and papers and cutting them apart?"

"I was a coward, too scared to appear out of nowhere when she was having success."

My guard rose at that statement. "But that's what you've done. Have you overcome your cowardice now that Charlotte was given the estate and you don't have any money? Is that really why you wrote me the first time?"

Mama lowered her head. "Yes. That was the reason. I panicked when I found out what Mother had done. Reclaiming a part of your life seemed my only chance not to lose everything."

"Marie, how could you do that?" Papa placed his arm around my shoulders.

Mama stood and paced the room. We watched her, waiting for an explanation.

Finally, she sat down and folded her hands in her lap. "I called my friend, actually the man who wanted to marry me, and made him a proposition to join me in a business venture."

Papa, Andre, and I glanced at each another, but didn't interrupt.

"He is very wealthy—from a newspaper family in New York. He flew to Paris and met with Madame DuBois in hopes of making a deal to represent your work in America."

"Mr. Hudson?" My hands covered my gaping mouth.

Mama nodded. "Theodore Hudson. My close friend, and perhaps more."

"All this time, you're the mysterious American woman? And you've been selling my paintings in New York and sharing the profit with Emelia?"

"And with you and Theodore. The split goes four ways, but it was enough to get me back on my feet and prove there's a demand for your work overseas."

Now it was my turn to pace the room as the shock of Mama's revelations sank in. "You could have kept this a secret and stayed in New York." I locked eyes with her. "You still haven't said why you came home."

"We needed more paintings. We thought if I met with Madame DuBois, I would be able to secure more pieces for the gallery that Theodore and I opened in the city. We have buyers wanting your work and nothing to sell to them. Madame DuBois ... Emelia ... drives a hard bargain. We didn't know if she was holding out on us, trying to negotiate a better percentage. I had to come see for myself if more of your work existed. Madame DuBois confirmed that to her knowledge, you hadn't painted since you left Paris, and she was in the same predicament."

"And when you saw the paintings tonight?"

She took a deep breath and blew it out slowly. "I discovered a gold mine. Pieces that are unlike any of your others. Paintings that expose your soul."

My cunning mother blinked at me with tearful eyes and whispered, "But I couldn't do it. It would be like selling the small part of what's left of my soul if I tried to profit from those pieces." She cradled her face in her hands and wept. "How will you ever be able to forgive me?"

I stood next to her and watched the slouched figure reduced to a fragile human just like the rest of us. Hesitantly, I ran my fingers through her hair and whispered back, "Because God forgave me."

* * * * *

Papa invited Mama to stay in Charles and Jack's old bedroom for the night. In the morning, after some sleep and the welcome sunshine of a new day, we would talk more.

"*Bonsoir.*" She started down the hallway and I touched her shoulder.

"Mama, may I kiss you goodnight."

She turned and paused. "A long overdue bedtime kiss. Let me kiss you as well."

We held each other in the darkness and nothing else mattered.

Forty

Jack's Revenge, 1952

We spent much of the next day walking in the sleepy vineyards and showing Mama the bounty of another good growing season that was bottled in the cellar. Later, Papa was wrapped in a heavy blanket and snoring loudly in a front porch chair while Mama and I snapped off the ends of string beans and tossed them into the grass. Aimee lay on her blanket next to us, kicking her feet and giggling.

"Andre should be back from town any time now. It's starting to get dark." I smiled as my baby rolled onto her stomach. She seemed surprised when she became reoriented and had a new view of her tiny world.

I raised my head and sniffed the air. "Do you smell that?"

She sniffed. "Smells like a fire."

One of the hired men ran full stride toward the house from the side field. As he got closer, I heard him yelling. "Monsieur Moreau. There's a fire in the shed at the south end of the vineyard."

Papa roused and pushed himself from his chair. "What did he say?"

"There's a fire in the shed." I tossed the remaining beans. "Let's get down there."

Papa shuffled out of his chair and met the panting man in the yard. "Ella, stay here with Aimee. I don't want her near the smoke. Where's Andre?"

"He should be on his way—"

"Here he is." Mama pointed to the truck reeling into the drive.

Andre jumped out of the truck and stood with Papa and the man.

The worker gestured to the far vineyard. The three of them got in the truck and Mama scurried down the stairs. "I'm coming with you." Papa waved her away, but she opened the door and climbed in.

I lifted Aimee and stood alone as the truck sped out of the drive, turned right, and headed to the far end of the property. "Everything will be fine, sweetie. Everything will be fine." A black plume of smoke billowed across the field and my heart sank.

The air became chilly as the sun set. I decided to dress Aimee in warmer clothes, grab a jacket for myself, and return to the porch in hopes the cloud of smoke would subside. I started for the bedroom and heard a loud thump, and then glass shatter in the studio. My body became rigid, and I held Aimee to my chest as the sounds of glass crushing and items being moved came from the room. Aimee whimpered and I hushed her. *Get Papa's gun.* The thought raced through my mind, but I was helpless as I held on to my child. I took a step forward and then my instincts told me to run. Just then, a figure stepped from the room.

"Jack!" I clutched Aimee tighter. "What are you doing?"

He peered over a stack of papers and canvases held against his body. Even in the dim light, his eyes looked glazed. "Get out of my way, Ella. You and the baby."

"Why would you do this?" Suddenly, I thought of Mama needing more artwork. I shuddered. "Did Mama have you—"

"She's got nothing to do with my business." He glanced around. A strange paranoia defined his stubbly and dirty face. "Where is she?"

"Trying to help with the—" I moved toward him. "*You* set the fire." I wanted to slap him, and at the same time, run from this crazed man.

He held the stack firmly to his chest. "Pretend you never saw me, Ella. Go put the baby to bed and let me walk out of here. I don't want anything to happen to either of you." His head twitched and I knew he was serious.

I stepped backwards and moved toward the front door. Jack followed me.

"Put the baby in bed," he hissed like a venomous snake.

There was no way Aimee was leaving my arms.

"I'm letting you out the door." I backed myself to the front door, turned the knob, and opened the door. The truck turned into the drive and Jack cursed, shoving me aside. I tripped and fell as I tried to keep Aimee from hitting the ground. She began to cry and I screamed for Andre.

In the light of the headlights, Andre jumped from the truck and leapt onto the porch. He wrestled Jack onto the stones. As if in slow motion, my paintings were tossed into the air, and then floated to the ground like I had watched them do the day Mama left.

"I should kill you." Andre held Jack by his throat, shoving his head into the hard surface.

"Andre, don't!" I had never seen him so fierce. I huddled Aimee closer and prayed.

Papa appeared with Mama at his side. He held onto the railing and steadied himself. "Let him go, Andre." His breathing was labored.

My enraged husband tightened his grip and Jack gasped for air.

"Andre!" Papa barked. "No more!"

Andre released his hold and fell back on his heels. Papa hoisted himself up the stairs and stood over his son who was coughing and gagging. "You've committed one too many sins against this family, Jack. My men could have been killed in that fire, which was clearly set on purpose. And if you had harmed Ella and my granddaughter, I would have killed you myself."

Mama held Papa's arm and looked down at her son. "Jack, what's happened to you?" She knelt toward him, but he pushed her away.

He sat up and curled his lip into a sneer. "I could ask *you* the same question."

Mama teetered backwards and remained silent.

Andre grabbed Jack's collar. "Ella, go inside and call the police."

"No, let him go." Papa was breathing harder now. "But I never want to see you or hear from you again. You're no longer my son."

My heart ached for Papa. Despite what Jack had done, I knew my father was tormented by his decision.

Andre released Jack and stepped way. "And you're not my brother."

Jack snickered and pushed himself to a stand. "I never was." He looked from Mama to Aimee and then to me. "And the women have each other now. Isn't that just lovely?" He kicked at a few scattered paintings and leapt from the porch. We watched him disappear into the darkness, enveloped by the same blackness of his heart.

Forty-One

Papa's Farewell, 1953

Papa slept much of the winter, just as his vineyards rested in anticipation of returning in the spring. But as the buds began to unfold, he withered, and we knew this would be his last season.

Mama remained with us, helping care for him and watching Aimee while I painted. Working in the studio kept my mind busy as Papa's illness progressed. None of us could change its course.

The woman who once filled his life, then left him alone, now sat on the edge of Papa's bed. I held Aimee in the rocking chair.

Papa's voice was weak but he retained his wit. "It still makes me laugh when I remember the expression on your face when I told you."

"Told me what?" Mama rubbed his arm.

"That Emelia was the woman I had met in Marseilles." He chuckled and then coughed.

"Yes, I admit that was quite a surprise. I should have believed that you didn't love her."

"She looked much different when she was younger." He smiled and winked at me.

"Papa, that's not nice." I gave him a reproving look, but smiled back. "I wonder how she's doing, knowing she won't be representing me any longer."

"She'll land on her feet as always." He grunted. "She's probably found an unsuspecting victim already."

"Emelia did get me started. Without her, I never would have been taken seriously as an artist. For that, I'll always be grateful."

Papa's eyes drifted shut. "She did, didn't she? Life has a funny way of surprising us."

Aimee had fallen asleep in my arms, and I rose to put her in her bed.

Papa opened one eye. "Ella, I want you to hear what I'm going to say so I have a witness before the Lord."

Andre stuck his head into the room. "Here you are."

Papa motioned him to the bedside. "Now I'll have two."

"What about me?" Mama pointed to herself.

"They need to hear what I'm going to say to you, Marie." He took her hand and held it on his chest. He opened his other eye and stared at her. "I meant what I said years ago, that I'd always loved you, only you. I regret ever hurting you and would do anything to change the past." His eyes clouded with tears. "I've loved you all these years, and seeing you again makes me want to start all over. But I can't. It's time for me to go home."

"Henri." Mama tried to hold back her tears, but they came at their own will.

"The Lord forgave me a long time ago, but now I'm asking you. Will you forgive me, Marie?" Tears trickled down Papa's ashen cheeks.

She squeezed his hand. "I forgave you a long time ago when I realized I would never stop loving you." Mama bent over and kissed his tears away.

Andre wrapped his arm around my waist and held our family close.

"Henri." Mama paused and lowered her eyes. "I suppose forgiveness needs to go both ways." Placing her palm on Papa's chest, she spoke in a whisper. "You have always had a beautiful heart. You've been a good man since the day I met you."

"Not always." Papa chuckled and then a terrible coughing fit followed. Mama gently rubbed his chest until he was able to relax on his pillow.

"I surely haven't been perfect either." Mama shook her head. "But, Henri, I'm asking you to forgive me too. I should never have left you and the family. I regret every lost moment."

As though they were the only two people on the planet, my parents locked eyes—desperately reaching for one another across a vast span of time, loneliness, and pain.

Finally, Papa reached up and took her face in his hands. "Marie, I love you and I forgive you." In that moment, they seemed to find each other as Papa gently pulled her closer and they met each other's lips after so many years.

* * * * *

Papa was laid to rest alongside Charles as the poppies bloomed, waving good-bye in the gentle wind. I tucked a vase of burgundy peonies into the soft earth and cried beside my mother.

Andre held Aimee as the last of the people left the small cemetery. When I stood to leave, his shoulders were heaving. Andre wept for Papa and himself. He had lost his father a second time.

I went to him and wrapped my arms around my small family. We remained huddled together for a long time, and then a fourth nudged into our circle.

We pulled Mama in and prayed.

Forty-Two

Releasing the Butterfly, 1953

"I've been thinking, Mama." I sipped my tea and licked a sprig of mint leaf that had grown thick in the garden over the summer.

"About what?" We rested on the porch, shaded from the intense, end-of-summer heat.

I know you miss New York, and I've heard you talking on the phone to Mr. Hudson."

"Theodore."

"Yes, Theodore. You should consider going back to America."

She looked surprised. "You're getting rid of me?"

"No, never again. But do you love him?"

She lifted her drink and took a long, thoughtful sip. "I do. He's a good man—treats me well, and …" She tossed her head back and laughed. "He's patient. After all, he's waited for me a long time. That's the only reason he continues to help me finance the gallery."

"Is it still open? I mean, whose artwork is in it?" I tucked my legs under my skirt and turned toward Mama.

"There are a few local artists, plus one from California whose popularity has spread across the continent. Theodore wants to represent one of the abstract artists like Jackson Pollack or Franz Kline, but that will be difficult. I don't really understand their pieces, but others apparently do."

"Well, I've decided to represent myself for the sales in Europe. I can run the business end of things and continue painting from here. If buyers want my work, they'll find me."

"What about in the United States? You have a presence there too." My mother leaned forward, putting on her business face.

"You and Theodore could handle that for me." I grinned like a schoolgirl. "Would you like to represent your daughter, but this time legitimately?"

Mama leaned back and sighed. "I'd be honored, Ella. Truly honored."

* * * * *

The heat waned and the vines showed off their autumn colors. Mama would catch the train to Paris at noon and fly home from there. We had meticulously framed, wrapped, and packed twelve of my best landscapes, and Andre delivered them to the shipping docks in Marseilles. They would soon be on their way to be displayed in New York City at the recently renamed gallery, *Henri*.

I looked out the kitchen window as I finished preparing an early lunch before we headed to the station. Aimee toddled beside Mama at the edge of the vineyard. She had turned one year old in the spring, and now she scurried and stumbled every which way, eager to explore her bigger world. I laughed aloud as Mama pretended to chase her through the rows of red and orange-tinged vines. Aimee's tiny head with dark, curly hair emerged at the top of a row, and then Mama appeared a few steps behind. I realized God was allowing me to see Mama at peace in the vineyards. She was joyful and had truly come home.

A large butterfly glided from above. Aimee reached for the fragile wings as it flitted between wildflowers. She giggled as it remained out of her grasp. My eyes followed the sun-kissed creature as it flew away and out of sight. All the lingering fear and guilt from my past floated away with it.

Mama finally snatched her granddaughter into her arms and kissed her pudgy cheeks. I grabbed the tray of sandwiches and went to meet them in the garden. They stood in front of the largest sunflower, the seeds partly eaten, its head beginning to droop. I joined them and, instinctively, the three of us turned our heads the same direction as the majestic flower.

And I silently thanked the Lord.

Forty-Three

My mother was happy in New York. The gallery was a success and Theodore had proposed to her on Christmas Day. This time, she accepted. We would attend the wedding in the fall.

Andre and I walked through the forest near the base of the path leading to Remy's Castle. When Aimee was older, we would take her to the top of our world and show her our kingdom. For now, we wandered under the veil of the tall trees as our daughter explored each new sight and subtle movement in the thick forest.

I crouched and lifted a thin vine. My fingers followed its path to the end.

"Andre, look what I've found." He knelt next to me, and a small body nudged herself between us to see our discovery. "It's the first strawberry."

"Papa used to tell us it's an old French tradition to honor the season and celebrate rebirth. It's for renewal—it connects the past to the present."

"Go ahead, Ella, say it."

I closed my eyes. "This is the first strawberry of the season, so I'm going to make a wish." Then I opened my eyes and looked at my husband and child.

"There's no need. All my wishes have already come true."

Epilogue

Roussillon, France, 1960

Last week, I watched my daughter make a wish and blow out seven candles on her cake. It was her favorite—vanilla, layered with pink frosting and fresh strawberries. She laughed and licked the frosting from the candles. Kissing her father on the cheek, she gave him the best gift of all—her love, sealed with a pink print.

I studied her, sketching each detail of her beautiful face and body into my memory. I rehearsed in my mind, her dark, wavy hair falling over her right shoulder and her turquoise-colored eyes dancing when she smiled. The next morning, I would paint this scene, a celebration of my daughter and husband—my way of glorifying God and praising Him for all He had done for me.

Made in the USA
Lexington, KY
10 November 2014